ISLAND
OF MYSTERY

Also Available in Large Print
by Arlene Hale

Home to the Valley
A Glimpse of Paradise
One More Bridge to Cross
The Other Side of the World

ISLAND
OF MYSTERY

Arlene Hale

G.K.HALL&CO.
Boston, Massachusetts
1978

Library of Congress Cataloging in Publication Data

Hale, Arlene.
  Island of mystery.

  Large print ed.
  1. Large type books.   I. Title.
[PZ4.H1618Is 1978] [PS3515.A262] 813'.5'4 77-27943
  ISBN 0-8161-6552-1

Published in Large Print by arrangement with Little, Brown & Company

Set in Photon 18 pt Crown

FOR

*Woodrow, the best brother a girl
ever had, and Freeda, his wife*

1

They had met on campus at Mitchell Grove, where Alison Blair was taking a summer course in music appreciation. Regan Williams, who taught at a local junior high school, was studying for his master's degree. For nearly a year, they had been seeing each other, and while Alison wasn't sure if her feelings for Regan could be called love, there was no doubt in Regan's mind how he felt about her.

"We belong together, Alison, I've known that from the beginning."

"Always the positive one," she teased. "Honestly, Regan, sometimes I wish something would happen to lead you off the straight and narrow path."

He frowned at that. "I know what I want to do with my life and why. I couldn't live like you, Alison. You flit from one thing to another and never settle down. You could become a great music teacher, do you realize that?"

"So you've told me countless times before. But I know my limitations, Regan. I'm not a teacher. I'm a writer. Of all the things I've done, writing is what I enjoy most."

"And you're darned good at it, I admit, but you're almost as good with music. Writer, musician, composer — what are you, Alison Blair?"

"Who knows?" She laughed with a shrug. "But I think writing is really my deepest interest and always will be. That's why I have to go away to find out all I can about Leighton Thordsen."

"You've already gathered reams of material," Regan countered. "What more do you need to write a book about him?"

"All I can get. He lived on Windswept Island, where he built a huge house. He was working on his last composition before he left abruptly for Venice, where he died shortly after. That last composition has never been found."

2

"And you have some illusions about finding it?"

"No illusions, just good research."

They talked like this on many occasions as spring came to Mitchell Grove. But when the last days of Regan's school year arrived and he was due back at graduate school, the real arguments began.

"You could write your book right here at home," he pointed out. "We'd be together that way."

"I'd like that but —"

"You know you're driving me crazy, don't you?"

They had gone out to supper, lingering long over their food but all that time skirting the issue, knowing that it was sure to lead to disagreements. Later, sitting on their favorite bench overlooking the river, Regan reached out and held her hand tightly in his.

"Regan, I have to go," she said quietly. "I don't know what more I can say. It's a kind of compulsion — I wake up at night knowing I *have* to go. I saw the island once, years ago, and I've never forgotten it. It keeps tugging at me, pulling me back

— I have this uncanny feeling that something tremendously important waits for me there."

Regan frowned. As a teacher of science, he paid little attention to whims or any kind of sixth sense.

"Alison —"

She put a finger against his firm lips and shook her head. "Don't argue, Regan. It won't do you any good and we'll only have a terrible fight —

"I don't want you to go," he said bluntly.

"I must."

"Nonsense!'

She held her tongue and choked down all the defensive words she wanted to hurl back at him. He didn't know about the island, had never seen it, never felt its cool, moist air against his face, seen the clear depths of the lake, experienced the feel and mood of it as she had. Perhaps knowing that Leighton Thordsen had lived and worked there, only to leave under mysterious circumstances, had enhanced the place for her, but then again, perhaps it was not that at all. It was her destiny,

4

that island, and it didn't matter what Regan said or thought or felt, it wouldn't change anything.

"Why must you become obsessed with things? Once you were wild over decoupage, another time you went around collecting every native flower you could find, and I remember another time you went out of your skull over Picasso's work and you played Vladimir Horowitz records until I thought my head would burst! Now, it's Leighton Thordsen and some moldy old island out in the middle of nowhere —"

"I am what I am and I can't change that either, Regan."

"The hell of it is, I love you, despite everything." He lifted her hand and pressed his lips against her fingers. "You're all wrong for me, you know. I've always known that, but I just went along —"

"I'm sorry. I should never have let it get this far with us. I'm just not ready to settle down as a schoolteacher's wife. There's too much waiting for me out there. Which isn't to say I won't ever change. When I find the right place, the right time, the right *everything,* I'll become as settled as anyone else you know."

"And you think you're going to find it on Windswept Island, don't you?"

"Maybe. In fact, yes, I *know* I will. There's something about the place, Regan. Anyway, I have to go and see. Let's not have it end badly between us."

Regan pulled her into his arms, reluctant to let all the good times go, but he was practical and knew when his luck had run out.

"I'll never forget you, Regan," she said.

"You make this sound like a final good-bye. I won't let it be that, Alison. I'm not letting you out of my life completely —"

"You know where I'll be. The house that Leighton Thordsen built and lived in has been turned into an inn. I plan to stay there, as close to my subject matter as I can get."

When they left the park bench a few minutes later, both were silent, and on the way back to Alison's house Regan scarcely said a word. They said good-bye and he gave her a curt nod of his head. She watched him drive away, unhappy that they should have parted in anger.

Inside her parents' house, where she had been staying for some time, she found everything dark and quiet. She went upstairs to her room and flipped on the light. Her things were nearly all packed and her plane would leave at ten in the morning. By now her parents were used to her disappearing for months at a time. They wanted her to be herself, to find her own destiny. She loved them for that and for the solid family background they had given her. But it was time to move on again and, thinking ahead to Windswept Island, she trembled with anticipation.

The next morning, Alison's mother made breakfast a farewell occasion. She guessed at once that Regan would not be coming, although she had particularly invited him to join them.

"Did you quarrel?" Mrs. Blair asked.

"Yes. Regan is shortsighted. I like him very much, except for that."

7

"Well, don't worry. Once you leave here, you'll forget about it. I only hope your trip to the island isn't a disappointment. You're counting on it so much."

"Don't I always?" she asked with a short laugh. "I'm an uncontrollable optimist. Where's Dad?"

"He'll be down shortly."

"And you promised to come for a visit."

"We will if we can," Mrs. Blair said. "It will depend on your father's work. You know, Alison, you're a wonder to me. I admire your courage and your determination. When I was a young woman like you, I was expected to stay at home and be ladylike and join local clubs or work for the church. To go gallivanting all over the country was not considered the proper thing to do."

Alison laughed. "Thank God I came along a generation later. I'd have died."

"So long as you put down roots soon, Alison. But there's still time. You're young and have so much ahead of you. I just don't want you to be cheated of anything."

"Ah, Mother, don't you know that's why I'm bound for Windswept Island? I'm going to heap up my basket with riches, just as you heap up the leaves in the autumn."

Breakfast was cheery and filled with laughter, and Alison knew her parents were making a special effort to gloss over Regan's absence. Then it was time to leave for the airport with the usual last-minute scurry to find all her things.

At the terminal they talked of small matters and reminded each other of errands that had to be done. Then, with a wave, Alison hurried away with the other travelers. Even up to the final moment she thought Regan would come, but she should have known he wouldn't.

The trip required one stop with a brief layover, and in three hours she had arrived, at the south end of Thunder Lake, only a few miles from the Canadian border. From the window, she had caught a glimpse of the immensity of the lake, which reached more than sixty miles to the north and spread twenty miles at its widest portion, tapering off to narrow

9

strips of water at each end.

The nearest city to Thunder Lake and Alison's destination was Donnerville, a sprawling city with an active tourist trade aimed mostly at enthusiastic campers and fishermen. It also sported a large paper mill that was part of its thriving lumber business.

Alison had made arrangements to be picked up at the dock at five that evening, so she had plenty of time to get reacquainted with Donnerville. She had hardly done more than pass through the last time she had been there.

She spent an hour or so browsing in a bookshop and discovered a little gift store filled with handmade articles that delighted her. The owner introduced herself as Lois Martin.

"I'm bound for the Greenwood Inn on Windswept Island," Alison said. "Do you know it?"

"I'm afraid it's not what it used to be. It was left empty for several years and the vandals had a field day. But Reba Zeller has done her best since she took it over, and she rents a few rooms now. Will you be staying long?"

"For the summer," Alison said.

"Oh, I see!"

The tone in Lois's voice made Alison give her a quick look.

"Something wrong?"

"No, of course not, if you like islands. I buy some of my merchandise from someone who lives over there. It's a strange sort of place."

"Why do you say that?"

"Joni's told me about those odd Meadows people that live there, and then there's Reba's brother, Roy, who isn't quite bright sometimes . . . Oh, I shouldn't be saying all of this! It's just local talk and probably doesn't mean a thing."

If the girl thought she was putting Alison off, she couldn't have been more wrong.

"You make it seem all the more interesting," Alison said.

"Oh?"

Alison laughed, and with a wave and a promise to stop in again, she said good-bye and left.

11

At five o'clock Alison was at the dock with her belongings, waiting for the man who worked for Reba Zeller to pick her up.

The sunlight had faded suddenly more than an hour before and a chill wind had come up. The fog had rolled in, lifting up off the water, enshrouding everything.

She sat shivering on one of her suitcases, wishing she could remember which bag held a warm sweater.

At the sound of footsteps somewhere behind her, Alison turned about sharply.

"Hello," she called out.

The footsteps stopped. Through the fog she saw a tall man in a gray raincoat turned up at the collar. He seemed startled to see her, although she couldn't get a good look at his face or his eyes. It was the way he stood tensely, staring at her.

"I'm waiting for the boat over to the Greenwood Inn," she said. "Are you waiting too?"

There was no reply. Instead, he moved away from her and stood at the far end of the dock, peering out into the murky water.

Alison shivered in the coolness of the fog and this stranger's manner. She wondered who he was and why he was there, and she began to wish that the boat would come or that another person would happen along. But only the two of them remained. The city of Donnerville was lost to view and no one was venturing out in the fog. Perhaps the boat wouldn't be running because of it. She didn't relish the thought of waiting here longer than she had intended, especially with this strange man standing just a few feet away.

She looked at her watch. The boat was already twenty minutes overdue. Perhaps there had been a mix-up and she wasn't expected. If only there was a phone nearby.

She was about to go and search for one when she heard the boat. It was coming fast and she caught her breath. If it was as near as it sounded, it would crash into the dock! Then it suddenly cut its motor, and she saw the wake of the water slapping at the pier before she saw the boat.

It was not a fancy vessel, but rather rundown, with the name *The Maiden* painted on its side in faded letters. The man behind the wheel eased the boat expertly to the dock and leaped out to make it fast. He was a small man, dressed in casual clothes and deck shoes. A stained captain's cap was perched rakishly on his red hair, and a scar ran along the right side of his face. He was not nearly as young as she had first thought.

"Are you from the inn?" Alison asked.

He nodded curtly. "I am. Are you Miss Blair?"

"Yes. Thank goodness you've come. I was getting anxious —"

"Fog's worse here than at the island, so it slowed me down. I'll stow your things aboard."

He put all her luggage inside the shabby boat and then reached for her hand.

"I'm York. Tom York. People around here call me Salt. I don't answer to anything but that, if the truth's to be known."

"Nice to meet you, Salt."

He was about to toss the mooring lines inside when the man Alison had seen earlier came striding toward them. He was smoking a pipe, his collar still turned against the fog, and she caught sight of his face with its dark and brooding eyes, firm mouth, and stubborn chin. There was something about him that was remote and gloomy.

"I'm a passenger too," he said quietly in a muffled voice.

"Oh? Are you bound for the Greenwood Inn?" Salt asked. "Reba never told me."

"She doesn't know I'm coming."

"Oh, well, then, I'm not at all sure —"

But the man tossed his things aboard and climbed in. He sat down as far away from Alison as possible, and there he leaned over the side of the boat to stare out to the lake, as if he could penetrate the fog and see the inn.

Salt glanced at Alison and then with a shrug turned the starter and nosed the boat and its two passengers into the fog.

2

It was apparent that Salt knew the lake like the back of his hand or the fog would have landlocked him. At times they reached pockets of clear weather, when Alison could glimpse the breadth of the lake; then abruptly they would be swallowed up again in a cloak of mist.

The stranger sat very still, looking out across the bow of the boat, trying to catch his first glimpse of the Greenwood Inn. Salt handled *The Maiden* with a dash that could have been recklessness but which Alison decided was really a kind of practiced confidence developed over the years.

"How far is the inn from Donnerville?" Alison asked over the engine's roar.

"Five miles," he said.

"Seems much farther."

"Yes," Salt nodded. "Especially in all this muck."

The rush of air pounded against Alison and stirred her silky dark hair, swirling it around her face. She absorbed the sound and feel of the boat, the slap of water against the hull, and the presence of the quiet stranger smoking his pipe. Could five miles make it seem she had gone to another world?

Then Salt was bringing the motor down and it groaned in protest. They cleared a patch of fog and for one startling moment Alison saw the Greenwood Inn, perched on the edge of a stony cliff a good fifty feet above the surface of the water, where it had a commanding view of Thunder Lake. She remembered the one other time she had seen it, and how it had seemed to her like a sprawling castle lifting its face to the sky.

"It's beautiful!" she said.

"In its day it was," Salt replied. "Lately . . ."

His words died away, and the melancholy in his voice touched her.

They skimmed by the inn, and Alison

saw that the dock was at the foot of the cliff. There Salt eased the boat to the wooden platform, and the stranger reached out to help make them steady.

With *The Maiden* tied up, Salt helped Alison ashore and told her he would bring her things up.

"Roy will give me a hand," he said. "Now where in thunder is that man? He's never here when I need him. Roy! Roy!"

Finally, at Salt's shout, a big man came shuffling toward them out of nowhere.

"Reba's brother," Salt explained in a low voice. "Not quite right, but harmless —"

Roy came to take some of the luggage, stuffing it under his huge arms as if they were pillows instead of heavy suitcases. He stared at Alison and gave her a foolish grin.

"Alison Blair," Salt said. "Alison, this is Roy Zeller."

Alison gave him a polite nod.

"Just follow the path up to Greenwood," Salt said. "It's a bit of a hike."

"Yes, I remember," Alison said.

The skies overhead were gloomy, but the fog was only a wisp, and as Alison started toward the inn the stranger fell in step beside her.

"Are you planning to stay long?" Alison asked, eyeing the two small bags he had insisted on carrying himself.

"Perhaps. I don't know."

"Have you ever been here before?"

He gave her a quick look. "Yes. I have."

"My name is Alison Blair. I'm staying the summer."

"Chris Dumont," he said.

She had to hurry to keep up with his long, impatient strides — he seemed terribly eager to reach Greenwood. But he said nothing the rest of the way. Behind them, Salt and Roy followed with Alison's luggage.

A large dog of uncertain pedigree came barking to greet them. He sniffed at Chris for a moment and then charged at Alison.

She laughed at the welcome. "Easy, boy."

"He likes you," Salt called up the path to her. "Old Duggan doesn't do that often."

Old Duggan fell in step beside Alison, touching his nose to her hand and lolling his tongue from his mouth with a playful expression. She stroked him occasionally and he barked with pleasure.

Halfway to the inn they passed a small house a few steps off the path. When Alison asked about it, Salt told her that Reba Zeller lived there.

"Me too," Roy spoke up.

"She owned it before she bought the inn," Salt explained.

At last, puffing a little, they reached the Greenwood Inn. Chris Dumont held the door for her and Alison stepped inside a cozy living room - lobby with a stone fireplace and comfortable rustic furniture. The room offered a view of the lake and set the tone for the place. Lamps burned low, an old musket hung over the mantel, and the walls were a rich, dark paneling. The floors were of native pine, scrubbed and waxed and covered here and there by throw rugs.

"Reba will be along in a moment," Salt said. "But I can show you your room now if you like —"

"Yes, thank you."

She followed Salt into one of the wings, down a narrow hall that branched off from the center of the inn, Roy following. After making one sharp turn down another corridor, Salt stopped at the last door on the left, twisted the knob, and went in ahead of her. Roy deposited her luggage in a lump on the floor. The room was medium-sized and would do nicely. One window gave her a fair view of the lake and the other looked out on the island itself. She saw that another house was very near, nestled in the trees that grew so abundantly on Windswept Island.

"Who lives there, Salt?"

He straightened for a moment and gazed at the house before answering, "The Meadowses."

"Oh, yes, someone in town mentioned them to me."

"Did they?"

"Does anyone else live on the island?"

"Precious few. It's not a large place and there are problems connected with living on an island. You can't go anywhere except by boat. Most of the island is

21

owned by a man in New York who never comes here and doesn't bother to develop it. So we're sort of remote, Miss Blair.''

"What are the Meadowses like?''

"An older couple — at least, David Meadows is in his eighties. His wife is about my age — in her sixties, I should imagine. Now if you need anything, you can find Reba around somewhere. I'll tell her you've arrived. And if you're wanting supper, Reba will feed you in a half an hour or so. The dining room is left of the lobby where we came in.''

Salt moved to the door and motioned to Roy. "Come on, Roy.''

The man had been staring at Alison ever since they had come into the room, and she had given him an uncertain smile that he had returned readily, boyishly.

Roy took his time in leaving and Salt finally tugged him away and closed the door behind them. Alison looked around with interest. Her room was situated so there would be some measure of privacy, but she saw at once that she'd need something to use as a desk. She would ask Reba Zeller for a card table.

The room had apparently been redone recently, for the walls were paneled with modern materials. One closet was so large she could walk inside it, and there she found old, cracked plaster and rusted rods and hooks. But the other closet was new and near a small, modern bath. The bed seemed comfortable enough and she felt that her stay should be very pleasant. What really interested her was the rest of the house, for Leighton Thordsen had built the place for himself, and she was extremely anxious to see the music room where he had done his work.

The other time she had visited the island, the building had been closed and she had been able to catch only a glimpse or two through a window. Now she had the summer to explore and probe the memory of Leighton Thordsen.

Reba Zeller knocked on her door five minutes later. She was a buxom woman with gray hair in disarray and the clean, open face of a person who worked long and hard and spent much of her time over a hot stove.

"So glad you came, Miss Blair."

"Alison," she said. "I'm looking forward to my stay."

"I know you want to see the place and I'll be glad to give you a tour tomorrow. Right now, I have supper to serve."

"Do you have a lot of guests?"

"Two couples who are leaving tomorrow and then, of course, Chris and yourself. I really don't have the place ready for very many people and I've been very selective about guests. But you seemed so anxious to come."

"Yes. I've told you how interested I am in collecting material about Leighton Thordsen."

"I'm afraid I can't help you much there. What I know has just been handed down. I wasn't living in Donnerville or anywhere around here when Thordsen had this place built. That's been several years now."

"And he lived here until —"

"About seventeen or eighteen years ago," she said. "The place went downhill fast. There was a man from Chicago who started it up as an inn, but he ran into financial difficulties. It set empty for several years after that and the vandals went to town. You wouldn't believe what a mess it was when I took it over. They stole everything they could haul down the cliff and put into a boat.''

"What a shame!"

Reba shrugged. "They told me I was crazy to take on a place like this, but it was something I thought I'd like to try. I own that little house just down the path and to the left, and when this place came up for sale, I decided to take a chance. Then, too, I thought it was something Roy could help with. I guess you've met my brother."

"Yes."

"Poor Roy! He really does try. Anyway, I wasn't here more than a couple of days before I knew that the people who said I was crazy to buy it were probably right."

"I'm interested in the music room where Thordsen worked."

"That's one place the vandals never bothered as much as the rest. Even his piano is still there — scarred and out of tune and needing repairs, but there —"

"I'd love to see it!"

"Help yourself. Turn right at the lobby and you'll find a round room with many windows. That's it. It's probably got the best view in the place. The door's closed, but go right in and look around all you want."

When Reba had gone, Alison wasted no time in locating the music room. Pushing open the door, she paused for a moment, eagerly taking it all in.

The room was bare except for the piano and a few straight chairs and some empty cardboard boxes, but her imagination was vivid, and what little she had been able to read about the room transposed out of her memory to the scene before her. She closed her eyes and imagined the room as it must have been once — a grand room, with silk hung at the windows, paintings over the mantel, and polished floors reflecting the gleaming wood of the piano. She could even imagine the smell of candle wax, the smoke of the fire, the glow of red wine in a crystal decanter, the sound of laughing voices, and above all, music as only Thordsen could compose and play it.

Maybe it was the gloomy weather outside, or perhaps it was ghosts, but for one uncanny moment she *knew* what it was like to see Leighton Thordsen in this room, to hear his piano. The tremendous feeling of being close to him made her chest tighten and brought a lump to her throat.

She went to the keyboard. With a feeling of awe and wonder she lifted the cover and through the film of dust found the yellowed keys. Some of the ivory was missing, but surprisingly, when she struck a chord, the sound was better than she had expected. Could it be that Leighton Thordsen had actually sat at this piano and composed his last work — here at this very spot?

Another ripple of excitement went through her. If she'd had any doubts at all about coming, they were gone. If only Regan could be here this moment to feel what she felt, she thought, perhaps he would understand.

Alison would have stayed in the room much longer if Salt hadn't appeared to remind her that supper was being served.

She left the place reluctantly and found the dining room, a large area that extended out to a cozy glassed-in porch where Reba preferred to serve the meals.

Chris Dumont was there as well as the two other couples, who spoke politely but seemed interested in only themselves. The food was tasty and ample. Reba did it all, and Alison wondered at the woman's indefatigable abilities.

As Alison ate, spreading homemade bread with thick jam and enjoying a last cup of coffee, the fog deepened. At the table next to the window, Chris had finished his meal and sat smoking his pipe, staring out toward the lake, a man lost in his own thoughts. He struck Alison as being moody. Was he terribly lonely or just seeking peace and quiet? Who could tell?

"More coffee, Alison?" Reba asked, appearing beside her.

"Thank you, no. Would you sit down and join me?"

"If only I could! I usually have some help in the evenings, but my waitress quit on me. So I have it all to do."

28

"The piano in the music room — are you certain it's the same one Thordsen used?"

"So they tell me. Moving pianos into a place like this isn't an everyday occurrence, you know. Moving it out would present the same problems. So I guess it was easier for Thordsen and the vandals to just leave it where it was."

"But it's priceless! It should be preserved."

Reba gave her a tired smile. "So should everything here, but unfortunately, it takes a lot of time and even more money."

Reba moved away to tend to other matters and Alison finished her coffee. She wanted to go back to the music room, but the trip was beginning to catch up with her and the excitement of finally arriving on Windswept Island was wearing on her nerves. With the damp fog closing in around them, the coziest thing she could think to do was go to bed and fall asleep.

But somehow Alison couldn't make herself go back to her room just then.

Beyond the porch was a kind of patio that reached out to the very edge of the cliff. She went to lean against the damp railing, the water below barely visible through the thickening fog.

Chris came to stand nearby, his pipe clenched in his teeth, and she flashed him an uneasy smile.

"I hope it's not like this often. I'm no lover of fog."

"Tomorrow will be beautiful. It's like that here."

"You seem to know quite a lot about this place."

"I spent the best two weeks of my life here once. In a stretch of perfect weather. It's not a place a man forgets."

"You've never been back since?"

There was a look of pain across his face, as if he had remembered something he'd sooner forget.

"No, I haven't."

"Where are you from?"

"The Midwest. A suburb of Chicago."

"Is this just a vacation?"

He rapped his pipe against the iron railing and thrust it into his pocket.

"More or less," he murmured.

Then he was gone, walking away quickly, and Alison had a feeling that she had asked the wrong questions. He was not a friendly man and yet, for some reason — perhaps the haunted look in his eyes — she felt sorry for him.

The dog, Old Duggan, came to sit at her feet and lean his head against her. Alison decided that it was, indeed, time to go to bed as a tiredness overcame her that couldn't be put off.

Closing the door to her room behind her, she discovered it had no workable lock, so she propped a chair under the knob. She unpacked and took a warm bath. To lull herself to sleep, she dropped a cassette of Leighton Thordsen's music into her small tape recorder, and with his lovely haunting notes ringing in her head she dropped off.

The recorder shut off automatically, the night fog kept rolling along the lake, and the inn settled down for the night. Alison awakened once to hear Old Duggan barking at something or someone, but she turned over and slept deeply again.

She had no idea how long she had been asleep before something was tugging at her consciousness, demanding she awaken. At first she thought the television had been left on until she remembered there wasn't one in her room. As she sat up with a sleepy yawn she heard the sound again.

Could it be coming from the next room? But no one was there, she was certain. Chris's room was directly across the hall, but the sounds, the voices, the strange vibration of it all, was not coming from there. It was right there in her room!

"I don't like this!" a voice said woefully, echoing. "I don't like this. I want to be free . . . free . . . free . . ."

There was the muffled sound of another voice, a stern, angry voice, followed by a kind of sob and then metal clanging on metal, echoing into the room, grinding on Alison's nerves, but it was impossible to determine the source. It was all around her like a cloak, a nightmare that had her in its grip.

All of a sudden a high, screeching scream scraped across her already jangled nerves. It was too much. She leaped out of bed, snatched her robe, and ran barefoot to the door. She struggled to open it, forgetting about the chair propped under the knob. The hall was quiet. A dim light burned at the far end. She had no idea if Reba stayed at the inn or down at her own small house, but she went in search of her anyway.

The inn was stingy with night lights, and Alison bumped into the lobby furniture. She found the kitchen, but still had no idea where to find the manager.

Rubbing at the gooseflesh on her arms, she wished that Old Duggan would appear to keep her company. Finally she decided simply to knock on the first door she could find and get someone up, but as she raised her fist to do so, she realized how wild and ridiculous her story would sound. Could she have been dreaming? She brushed back a lock of dark hair and tried to reason with herself.

The thing to do was to return to her room and face whatever it was in there. She swallowed hard and started back. Making the sharp turn in the corridor to the left, she ran into something solid, something that had arms and strong hands and breathed.

She screamed.

"Easy, easy," Chris Dumont said. "It's only me."

But remembering Chris's unfriendly face with its burning, haunted eyes, she found little comfort in being held tightly in his grasp.

3

"Let me go!"

Chris held her tighter. "What is it? What's wrong?"

"Nothing," she said. "Just let me go!"

"Sure," he said. His voice went cold and hard.

Alison didn't explain why she was prowling around at that time of the night and didn't give him a chance to ask. She wrenched herself loose and hurried back to her room. Timidly, she pushed open the door. It was all very quiet inside. She stood for a few seconds, listening intently, but there were no more strange noises. She began to think it had been only a dream after all.

She put the chair under the knob again and went back to bed, where she lay wide-eyed and intent, straining to hear the least unusual sound. But there was nothing. She began to relax and, finally, sleep overcame her. When she awoke again, it was morning.

The fog had lifted, and she was glad to see a deep blue sky mirroring the clear aquamarine of the lake. Dressing quickly, she went down to breakfast in the empty dining room.

"You're up early," Reba said.

"Not really. I'm anxious to explore the island. When I visited here before I wasn't able to see much."

"There are paths all over the place. And you can't get lost. You can see Greenwood from almost anywhere on the island," Reba said. "I hope you had a good night's sleep," she added.

Alison started to tell Reba about the strange noises she'd heard, but just then Chris Dumont appeared, wearing casual slacks and a shirt open at the neck. He glanced at her for a moment and she gave him a curt nod.

"Coffee, Chris?" Reba asked.

"Yes, please."

Reba hurried away to wait on him and

Alison quickly finished the rest of her breakfast. Then she left the dining room and set out for a walk around the island, where the brilliant sunshine and fresh air dispelled the last lingering memories of the frightening night she had just experienced.

She paused often to look at the serenity of the lake. Pine trees grew abundantly, giving off a sweet scent as the sunlight poured down on them. Squirrels and bright-winged birds were everywhere. Circling the island, starting to the left, Alison came unexpectedly upon a small cottage nestled among some stony boulders and shaded by an ancient oak. A young girl sat on the front step, drying her long blond hair with a towel and a brush.

"Hi," she called.

"Hello," Alison said. "Sorry, I didn't mean to come bursting in on you like this."

The girl shrugged and gave her a smile. "No matter. You're fron Greenwood?"

"Yes. I'm exploring the island, taking this path and that. I didn't realize this one would bring me to a house. I didn't see it until I was upon it."

"I'm Joni King," the young woman said. "I'm just back from my morning dip in the lake. There's a path over there that goes down to a little cove. Perfect for swimming."

The cottage looked very spartan from the glimpses she had through the open door, and Alison suspected that Joni King lived very simply.

"Are you a native of the island?" she asked.

"Just for a little while," Joni answered. "I like it here though, and I might decide to stay. I can't seem to find my spot, but I keep looking." Her blond hair glistened in the sunlight. "I dropped out of college," she continued. "Now I do a little craft work — crazy things with wood and feathers and seashells and anything else that interests me. I have a friend in Donnerville who sells some of it for me."

"Well, it's a small world! You're talking about Lois Martin, aren't you? I met her yesterday and I saw some of your things. They're fabulous!"

"Thanks. Lois has been able to sell

enough of my stuff to keep me going. I don't need much — maybe that's why I like Windswept. It's good to get down to basics and you can do that here."

Joni King finished brushing her hair and tied it back with a bright ribbon. Alison heard someone else coming down the path and turned around to find a young man with a camera bag slung over his shoulder wearing chopped-off jeans, sturdy hiking boots, and a grin that was quick and friendly. He had blond curly hair and warm brown eyes.

"Ah, you have company, Joni," he said.

"Good morning, Bob, you're out early. Have you been shooting already?"

"I caught the sunrise — perfect. The fog was lifting, the sun came up blood red — even the gulls made their entrance on cue. Perfect clips!"

"Bob, this is — sorry, I don't know your name," Joni said.

"Alison Blair."

"Bob Beale," the man said. "You've just about met the entire population of the island. There's hardly anyone here but Joni and myself and, of course, the

Meadowses — and the couples at Greenwood."

"Oh, don't forget Stone," Joni said with a wry smile. "No one could overlook him!"

Bob laughed, showing a row of straight white teeth. "Stone looks after the Meadows couple and he surely has a first name, but no one seems to know it. Everyone calls him Stone and the name suits him."

"Are you a filmmaker?" Alison asked with interest.

"I've done some documentaries, even won a few awards in Hollywood, but then things went sour and I came here looking for something fresh. Windswept seemed like a good candidate."

"It's a lovely place!"

"And you?" Bob asked.

"Writer. I'm here on a summer project."

"Ah, that's great," Bob said. "Frankly, Joni and I are starved for companionship with someone besides the usual lot that come to the inn."

Bob draped an arm around Joni's

shoulders in such a way that Alison suspected they were more than casual friends.

"We'll have to have a real rap session one of these days soon," Bob said. "Right now, I've got to go and develop my film. I'm anxious to see how it came out. See you two around."

Bob Beale was gone almost as quickly as he appeared. Joni lifted her arms over her head and stretched lazily.

"I think I'll sack out for a while. I couldn't sleep last night —"

"Matter of fact, I didn't sleep well either," Alison said, remembering the strange sounds in her room. "I'll see you, Joni."

Alison returned to her tour of the island, spotting the cottage where she was certain Bob Beale must live and coming around the point once again toward Greenwood. As she passed the little house that Reba owned, she waved to Roy, who gave her his childish smile. Roy had to be in his fifties, judging from his salt-and-pepper hair and the lines in his face, but he acted like a young boy.

Returning to Greenwood a little tired from her hike, which had been longer than she had anticipated, Alison went in search of Reba and found her in the kitchen, already at work on the noon meal.

"Reba, I've got a request."

"Sure, what can I do?" Reba asked.

She explained her need of a small table for her typewriter and Reba promised she would provide something.

"Another thing. I know this must sound crazy, but I heard funny noises last night — they seemed to be in my room."

Reba straightened and stared at her. "What did you say?"

She explained what had happened and Reba shook her head. "You must have been dreaming, Alison."

"I don't think I was."

The phone was ringing and Alison felt that Reba was glad to have an excuse to hurry away and answer it. Had she been evasive about the noises? Somehow Alison sensed that Reba had received similar complaints before.

While Reba was busy on the phone, Alison found herself drawn again to the music room. Bright sunlight streamed through the windows, and she had an overwhelming sense of what the room had been like once. Coming here was going to set the mood and help her bring all the material she had already collected into something solid and meaningful. As she stood there in the shafts of sunlight, touching the old piano, she suddenly knew what she wanted to do.

She rushed away to find Reba again, and when she explained her idea, Reba stared at her with surprise.

"Oh, I don't know —"

"I'll handle all the cost myself."

"I don't see what it would hurt, but it will be expensive, I'm sure. But if you want to, go ahead."

"I'll need to find a piano tuner. Is there one in Donnerville?"

"I'm not sure. Check the phone book. And if you want to go with Salt today, he's already gone down to the dock."

"I'll see if I can catch him."

By the time Alison had reached the dock, rushing down the steep path, Salt was just tossing in the mooring line and she shouted, "Wait up, Salt."

"You darned near got left," he said.

"Thanks for waiting," she panted as Salt helped her aboard. "How long will you be on the mainland?"

"Takes me an hour or so as a rule to run all the errands, and I'm to bring a passenger back with us. He's to be on the dock at eleven o'clock."

"That should give me enough time. Salt, you don't know a good piano tuner, do you?"

Salt arched his reddish brows with surprise. "Used to be an older man, Reeves, Herman Reeves, that did that kind of work. He and his son run a music store in Donnerville. You might ask there."

"Thanks. I'll do that."

That boat ride to Donnerville was in sharp contrast to her trip to the island the night before. The water was smooth and brilliantly blue, and Salt wasted no time skimming the five miles to Donnerville.

Alison walked the short distance from the dock to the shopping area of the city, and it was easy to find the Reeves Music

Shop. A bell jangled overhead as she went inside, where there was a good assortment of instruments, ranging from baby grands to clarinets. There was also a sheet music department as well as a supply of records. A man in a neat business suit came toward her, his brown hair carefully brushed. He smiled at her from behind horn-rimmed glasses.

"May I help you?"

"I'm looking for a piano tuner," she said. "I was told that someone here —"

"My father," he said with a nod. "He's out right now, but if you'd like to leave your name and phone number —"

"I'm staying at the Greenwood Inn. There's a piano there in a very bad state and I wonder if he would look at it for me."

"Leighton Thordsen's piano?" the young man asked with interest.

"Why, yes, do you know about it? But of course, you probably would —"

"I heard it was left behind when Thordsen left so unexpectedly. My father tuned that piano when Thordsen lived there several years ago."

"Your father knew Leighton Thordsen?"

"Yes. At least as well as a piano tuner knows a man like that."

"How interesting! I'd like to talk to your father about Thordsen."

"I'll ask him to come over. Perhaps tomorrow. Would that do?"

"Wonderful!" she said. "I'd really appreciate it. My name is Alison Blair."

"Let me guess, you're a musician yourself."

Alison laughed. "Not really. I'm a writer, doing research for a book about Thordsen."

"Oh?"

"Then I can expect your father tomorrow?"

"Yes, unless we phone otherwise. By the way, here's my card with our phone number and address —"

She saw the man's name was Ed Reeves. He gave her an appraising smile that she took as a compliment. It had been so long since she'd paid any attention to any man other than Regan that she found the glance stimulating.

Ed kept her in the shop longer than she intended to stay, but his conversation was interesting and she was anticipating seeing his father. Finding people who knew Thordsen was one of the reasons she had wanted to come here, and already her trip was bearing fruit. By the time she could politely wrest herself away, she barely had time to do some shopping and return to the dock.

Salt was already there, pacing the wooden platform restlessly.

"Damn," he muttered. "It's like him to be late. He can be the most insolent man alive!"

"A guest at Greenwood?" Alison wondered.

"No. Stone. He looks after the Meadows couple. He's been away for a few days, some kind of emergency, I gather. He asked me specifically to take him back to the island this morning and he's not here!"

"Schedules do have a way of going awry, Salt," she said.

She sat down to wait, feeling in no real hurry, happy to soak in the atmosphere.

How had Thordsen found this place, how had he come to build such a house on this remote island? Had he wanted peace and quiet for his work? He was an eccentric man — Alison had managed to learn that much. He was moody and temperamental and superstitious about odd things. One of them was the number three. He refused to dine at a table laid for three, concert programs listing his performances skipped the third selection and went simply from the second to the fourth. He feared earthquakes, and loved women excessively — he had always had a female manager and secretary. These were just a few of the things Alison had already learned. On Windswept Island she hoped to learn still more.

A cab pulled up to the dock and Salt straightened, tugging his cap down sharply on his head.

"Here he is, finally," he said.

The man was slight of figure, wearing a gray suit and a gray tie. He carried one small suitcase and an umbrella that he used as a walking stick as he came toward them at an unhurried pace. Alison thought he looked English. He barely glanced at her and ignored Salt completely as he went straight to *The Maiden* and got aboard.

Salt swore under his breath, motioned to Alison, and tossed the mooring line clear.

"This is Stone," Salt said. "Stone, this is a guest at Greenwood, Miss Blair."

Stone gave her one appraising glance and she saw at once why Bob Beale felt the man had been aptly named. There was a hard look to his face and his cold eyes chilled her. He barely nodded and then turned his head and looked out across the water to their destination, standing stiffly, ignoring the comfortable seats. Alison might as well not have been there. She glanced at Salt, but he too had grown aloof. There was a strange mood in the boat, three people sharing the same vessel and yet miles apart. She sensed that Salt truly disliked Stone and it was possible that Stone, if he had any feelings at all, disliked Salt in return.

Alison was glad when the Greenwood Inn came into sight.

4

Chris Dumont had spent the day quietly studying the inn, watching and listening to all that went on. It was obvious to his business mind that it would take a great deal of work and even more capital to turn the place into something special. It was also painfully obvious that Reba Zeller had neither. How she had managed to acquire the place at all was a puzzle to Chris. But that part of it didn't really matter. He had to decide what he was going to do. The thought of coming had been flitting in and out of his head for the past several months, and the decision to come had not been easy to make.

Probably because he remembered all too well the last time he had visited Greenwood. Those two golden autumn weeks still burned like fire in his heart, even though all his common sense told him to forget them. It was behind him, and only bitter ashes remained.

Chris eased himself into one of the comfortable chairs on the patio and did some quick mathematics in a small notebook. Reba came up beside him.

"Oh, here you are, Chris. You're wanted on the telephone."

He looked at her with surprise. Only one person knew where he was — his secretary, Natalie. He went inside to take the call.

"Chris, you old devil! Why did you run out on me like that without a word?"

Chris gripped the phone tighter, not especially happy to hear his partner's voice on the other end of the line.

"How did you track me down, George? Did Natalie —"

"Don't be sore at her. I twisted her arm pretty hard, Chris. Look, we have to talk. This thing is getting to me. You just can't mean all the things you've been saying."

"I meant them, George. I'm selling out my interest in the company. Either you buy me out or someone else will. I'm

51

leaving the firm for good."

There was an angry silence on the other end of the line and Chris felt a headache beginning somewhere behind his eyes.

"I know you've had a rough year, Chris, but that's no reason —"

"It just won't work anymore, George. I want out. I have a lawyer already busy on the paperwork and it doesn't matter what you say."

"Listen, Chris, for God's sake —"

"I've heard all your arguments, I've considered them carefully, and I simply want out. Nothing's going to change that, George. For a while I liked what we were doing, but lately —"

"Okay, so I made a few bad investments, made a couple of wrong turns, are you going to hang a guy for that?"

"Let's be realistic, George," Chris said with a set jaw. "You pulled some shady deals without my knowledge and it was only by the skin of our teeth that we got out safely. I don't want any part of it!"

"Hell, Chris, it won't happen again. I gave you my word, didn't I?"

"Sorry, George. Now, if there's nothing more —"

"Don't hang up! Chris —"

Chris drew a deep breath. George Warner had been his friend since school days, right on through a stretch in the service. But then the bad times started. Everything Chris touched went sour. There was the long period of time as a POW and the vacant, empty man he had become when he was finally released and sent home. There was losing Amy — he winced at that thought. But the last straw was the company. Their business, a wholesale electrical supply house, had done well enough. Chris had been satisfied with the profit margin, but George had come down with a streak of greed. There were always shady deals involved in any business and Chris was not unaware of them. But when he discovered that George had betrayed him, he had been stunned and outraged and finally sick at heart and defeated.

"George, I don't want to argue anymore. It's finished as far as I'm concerned and I'm not changing my

53

mind," Chris said.

"You let Amy do this to you, Chris. You let her make putty out of you!"

Chris hung up angrily. Amy. His head reeled for a moment, the old hurt coming to tear at his heart with spears of pain. What made it even worse was the two weeks spent at Greenwood with her when he'd come home from the POW camp, those two weeks that she had made so ecstatically happy had been a mockery. She meant nothing of what she had said or done. Why else would she have told him six weeks later that she wanted out of his life?

Chris ran a cold hand across his brow and it came away moist. He had hoped not to have to talk to George again, but he should have known it wouldn't be that simple. Nothing was going right for him, nothing seemed to jell.

"Chris. Something wrong?"

He spun about to find Reba. She had been in charge of Greenwood for almost three years. She had sensed how much he and Amy loved each other when they had visited earlier and had gone out of her way to be nice to them. When he had suddenly reappeared unannounced the day before, she remembered him at once. But she could tell by the look on his face when she asked about Amy that Chris had lost her.

"I'm all right, Reba," he said.

"I'm not so sure about that. The way you looked last night when you came, all caved in, and now — do you want to talk about it? I'm a good listener."

"Thanks, Reba. I don't much want to talk about it. But there is something else —"

"Let's go sit on the patio. I've been on the run ever since early morning."

"All right."

In the bright sunlight, Reba sank in her chair and stretched out her aching feet.

"This place is too much for you alone, Reba," Chris said.

"Don't I know it! Roy helps, but you know how Roy is."

"How would you like to sell out, Reba?"

She gave him a quick, startled look. "I've invested a lot here — all of my savings plus much more. I'd have to price it for more than most would think it was worth. Why are you asking such a question?''

Chris fumbled in his pocket for his pipe and filled it, and when he had held a match to it he gave Reba a long gaze.

"I'd like to buy Greenwood, keeping you and Salt on as employees, and see if I can get the place going like it should be operated.''

Reba's mouth dropped and, with a laugh, she smoothed her ruffled gray hair and shook her head. "You're crazy, Chris. Do you know what you'd be getting into?''

"Yes, I think so.''

"I'm interested, of course. But what about Roy?'' she asked with a frown.

"I can't take him on as a full-time employee, Reba, but maybe I could find part-time work for him. There's a lot to be done here, but I'll do most of it myself. I'm a fair carpenter and I'd start right away getting more guest rooms ready. I'd redecorate and do whatever I could to preserve the flavor of the place. I don't want to spoil the mood —''

"You are serious, aren't you? Does this

have something to do with the fact that you've come alone this time?''

Chris clenched his pipe tightly between his teeth. ''That may be true, Reba, but I'd rather not discuss it. My business partner and I have had a parting of the ways and I'm looking for a fresh start. This time I want to do something different, something for myself. I love this place. I've never been able to forget it.''

They talked a while longer and Reba named her price. It was a few thousand more than Chris had hoped, but he expected to be able to get a loan for what he couldn't raise himself. He drew a deep breath.

''I'll take it, Reba.''

She stared at him. ''You really mean it?''

''I'd like you to run the kitchen. I want to get more people to come here to eat. We'll find you more help and we'll make some changes in the menu. Most of the guest rooms need work. Except for reservations already made, I think I'll close the rooms and concentrate on the dining end of it, at least for the rest of the summer."

They talked on enthusiastically for more than an hour. Then Reba left, promising to see about the legal end of turning Greenwood over to him. Chris sat very still for a long moment. He wondered if he had gone mad, taking on a project like this.

He knew that Alison had gone to the mainland with Salt, and when he heard the boat returning shortly before lunch time he watched for her. She strode up the path, the wind stirring her dark hair. There was something about the quick way she moved, the tilt of her head, and her searching glance that interested him. Was it because she was the direct opposite of Amy, who had been rather helpless and shy, whose hair was never out of place, who seldom looked anyone directly in the eye? He had found that refreshing once. Now . . .

"Hi," Alison said. "Isn't it a lovely day!"

"Much better than last night."

He saw a hint of color come to her cheeks.

"Exactly what *was* wrong last night?" he asked.

"Bad dreams," she replied too quickly. "Does Reba have lunch ready?"

"Soon. There's time for a walk. If you'll join me, I'd like to talk to you."

"Oh?"

He was aware that he had piqued her curiosity, but at the same time he sensed her hesitancy.

"It's rather important, since you're to be a guest all summer."

"What does that have to do with anything?" she demanded.

He took her arm and propelled her away from the inn down a short path where a bench leaned against a tree.

"I've bought out Reba Zeller," he said. "I'm going to run Greenwood. We've agreed on immediate possession."

"What!"

"I'm your new landlord. I'll be making some changes, but I'll do what I can to make your stay a pleasant one here."

She shook her head with surprise. "I hadn't expected anything like this! What about the piano in the music room? Reba agreed to let me use it this summer. In fact, I've hired a piano tuner to come tomorrow and fix it."

"If Reba agreed to that, so will I," he said. "Eventually, though, I'll want to do something with that room."

"It's an important room, you know! Leighton Thordsen worked there. Do you know its history? You wouldn't ruin it, would you? I mean . . ."

He shook his head. "I intend to restore the inn as much as possible the way it originally was. We both know it needs attention."

"My word!" she said again, staring at him. "You *are* full of surprises. But what about Reba and Salt?"

"I'll keep them on. I'll need all their help."

"I guess congratulations are in order."

Chris smiled. "Thank you. Either that, or I've taken leave of my senses!"

They talked a little longer before returning to the inn. Chris watched Alison disappear down the hall and he remembered the night before, when he had bumped into her in the dark and how frightened she had been. For one moment he had held her, felt her trembling, drank in the scent of her dark hair, her sweet breath on his face. There had been no one since Amy, and it had seemed strange to hold a woman in his arms again.

The news about the transfer of ownership buzzed around the small island quickly. At about four o'clock that afternoon a casually dressed man with fiery brown eyes came to seek Chris out, extending a hand.

"I'm Bob Beale. I live on the island and I just heard the news. Are you really taking over Greenwood?"

Chris stared at him with surprise. "How on earth did you hear that?"

"Oh, we have our own little grapevine here," Bob said. He peered around the inn for a moment, taking it in with eyes that were like radar, sensing out every last item.

"You'll make changes?"

"Some."

"I'd like to do a series of photographs on this for a travel magazine I work for occasionally. A sort of before-and-after story."

"I don't understand."

"I'm a photographer. Free-lance right now. I'm looking for good subject matter and I've a hunch you'll do right by this place. I'd just like to take a series of pictures, add a little article, and send it in. Okay?"

"I'm not sure —"

"It would be good publicity and, listen, fella, you'll need it. Things like this don't take off overnight, you know."

"I suppose I can consider it. We'll talk about it later."

"I should start very soon, even tomorrow. If you don't mind me nosing around with my camera —"

Chris knew that no matter what kind of arguments he came up with Bob Beale would outtalk him. It seemed simpler just to give in and agree.

Reba turned over some ledgers to him that afternoon and Chris left Bob to go over them. He and Reba would have a session together later and discuss things at length. There were many details to iron out, but he knew that Reba was eager to sell and he was certainly eager to buy.

All afternoon, his head still spun with what he had done. There were moments of utter despair when he knew he'd made a horrible mistake. Then, the next second, he was convinced that he belonged here and needed this challenge.

Supper was over. The night was filled with stars and the water had turned black, touched with bits of silver. He saw Alison on the patio again. She was leaning on the railing, staring out into the darkness, and there was something so lost and lonely about her that he felt drawn to her. He went out to stand beside her.

"The stars are thicker here," he said.

She started and seemed to pull herself back to the present. But he saw a glint of tears on her cheeks, and it was so unexpected that he instinctively stepped back.

"Perhaps you'd rather I didn't bother you —"

"I'm not very good company, I'm afraid."

"You're far away," he said. "Back

home perhaps?"

She lifted her chin and he saw the fire come back to her eyes for a moment.

"I was thinking of someone."

"Someone special," he said. "I know the feeling."

"You do?"

"Let me buy you a drink at the bar. That might help."

"Doubtful," she said in her practical way. "But thanks for being . . . kind . . ."

There was nothing for him to do but walk away and leave her alone. Salt fixed him a long, cool drink at the bar and he sipped it slowly. There was sweet, melancholy music playing on a tape deck, a perfect match for the evening, but he felt restless and uneasy. It had been a day to remember, a day when he had plunged into something new, probably over his head, but it was a fresh beginning.

He looked beyond the open French doors to the patio where Alison was still standing, the wind stirring her hair. His thoughts turned to the night before, when he had bumped into her in the dark hall, and he felt once again a stirring inside, a little nudge against his heart, just enough to tell him that he wasn't completely numb after all.

5

Alison didn't know why she felt so melancholy, but she did and most of it centered about Regan. She was sorry that they had parted in anger and she wished he had understood her need to come to Windswept Island. But there was no point in shedding tears over it. The sooner she put it behind her, the better. She only hoped that the changes due for Greenwood weren't going to affect her summer. But Chris had promised her the use of the piano and her thoughts turned excitedly to the reason she was there. Her anticipation at seeing Herman Reeves, the piano tuner, grew sharper.

Herman arrived the next day at about ten o'clock, coming in a small boat that he apparently used for fishing. Alison was surprised to find his son, Ed, with him. She waited for them at the lobby door as they came up the steep path, Herman puffing a little, Ed carrying his father's tools.

"Good morning," Ed said with an easy smile. "I decided to bring Dad over. I got to thinking about Thordsen's piano and was curious to see it."

"I just hope you're not going to tell me that it's beyond repair." Alison frowned.

"I'll have to take a look," Herman replied. "I don't expect to find it in very good shape."

Alison took them to the music room, and Herman stood for a moment looking about, a wistful expression on his face. He was a white-haired man with round shoulders, a gentle face, and weary eyes behind wire-rimmed glasses.

"I remember so well coming to this room when Leighton Thordsen was here," he said.

"Dad has a memory like an elephant," Ed said with a grin. "He can probably even tell you what color ties Thordsen wore."

"Red. He had a passion for red," Herman said. "He was a man with a very vibrant personality. More so before he came here, they say. Well, let's take a look and see what we have."

Ed paced about restlessly as his father probed inside the piano and Alison held her breath. Having Thordsen's piano in working order was something she had never dreamed of, and she was anxious for Herman's diagnosis.

Finally Herman lifted his head and gave her a nod.

"I can fix it. May be a little expensive, but I think I have most of the parts in stock."

"Oh, wonderful! How long will it take?"

"A few days," he said. "I'm not a fast worker, Miss Blair."

"But he's very painstaking," Ed said. "I'm sure you'll be pleased."

"Always the salesman," Herman muttered rather sourly. "I'll stay today and tomorrow I'll bring some of the parts I'll need. You'd better get back to the store, Ed. Pick me up at about four-thirty."

"Okay," Ed nodded.

But he didn't seem to be in any hurry to leave. He chatted with Alison, and she was aware again of how attractive he was. A kind of chemistry seemed to spring up between them.

It was apparent that Herman loved his work. His fingers were nimble and sure as they began to work inside the piano once again.

"Tell me more about Thordsen," Alison prompted. "I'm eager to hear anything you can remember."

Herman smiled. "I'll never forget the first time I saw him. He wasn't anything like I thought he'd be. He played so robustly, though he was rather a small man. And frailer than I had expected."

"Perhaps because he was in bad health?"

"Not that anyone could really detect. It is true that he died shortly after he left here unexpectedly and went to Venice. But when I knew him he was energetic, high-strung, and brimming with life."

"No one seems to know why he went to Venice. Was it a whim?"

"All I know is that he decided one day he was going and he simply picked up and went. There was some talk —"

"Gossip?"

"Thordsen was always involved with some woman and there were whispers of a scandal. I don't know if this was true or not."

"And the woman in the picture?"

Herman shook his head. "They said she was married to a very prominent man in Donnerville. Personally, I always thought he might be sweet on his secretary. He looked at her in a special way and she at him and . . . well . . ."

"Dad's a romantic, Alison," Ed said. "Sometimes I think it affects his imagination."

"What was the secretary's name?" Alison persisted.

"As I recall, it was Miss Benson. I can't think of her first name — perhaps I never heard it. Thordsen always called her by a pet name, Little Mouse."

"Do you know anything about his last work?"

"Ah, yes, 'The Rains of Spring,' "

Herman said. "He wasn't happy with it but was determined to finish it."

Ed came to lean on the piano and stared at his father curiously. "You never told me you knew anything about Thordsen's last work!"

Herman shrugged his thin shoulders. "Maybe because you have a way of not listening when I talk, boy," he said.

"Are you saying that Thordsen completed that last composition?" Alison asked eagerly. "Are you positive? I've been trying to find out about this, to be sure —"

"I can't be sure and there have been rumors both ways. Some say he destroyed it in a fit of temper. He was the sort that could do it."

"But he was a proud man and proud of his work," Alison pointed out.

"That's why I don't think it was ever destroyed. That's somebody's wild idea. Another rumor says that Miss Benson has it and will release it someday when the value of it has gone way up."

"Wait a minute," Ed said with a scowl. "If that music really exists, it would be worth a fortune!''

"I couldn't guess how much," Herman said. "But the question is, where is it? Probably lost for good. But who knows, Thordsen might have pulled some crazy stunt and hid it somewhere — maybe in this very house."

Alison straightened with surprise. "Would he do such a thing?"

"I wouldn't put anything past him. The longer he lived here, the more eccentric he got."

"Dad, that doesn't stand to reason. If he'd hidden the manuscript here, it would have been found by now."

"Who says?" Herman demanded, looking at his son over his glasses. "Thordsen didn't always put his music on paper. He kept it in his head, especially new work. Maybe 'The Rains of Spring' was never written down."

"He was a genius," Alison sighed. "A real genius. I wish that music *could* be found. His very last work —''

"It would be the find of the music world!" Ed said with fervor. "It would be welcomed with open arms in all the important concert halls. Think what kind of money would be involved —"

"Ed, you put dollar signs on everything," Herman said reprovingly. "Anyway, it's not likely to happen. More than likely it died with Thordsen over there in Venice."

"Still . . ." Ed said, a kind of awe in his voice.

"You'd better get back to the store," Herman insisted.

Ed nodded. "Okay, Dad, I'm going. I'll be down at the dock at four-thirty to pick you up."

Alison followed Ed out of the music room, leaving Herman to his work. Ed had grown thoughtful and she knew he was thinking about the lost manuscript.

"You will make a search for it, won't you, Alison?"

"Perhaps, if Chris will permit it. But I really don't expect to find anything."

"Listen, maybe I could help."

"Ed, I'm afraid you've let yourself get carried away."

Ed laughed and pushed his glasses back with a forefinger. "You're right, of course. Well, I'll see you later. And good luck with your book, Alison."

He hurried away down the path toward the dock. Alison watched him reach the boat, where he paused to talk to Roy Zeller, who often loafed there, swinging his feet over the water. Ed seemed to be talking seriously to him and Roy was nodding his head eagerly, almost with excitement. She wondered what their discussion could be about. They seemed unlikely candidates for just a friendly chat.

Roy always made Alison a little nervous and had from the moment she met him. He had a way of staring at her as if he had developed a crush on her. Reba told her to pay no attention to him, but it was hard to ignore a man who stood well over six feet and weighed in at two hundred and fifty pounds.

But she forgot about Ed and Roy when Chris came to join her for a moment.

"How did it go with the piano tuner?" he asked.

"Herman says it can be fixed," she replied.

"I'm sure you're happy about that."

"Yes, very happy."

Chris gave her a long, searching look and she remembered the way he had come to stand beside her the night before. She had sensed a kind of compassion in him that surprised her. The haunted look was still in his eyes, but he seemed excited about taking over Greenwood and it showed in the very way he stood, as if ready to spring into action at any second. He no longer seemed quite as lonely and forlorn.

"Have you officially taken over?" she asked.

"More or less. I've been poking around all over the place and making a few plans."

"I'd like to ask a silly question," she said.

He smiled. "Shoot."

"Is there a cellar here, or an attic?"

"Both," he replied with a curious look.

"I know this must sound a little crazy and I guess it is, but I'd like to search them for something that was left here years ago —"

"Something about Thordsen."

"Yes. It's a long story," she said. "Just before Thordsen left, he was working on a final composition. No one has ever found that work. He was an eccentric, and it's possible it's still hidden here somewhere."

Chris's gray eyes studied her for a moment. "You really believe that? It's hardly practical."

"I know, but would you mind if I looked?"

"Help yourself, but the cellar is a real clutter and it would probably be best to let me clear some of it out first. If I find anything in the process, I'll let you have it."

"Thanks. Who could ask for more than that?"

Herman stayed for lunch and Alison joined him. He talked more of Leighton Thordsen with a mixture of respect and awe.

"Thordsen was a very jealous man, especially where women were concerned. He didn't like anyone having more of the spotlight than he was getting, but maybe that's typical of people in the limelight."

"But you liked him, didn't you, Herman?"

"He had a certain quality, you see. I was just a lowly piano tuner, but he respected me. He seemed to admire anyone who could work with his hands. By his own admission, he couldn't fix anything."

Herman talked on about such little things, and Alison stored it all away in her memory. She might make use of it later when she wrote her book.

Herman stayed most of the day and then left at four-thirty, promising to return the next day.

"I'll have that piano working in no time, Miss Blair."

The thought of sitting down to Thordsen's piano was almost too much, but Alison couldn't stay away from it. She touched the keys and struck a few notes, some of them in working order, others dead and toneless. But Herman would soon have it so she could play it.

That evening she found Chris Dumont in

the dining room, occupying the largest table, but he wasn't eating. The table was spread with a large sheet of paper and he was busy with a pencil and ruler. His dark hair was ruffled, his tie loosened, and his shirtsleeves rolled at the cuffs.

"Could I ask your opinion on something?" he asked.

"I'm not sure what help I'd be —"

He showed her the drawings, and she was surprised to find a rather detailed sketch of Greenwood. He had penciled in the changes he wanted to make — mostly to get more rooms ready for occupancy and to add to the dining facilities.

"If I took out this wall, would it ruin the effect of things?" he wondered.

"I suppose it's all in what you really want to achieve. If you want to keep the place pretty much as it was in its heyday, I'd leave the wall. If you're going to modernize and put in a lot of tinsel and glitter, go ahead."

"No tinsel," he said flatly. "I don't want to ruin anything, Alison."

"I'm glad."

He flashed her a quick look. "Why do

you care so much about this place?"

"Because of Leighton Thordsen. I think the place should have been made a kind of monument to him long ago. I don't know why the people around here didn't do something about it instead of letting it go downhill."

"You resent the idea of this being an inn?" Chris asked sharply. "There's no money in monuments."

"Is money the only important thing in this crazy world?"

"I'm a businessman," he said. "And it's necessary to make money to exist. Or do you live on stardust and dreams?"

They glared at each other, eyes full of fire.

"You lead your life, I'll lead mine!" she said stiffly.

She turned away to her usual table and tried to eat the food Reba put before her. But it was difficult with Chris nearby, his face once more moody and dark. She wished she hadn't said what she had. Her practical side ruled her head most of the time, but her heart was subject to the romantic, the farfetched dreams.

Sometimes she felt as if she were two people, and this was one of those times.

It didn't help matters when Roy brought a plate of food into the room and sat down very near her, proceeding to eat without taking his gaze from her. Usually he ate in the kitchen with Reba, but she had heard them arguing earlier about something and apparently this was it. She finished her meal hastily and hurried away to escape Roy's devoted eyes.

The next day Herman returned, but he came alone and he didn't mention Ed. He seemed intent on getting the piano back into working order. He put in a long day, plunking monotonously at the keys to tune them properly. It finally drove Alison out of the inn for a walk late in the afternoon. It was another grand day and she found herself on the path to Joni King's cottage. As she walked, she sensed someone behind her, but when she paused to look back, there was no one in sight. By the time Joni's cottage came into view, she was positive she heard someone behind her and spun about again with a sense of fright. Had someone ducked into the brush to hide? Was it Roy Zeller? The thought did nothing to make her feel easier. Not that she was really afraid of Roy, but she wasn't comfortable around him either.

She hurried on until she saw Joni, and she began to feel easier. Joni was busy making candles of an unusual design, all very original.

"You're so ingenious!" Alison said admiringly.

Joni shrugged with a laugh. "I do my best. How are things at Greenwood?"

"You've heard about the new owner?"

"Yes. I hope he knows what he's getting into. That old place really needs work. They say the plumbing is terrible and the roof needs replacing. It's all rundown."

"I suppose so, but I still find it charming and quaint just the way it is."

"You don't like what's going to happen, do you?"

"If Chris Dumont changes it a great deal, I'll hate it!"

Joni finished with her candle and set it aside. Then she gave Alison a warm smile. "Why don't you stay and eat with me? It's just a simple beef stew I've been simmering over the fire all afternoon."

"Sounds delicious."

Joni led the way inside the small house. There were no carpets on the floor or curtains at the windows, but everything had a scrubbed, clean look. A fire blazed on the hearth, and she was surprised to see the stew bubbling in a pot hanging over it.

"No stove here," Joni explained. "I make do with what I have. It's primitive but rather fun. Everyone thinks they have to have all the modern conveniences to live, but they don't. I've found out the old ways are just as good if not better than the new ones."

They ate the stew from wooden bowls with heavy pewter spoons and there was no other food. None was needed. The meal was satisfying, the talk stimulating, and Alison knew that someday Joni King would probably emerge as a character in one of her books.

Before they had finished Bob Beale appeared. He put his camera bag aside and sat down with them at the table.

"There's more stew," Joni offered.

"Thanks, but I've had my supper. I was just out taking a long walk and thinking I should film the sunset. But I had a streak of laziness and wanted the joy of female companionship, so here I am. And what luck! *Two* women instead of one."

Bob gave Alison a long, friendly look.

"How is your film coming?" Alison asked.

Bob shrugged. "So-so. I lack a focal point. I have all kinds of footage and some of it has gone together quite nicely, but somehow it's a mishmash. Did you know I did some still shots at Greenwood today?"

"No, I didn't."

"I'm doing a before-and-after thing for a travel magazine. Chris didn't much want me to do it, but I talked him into it. He doesn't seem the type to own an inn."

"Why not?" Joni asked.

"He looks like a typical nine-to-five sort of man to me. Greenwood will ask for more — in money, energy, and sweat. He's bought a dead horse and doesn't know it."

"He might surprise you," Alison said.

"I'll make you a bet — name the stakes."

But Alison let the subject drop. Maybe Chris wasn't the man for Greenwood, but she wished him no ill luck. She couldn't shake the feeling that he was burdened with some deep unhappiness. Perhaps he needed the challenge of the inn and the busy, hard hours ahead.

Joni picked up a guitar and began to pluck the strings, and Alison leaned back to listen as she played folk songs, singing in a lively, happy voice. Now and then Bob joined in and Alison clapped her hands in time. They lingered on happily until darkness fell outside the window.

"Let me see you home," Bob said. "I know these paths as well as anyone around here."

"Thanks, I was wondering if I could find my way. Next time I'll bring a portable lantern or a flashlight."

"Come again soon," Joni said.

Alison called good-night and Bob came to take her arm and walk beside her. The night was balmy, and a sweet south wind blew against their faces as they walked along the path toward the lights of Greenwood.

"I'm glad you've come to our island," Bob said.

"I think it's going to be a very pleasant summer."

"Sometime soon, I'd like to show you some of my film."

"I'd like to see it. Have you known Joni long?"

"Ever since I came here. Joni's a free spirit. She's doing her thing, but she'll be the first to tell you that she might decide to pull up stakes and leave tomorrow. She's been here more than a year, and for her that's some kind of record."

"I rather envy her," Alison said.

Bob took her arm and laughed. "I think you're a free spirit too."

"Up to a point," Alison agreed.

"There's an art show on the mainland tomorrow. How would you like to go? We could stay over for dinner."

"It sounds interesting and fun — yes, I'd like that."

"Good!" Bob said and he tightened his grip ever so slightly on her arm. She was aware of his touch and his presence in the dark, and she was surprised at how much she anticipated seeing him the following day.

6

It was shortly after lunch the next day when Bob Beale appeared at Greenwood. It was the first time Alison had seen him dressed more than very casually, and she was struck by how handsome he was. He was without his camera bag and seemed intent on forgetting work and having a good time.

"My boat's down at the dock," he said. "If you're ready, Alison —"

Chris watched them leave, a scowl on his face, and Bob gave him a curt nod that Chris barely acknowledged.

"Brrr," Alison said. "What's with you two?"

"We seem to get on each other's nerves," Bob said. "He wants me to forget about photographing Greenwood, but a deal's a deal, and I could use a story like that right now."

"I would think the publicity would be good for his business."

"He's a loner," Bob said. "He'll never make it in a hundred years."

"You seem very positive about that."

"I know human nature, Alison. I've studied it from all angles and under all kinds of circumstances, and Chris Dumont is not cut out to be an innkeeper. Wait and see if I'm not right."

Alison and Chris struck their own kind of sparks. There was something about him that put her off and would perhaps put off others as well. Then there were other times when he seemed to come out from under his black cloud, and his smile became warm and sweet, and she liked him. But those times had been few and far between.

Bob's boat was small but fancy and put *The Maiden* to shame. He seemed to like the good things in life, and Alison sensed that for a while he'd had them and had probably been extremely successful in Hollywood. But by his own admission things had gone awry, and so he was on

Windswept Island, fighting for a comeback.

Bob started the motor and skillfully maneuvered away from the dock. In a moment they were skimming the surface of Thunder Lake, faster and more daring than Salt. Alison caught a glimpse of Roy watching them go, standing on the dock, with his hands in his pockets, a dull expression on his face.

"Salt would love this boat!" she shouted to Bob over the roar of the motor.

"I know," Bob said with a grin. "I've let him use it a few times when that old clunker of his broke down. He'd give his eyeteeth for it."

"Has he always lived around here?"

"I don't know," Bob said. "I haven't been here that long myself, but he seems to be a permanent fixture."

"This art fair we're going to, do you know any of the local artists?"

"No," Bob said. "But I'm always going to such things, hoping I'll find some budding genius, buy some of his work, hold it a few years, and sell it for a fortune!"

"Good luck!"

Bob smiled at that and spun the wheel to change their course across the water toward Donnerville. "I can use all I can get!"

The boat ride was exhilarating. It was another golden summer day that promised to be hot. It was apparent when they reached the dock that the tourist season was in full swing. Nearly every boat leaving the Donnerville dock was filled with various kinds of fishing gear and people eager to try their luck.

They walked two blocks to a garage where Bob kept his car, a sleek, expensive sports model.

"I drove here from California in this," he said. "Sometimes, when I get tired of the island, I come over and take a buzz down the Interstate to brush a few cobwebs out of my head."

"I take it this is part of your Hollywood style of living."

Bob smiled at that, his brown eyes dancing. "It was and it will be again one day soon. I'm not the kind that gives up, Alison. I scored there once and I will again, you can bet on it."

"I believe you," she said.

"What about you, Alison? What are your biggest ambitions? A best-seller? I bet you have one hatching in your head right now."

"All I can think about is Leighton Thordsen, his music and his life on the island. That's why I'm here — to soak up all the local color I can."

"It's been years since he lived on Windswept," Bob said. "What can you hope to find now?"

"Atmosphere if nothing else," she replied.

Bob shrugged. "Well, there is *that* on the island."

The art show was being held downtown on a street that had been roped off from traffic. There were a surprising number of paintings, and what was even more interesting was the range of talent displayed. Alison and Bob prowled up and down the street, arguing good-naturedly over their preferences, and Alison found Bob a likable and amusing companion. She hadn't had such a good time in a long while.

Bob bought three paintings that they stowed safely in the car. And Alison was ready to get out of the hot sun when Bob suggested they find something cold to drink. The bar was shadowy and cool. Piped-in music enveloped them, and in the deep leather booth they stirred the ice in their glasses and relaxed.

Bob talked a lot about Hollywood and his work there.

"You promised to show me some of your film," she said.

"And I will. I'm not at all shy about doing that," he said with a warm grin.

"If you don't believe in yourself, no one else will either."

"Alison, you're a girl after my own heart! Here's to you, new friend! Thank you for coming here. I look forward to the summer now — very much."

"What will you do when winter comes?"

Bob leaned back and looked pensive for a moment. She noticed the tiny lines at the corner of his mouth, the way his blond hair curled up from his forehead, his deep tan and his long, silky eyelashes.

"When winter comes, I'll leave the island. I could never winter there. It's too hard to get to the mainland, although some of the more adventuresome drive trucks or jeeps across the ice. I need to be where the action is. Summer's different — I can be out doing things. But winter —" He shuddered. "I think I'll go back to California. Whether I have work there or not."

"What about the other people on the island?"

"Joni wintered there last year and went weeks on end without seeing another soul. But she can do that — it doesn't bother her. She has her own special inner peace. I don't know what the Meadowses do. Reba closed everything and took her idiot brother to Donnerville. They have a small house there as well as the one they own on the island."

"I wonder what Chris will do?"

Bob leaned toward her, his straight, white teeth flashing. "My dear, Chris Dumont will be long gone — back to wherever he came from."

"Near Chicago."

"What's he doing here anyway? Who is he?"

"A lonely person."

Bob arched his brows at that. "How do you know?"

She could have told him that it took one to know one, but she didn't want to broach that subject. Their conversation turned to other things and the hour or so they spent in the cool room was pleasant. Alison was surprised to see how late it was when she finally glanced at her watch.

"Dinner is half an hour's drive away. Shall we get going? Or is it too soon for you?" Bob asked.

"I'd rather get back early, if you don't mind."

"I'd much prefer it. I hate to admit it, but I'm not the best captain on the lake in the dark."

The supper club was rather nondescript on the outside but surprisingly attractive inside. It was the kind of place that Regan would have liked and Alison was reminded that Bob Beale was not unlike him.

"Is Hollywood really as glamorous as

everyone says?" she asked as they waited for their after-dinner coffee.

Bob shook his head. "Certainly not now. Perhaps once it was. I would like to have worked there in the forties and fifties. Maybe even as far back as the thirties."

"Who knows," she said with an impish smile. "When they film my best-seller, perhaps you'll be the man behind the camera."

"It's a deal, Alison Blair. I'll wait for that."

"You'll probably have a very *long* wait."

His dark eyes smiled at her and there was something about his glance that set her nerves tingling. "It will be worth the wait, Alison."

They left the club at sunset and drove away in Bob's car. Alison marveled at the beauty of the sky, the brilliant colors, the clean soft air, the mirror of the lake.

She watched the sky change from reds to purples to grays as the boat bounced along across the water. Bob normally docked the boat over on his side of the island but this night he took her home by way of the inn's pier. They climbed leisurely up the path toward the lights, and when Bob draped an arm casually around her shoulders it seemed natural and nice.

"Whew! I always forget that this climb is so steep," he said. "It might have been best to have walked from my place back to Greenwood."

"Good for us after all that food," she said.

"Why are you always so practical?"

"Can't help it. I have a streak of that in me."

"And other than that streak?"

"Pure sentimentalist," she sighed. "And that's where the trouble starts."

"Why do you say that?"

Regan crossed her mind, and the bitter words they'd flung at one another, but she didn't want to remember now.

"Isn't that Joni?" she asked.

"What's she doing here?" Bob wondered aloud. "It's not like her. She avoids this place like the plague — too many people, too much civilization."

But Joni was very much present,

wearing her usual garb of faded jeans and moccasins.

"Hi," she called.

Alison had the distinct feeling that Joni's presence was no accident. She was waiting for them, but when they joined her she pretended otherwise.

"I'd promised Reba a candle, so I just delivered it," she said. "I'm on my way home. Are you going that way, Bob? Could I beg a lift in your boat?"

"Why not?" Bob said. "It was a great day, Alison, one I'll remember."

Then he bent his head and kissed her cheek and gave her a wink that said even more. She smothered a laugh. He too had seen through Joni's pretense, and if he was surprised by it, he was hiding it very well. Alison had suspected from the beginning that Joni cared for Bob and just then she was certain of it.

From somewhere inside the inn Alison could hear the sound of a busy hammer, then the buzzing of an electric saw. She discovered Chris Dumont in one of the empty guest rooms, busily applying paneling to the cracked plastered walls.

He looked up, a dusting of sawdust in his black hair, his gray eyes looking vacant, almost bewildered.

They stared at each other for a moment. "You're back," he said.

"You certainly have your work cut out for you."

He said nothing. His aloofness put her off and she decided not to linger and even try to be friendly. Before going to her own room, she went to the circular room where Thordsen's piano waited. Herman Reeves had come that morning and was still there when she had left with Bob. Touching the keys, she found several more had been put into working order. If Leighton Thordsen was looking down from heaven, he would surely be pleased.

Almost at the first sound of a note, Roy Zeller appeared in the room as if he had materialized out of thin air.

"You play pretty songs?" he asked.

"A few, Roy."

"You know that man's music that used to live here?"

"Thordsen?" she asked with surprise. "Did you know Thordsen?"

"No." Roy shook his head. "I didn't know him, but I heard about him."

"I see."

"I can play," Roy said. "Chopsticks."

"Oh," Alison said with a smile. "When the piano's all fixed, you'll have to play for me."

"Sure. I'd like to show you how good I am," he said.

She left the piano then, knowing that Roy would keep her there indefinitely if she let him. She excused herself and hurried away, deciding to go outside for a moment.

Reba had finished in the kitchen. She joined Alison for a moment at the railing that overlooked the lake.

"It's muggy tonight," she said. "We're due for a rain."

"Better rain than the fog."

"Herman said to tell you that he wouldn't be back for a day or two — something about ordering some parts."

"Oh, that's all right. I think it's a miracle that he can even *fix* that poor piano."

"I think he's had better luck today than

Chris. He's worked so hard and hasn't made much progress."

Greenwood was very still and only a light or two shone on the lake. Now and then the distant sound of a boat drifted up to them. The sky was studded with stars and the quiet was intense. Old Duggan, who trailed Alison whenever he could, had come to lie at her feet, and she stroked his head and rubbed his silly ears. He breathed heavily in appreciation.

"I can see why Leighton Thordsen wanted to come here," Alison said. "There's a kind of quality about the island, a magic, a strange feeling that something very special is waiting. Do you ever feel that, Reba?"

Reba gave a short laugh. "Frankly, when you're faced with bad plumbing, falling plaster, broken appliances in the kitchen and any number of other trials, the spell sort of fades away."

"I've a hunch Chris wants to get it back."

"Poor fool," Reba said. "He'll work himself sick and I'm not sure he'll find it. I've tried to warn him. I couldn't have it on my conscience not to, you know, because the place is really in bad shape."

Alison stifled a yawn. The night air and the long, busy day were getting to her. She said good-night, patting Old Duggan good-bye, and found her way down the corridor to her room.

As she got ready for bed, she played some of her tapes of Thordsen's music. She felt a consuming need to play it with plenty of volume so as not to miss one single note, but she must have turned it up too much because Chris appeared at her door.

"Oh, sorry. I didn't mean to disturb anyone —"

"Let it play," he said. "It's Thordsen, isn't it?"

"One of his compositions as only he can play it."

Chris leaned in the doorway, listening, caught up in it, as if Thordsen had struck some special nerves. When the tape finished, Chris straightened.

"It's beautiful," he said. "I hadn't realized —"

"I have more tapes that I'll share with

you sometime."

"I'd like to hear them." He looked at his watch. "I don't know where the day went — or the evening, for that matter."

He said good-night and she closed the door. She went to bed with the tape playing softly, a soothing sound that relaxed her and lulled her to sleep.

She awakened once and the tape was still playing. But when she stirred the next time, the tape recorder had shut itself off. But there was a sound that jarred her nerves and brought her upright in bed, with her throat tight and her eyes open and staring into the darkness. At first she thought the storm had come up as Reba had predicted and the wind was howling around the corner of the house, rattling her windows.

Then she knew it was no storm, no wind, no rain — only that haunting noise she had heard before, a plaintive cry, a kind of sob — it was all around her — and her first and only thought was to escape.

She bolted for the door, fumbled with it, and finally got it open. This time she went to the nearest person she could find, which was Chris, for his room was directly opposite hers. She beat on his door with her fists and the palm of her hands, calling his name.

Within seconds he had opened the door, his dark hair ruffled, pulling on a robe over his pajamas.

"What is it? Alison, are you all right?"

"It's in there again, Chris. I swear I'm not dreaming —"

"Sh, sh," he said quietly. "It's all right. I'm here."

He put his arms around her and pulled her close and tight against him. For a moment or two she clung to him and she was aware of his hard muscles, the scent of his clothes, the brushing of his chin against her forehead. Then she backed away.

"Please, come and look. Would you just do that much? If I don't find out what that noise is, I'll go crazy!"

"Of course I'll come, Alison."

He went in ahead of her and stood very still, listening. There was nothing, no strange sound, only the thud of her heart, the ticking of her clock on the nightstand.

"I don't believe this! Chris, I swear, there was a terrible noise. I know there was —"

"Maybe it was the wind. Clouds were rolling up when I went to bed about half an hour ago."

"The wind," she echoed dully. "Sure, maybe it was the wind."

He put a hand against her cheek and smiled at her, gently, tenderly.

"Will you be all right now?"

His fingers were warm against her face and the sound of his voice unknotted the fear that had tightened in her throat. She nodded. "Yes, I'll be all right."

He took his hand away and she felt suddenly alone again. But she couldn't call him back without seeming silly and helpless, and she wanted to be neither in front of him.

"Good-night," he said.

The door closed behind him and Alison went to lean against it, wishing he had stayed a little longer. It wasn't the wind. Never in a hundred years would anyone convince her of that. But of what it was, where it was coming from, and why it came to haunt her, she had no idea. Just then she didn't even want to think about it. All she wanted was sleep, sweet, safe sleep.

7

The next few days passed uneventfully at Greenwood, and Alison did her best to put the strange sounds she had heard in her room out of her mind. Chris didn't mention them again and she was rather glad. He had his hands full and kept the place humming with activity, apparently bent on doing as much as he could in a very short space of time. She seldom saw him without tools in his hands or plans rolled up under his arm. There seemed to be a pent-up energy in him and a consuming need to work until all hours of the day and night. She wondered what drove him so hard and whether or not Bob Beale was right. Had Chris bought a dead horse?

He didn't encourage overnight guests, as he had most of the guest rooms in some state of repair. He was concentrating on the dining room and, although a few more guests were coming, the place seemed to be slow to catch on.

Herman Reeves had finished with the piano. His bill was staggering, but Alison paid it gladly for the privilege of sitting down at Leighton Thordsen's piano and putting her hands on the keyboard.

Herman had done an excellent job and the tone came out beautifully strong and clear. Alison began to put in some long sessions, closing the door most of the time to keep Roy out. He made a pest of himself whenever he could and always wanted to know if it was Thordsen's music. She ignored his questions and was always relieved when Reba sent him off on an errand.

Her music drifted out to the other rooms in Greenwood and sometimes Chris came to listen, pausing just inside the closed door, uncertain, drawn in at last, until finally he began to lean on the piano and watch as she moved her hands skillfully over the keys.

"You didn't tell me you were such an

accomplished pianist."

"I'm really not."

"You sound it to me. It's lovely. What music is that?"

"Thordsen's."

"Ah, I should have known," Chris said. "The man really has you in his grip, doesn't he?"

"I want to know everything about him, and his music is revealing. You can't help but sense the kind of person he was."

"You wanted to search this old place — I'm sorry I haven't had time to take you around."

"Soon?"

"Soon," he promised. "Lately I've just been run ragged —"

"When will you start in here?"

Chris looked around and went to peer out the windows and shook his head. "I don't know. But I won't do much — just a little freshening up. I won't destroy its mood."

"I'm holding you to that promise."

Chris smiled at her and she liked what it did for him. It chased away the shadows in his eyes, lifted the corners of his firm mouth, and brought a warm glow to his face.

"Well, here you are," a voice called to them.

Joni King appeared. She was dressed in her usual denim and the sunlight caught the sheen of her long, blond hair. She looked about with interest and gave Chris an appraising look.

"I just peeked into one of those rooms you're doing over. It's very nice."

"Thank you." Chris nodded.

"What else do you plan to do?"

"More than I can handle," he said. "I have some plans here —"

He spread them out on the top of the piano and told her in detail, his voice rising and falling with enthusiasm. Joni made a suggestion and Chris gave her an appraising look.

"That's a very good idea!"

"I studied decorating once. I thought about taking it up, but I didn't want to get that involved — you know, having the responsibilities of a shop and an office . . ."

"How would you like to help me?" Chris

offered. "I could use someone for the rest of the summer."

"You're kidding!"

Chris shook his dark head. "I'm dead serious. I'm trying to do this on a shoestring, and if you have some ideas about how to save money and still make this place attractive —"

"You know, I might just take you up on that."

They walked away, talking together, and Alison was more than a little surprised by this new development. Joni had made such a point of being out of the general run of things, of protecting her own privacy. Was working for Chris just a quirk, just something new to do? Or did she have some other motive?

Salt made a regular run to and from Donnerville every morning to bring the mail. Alison got a note from her parents, but there was nothing from Regan. Every day she felt sure that she would hear, and every day went by without so much as a postcard. She had written him when she first arrived, a quick, breezy kind of note

110

that she hoped would help ease the anger he'd felt at her departure. But Regan did not get over things easily, and apparently he wasn't yet ready to forgive her. She wondered sometimes if he ever would.

The days had begun to fall into a pleasant routine. Early in the morning, Alison took a quick hike around the island, often encountering Bob out on one of his camera expeditions. They usually ended up at Greenwood, having breakfast together. During the late morning she would work in her room, putting together notes she'd made on Thordsen. After lunch she spent hours at the piano and then lounged in the sunlight on the patio, Old Duggan at her feet.

She liked having Joni about, and they hit it off very well. Joni had been helping Chris at Greenwood for more than two weeks, although Roy didn't like the idea very much. But Roy simply was not able to do the work Joni did, although he had a hard time understanding that. After one particularly hectic day, Joni collapsed in a chair beside Alison.

"You know what we need?" she asked

with a tired sigh. "Some fun! Let's have a wiener roast down on the beach at my place. We can sit under the stars, swim, and relax. I'll ask Chris and Bob, and we'll make it a real party."

"Sounds great!" Alison replied.

Alison knew that Bob would be interested, but she rather doubted that Chris would come. But when Joni told him about it, he agreed it was a good idea.

So the next night Chris walked with Alison to Joni's place, swinging the basket of food that Reba had packed for them. He was determined to enter into the spirit of things, and for the first time since Alison had known him he seemed relaxed, almost happy.

"I haven't done this since I was a kid in school," he said.

"Then you've been missing out on the good things in life."

"I missed out on quite a few things," he said, and his voice went sad. She glanced at him, wishing she could read his thoughts.

"Why was that?"

"You wouldn't be interested in my life

story," he said.

"Why do you always shut people off?" she asked angrily. "Why wouldn't I be? I don't understand why you keep putting yourself down."

Chris bit hard on the stem of his pipe and seemed about to make an equally angry retort but thought better of it. They walked on in silence, and Alison was relieved when they reached the beach and joined Joni and Bob. A roaring fire crackled merrily. The sand was smooth and clean, the lake gleamed like polished marble, and the sloping beach was in sharp contrast to the cliff and the jagged rocks Alison saw so often at Greenwood.

"I hope Reba packed plenty of food," Bob said. "I'm starving."

"Reba usually isn't stingy," Chris said defensively.

"Look, I didn't mean it like that!" Bob replied.

"You usually enjoy taking potshots at me, in one form or another," Chris said in a calm but cold voice.

"Oh, shut up, both of you!" Joni broke in.

The two men exchanged glances, eyeing each other suspiciously. Alison had been aware of the friction between them before, but she couldn't figure out exactly why they disliked each other. For some reason, they simply rubbed each other the wrong way.

Joni took the basket from Chris's hand and smiled at him.

"It will be just fine, Chris. Thanks for bringing it and tell Reba thanks too, will you?"

Chris seemed to relax under Joni's warm voice.

"Sure."

Joni put the two men to work roasting the wieners. Passing boats made the water hit the beach with little slapping sounds. The sky was perfectly clear and promised another gorgeous sunset. There was a faraway feeling here, and Alison found her thoughts turning to Leighton Thordsen. Some of his music began to run through her head, the sweet clear notes echoing the mood of the island.

The fire blazed and snapped; the hot wieners burst their skins and were thrust into buns spread with mustard. Hot coffee was poured from Joni's pot, charred from many open fires. Never had food tasted as good. After dinner, Joni strummed her guitar and Bob sang lustily while Chris leaned back away from them and smoked his pipe.

"What are you thinking?" Alison asked.

He turned his head toward her, and in the firelight she saw the pain in his gray eyes, the stiff mask of his face. It was like looking at a stranger.

"I was remembering an army buddy of mine who made a guitar out of scraps and managed to get a tune out of it. He's dead now. They shot him when he tried to escape."

"Escape?"

"He was a POW. He always said he'd get home, that he'd fool them all, that he'd outlast anything they did to him, but he didn't. He wasn't a strong man and he wasn't as lucky as some —"

"I'm sorry," Alison said quietly.

Chris nodded. "So am I. Billy didn't deserve to die."

Joni stopped strumming the guitar and

put it aside. The stars were out and the warm wind caressed their faces. They all grew quiet, lost in their own thoughts.

Bob went to sleep with his head on Joni's shoulder. Chris barely stirred, and Alison's thoughts were locked into the island itself, the feel of it, the sound and smell of it, the gentle slap of water against the sand.

All of a sudden she heard something, a furtive footstep, the cracking of a branch underfoot. She straightened, listened, and heard it again, but no one else seemed to be paying any attention.

"Someone's out there." She gripped Chris's arm.

He stiffened and got to his feet. "I don't see anyone —"

"I tell you, I *heard* something."

By now Bob had awakened and he said, "Once in a while we get some crackpots over here, mostly vandals out looking for something to steal. Come on, Chris, let's investigate."

The two men struck off through the brush and trees that grew on either side of the path, and in a moment they were back with Roy between them.

"It's only Roy," Bob said. "What were you doing out here, Roy?"

Roy lifted his shoulders in a shrug and looked dumbly at them, from one to another.

"Just walking. I saw the fire. Just wanted to see who was here, that's all."

But Alison was almost certain that Roy had been spying on her, and the idea chilled her.

"Well, why don't you run along home now?" Bob said. "Reba will wonder where you are."

"Reba don't care if I walk around," Roy said defensively. "What's wrong with Roy walking around?"

Bob gave him a pat on his back. "Nothing, of course, but this is a private party, Roy. Go along now —"

Roy argued a little while longer and then shuffled away, staring at Alison before he went as if he were trying to record everything he saw on his befuddled brain.

"He's like a child," Bob said. "Harmless but curious."

"What happened to him?" Alison asked.

"Born that way," Chris said. "Reba sent him to special schools and educated him a little, but —"

"I wish he wouldn't sneak around like that," Alison interrupted with a shiver. "Still, better Roy than someone else, I suppose."

Bob gave her a teasing look. "What's wrong? What were you expecting, Alison? Leighton Thordsen's ghost?"

Alison flushed. "Don't be silly —"

The party lasted until nearly midnight. After a cooling swim in the lake, they made more coffee and Bob talked most of the time about Hollywood and his films. Joni said little about herself except that she had dropped out of school, wanted to do her own thing, and thought the world was coming to a bitter end. Chris just listened and smoked his pipe.

When Chris suggested they douse the fire and go home, Bob protested, and they nearly had an argument about it, but Chris got to his feet and reached a hand to Alison.

"If you're coming with me —"

Alison nodded. "Yes, it's time to go. It was fun, Joni. A wonderful idea. I'll see you tomorrow, Bob."

Chris led Alison up the path toward the inn, keeping a firm hand on her arm.

"How can you see so well in the dark?" she asked.

"Always could," he said. "Did you enjoy yourself?"

"Yes. And you?"

"I guess Bob just has a way with him that annoys me."

"He's going through a bad period right now. I suppose it's hard to be on top of the pile and then slide off."

"Yes."

"What about you, Chris? You've never told me what you did before you came here."

"I helped run a business with a friend."

"And you gave it up for Greenwood?"

"Yes."

"There's more. Would you rather I didn't ask?"

"That's right."

"You're an infuriating person, Chris Dumont, do you know that?"

He laughed shortly. "I really don't mean to be. Maybe I'm like Bob, going through a period of adjustment. Bear with me, will you?"

They had cleared the path, and with the lights of Greenwood growing closer, Chris paused for a moment to view the lake. He held a match to his pipe and she saw his eyes, the look in them, and something about his expression touched her.

"Who was Billy?" she asked.

"My friend — I told you that."

"No, you only told me part of it. Were you a POW too?"

He drew a deep breath. "Yes. But it's a part of my life I want to forget."

"It was that bad?"

"Worse than anything you can imagine. I don't know how I survived."

She felt instant pity, a need to comfort him now.

"I'm so sorry, truly . . ."

"Why should you be? You barely know me."

"I hate the very thought of prisons and war and men killing each other and locking one another away."

He thrust his pipe into his pocket and reached out to take her arms. His hands were trembling.

"You really mean that?"

"Yes."

"You're quite a woman, Alison Blair."

"How would you know? You haven't even looked —"

He drew her closer. "Haven't I? I've looked a lot more than you think."

He bent his head and his lips came down on hers, and she was so stunned that she simply stood there and accepted his kiss. When he drew away from her, she stayed very quiet for a moment.

"It wasn't very good, was it?" he asked.

"No."

"It might get better with practice."

"Would it?"

He kissed her again and his desire flamed high inside him, burning against her lips. She put her arms around him, and there on the island, in the starlight with the water glinting like black diamonds, they held each other. She was encircled in strong arms, pressed against his tall, hard body, and she couldn't tell if she was comforting or being comforted, for it seemed both were in need, both giving.

8

The work at Greenwood seemed to be moving at a snail's pace for Chris. He awakened every morning determined to get a great deal done, more than on the preceding day, but it never worked out as he had planned. There were unexpected complications, and the more he labored on the old building, the worse he found it to be. Outward appearances were bad enough, but inside, under walls and hidden in odd places, he found signs of deterioration, and he began to think he had indeed been mad to have taken on such a place. George and his shady deals might have been better than this!

But he was here, he had invested his time and money, and he was going to make it pay one way or another. If he didn't, he knew George would be the first to throw it up to him, and that was the last thing he wanted.

Although Reba had taken over the place three years before, she had really done very little in the way of improvements. Mostly she served good food and plodded along the best she could. If the truth were known, Chris suspected, once Reba saw how much needed to be done, she had just given up.

Every so often Chris thought of Amy, and the ache would spread through him, nearly immobilizing him until he would toss his tools aside and go out to sit in the brilliant sunlight and stare at the sky. With so few people around Greenwood, and only a few others on Windswept Island, no one bothered him. It was as if there was an unwritten code of privacy on the island. Even Bob Beale, the few times he had spied Chris stretched out in the sun, had made a wide swath around him and let him alone.

Slowly, the sun healed him, bronzed his skin while the hard physical work strengthened his muscles. For the first time since the war camp he began to feel fit again.

Despite the problems at Greenwood, his love for the place grew each day. He loved hearing Alison in the music room playing the piano and wondered why she hadn't pursued music professionally. When he asked her one day, she lifted her dark head and gave him a straightforward glance from her blue eyes and told him the truth.

"I don't have that special star quality. I recognized this long ago. I never will have it. To the untrained ear I might sound good, almost professional, but believe me, Chris, I'm not."

"And your writing —"

"Much better," she said with a happy smile. "And my book is going to take shape here on the island, in your inn. I feel it in my bones."

And what lovely bones they were! Chris remembered clearly the night of the beach picnic, the way Alison had come into his arms, the feel of her lips under his own. He had not wanted a woman since Amy, had never even thought about anyone else. It was too soon. But someday he hoped he could fall in love again.

Reba Zeller had become a good friend to Chris. She was practical and hardworking and Chris knew that she worried about his being lured unfairly into buying Greenwood.

"Put your mind at rest, Reba. I'm not complaining."

"I hope you're able to do all you want to do," she said.

"I will," he said with determination. "I only wish I could have seen the place when it was new, when Thordsen lived here."

"They say it was the showplace of Donnerville. Everyone used to talk about it. In the first place, no one had ever built such an elaborate home on any of the islands before. What most people wanted were weekend cottages."

"You never knew Thordsen, did you?"

Reba shook her gray head. "No. I wasn't around these parts then, but even after he'd packed up and moved away people talked about him. What most people remembered was his love of good times. He had lavish weekend parties and took trips up the lake to the old Grand Hotel."

"I haven't heard of that place."

"It wasn't a place to be proud of, not by decent people. It was notorious, to say the least. They used it for gambling and wild parties, and men used to take women there who weren't their wives."

"Is the hotel still there?"

"Yes. It's used by fishing parties now, and I guess the notoriety has gone. It used to be a remote spot, but with speedboats and airplanes, that little den of iniquity soon folded up."

"Did Thordsen ever marry?" Chris asked.

"No, not that I know of. But he never lacked for companionship. They say his one true love was his secretary, Miss Benson. He called her Little Mouse. Can you imagine that?"

"Thordsen sounds like quite a fellow."

"I suppose he was at that. But I'll have to admit his music is next to genius."

Chris thought about Thordsen from time to time and knew that he wanted to keep the inn as near to the original as he could.

It became a matter of pride and integrity with him and he knew that it pleased Alison. Joni went along with the idea as well, and while there were times she suggested making radical changes, she usually came around to Chris's way of thinking. Joni was ready to tackle anything. She had already painted two of the rooms for him and had suggested color schemes for carpets and drapes.

Alison was hard at work on her book and Chris knew that sometimes Roy senselessly interrupted her. He suspected that Roy had some strange attraction for their dark-haired visitor, and he had offered to speak to Roy for Alison, but she hadn't permitted it.

"He spooks me a little, but he's really done nothing wrong and I don't want to hurt his feelings," she said.

But Chris had decided to keep an eye on Roy and, if necessary, to step in and do something about it.

He often heard Alison's typewriter at odd hours of the day. At other times she seemed to seek refuge at Thordsen's piano. He had secretly examined her room when she was out for some logical explanation for the strange sounds she had been hearing, but he had found nothing. While he hated the thought of her being frightened, it pleased him to have her fly to him for help.

On one of those fine, summer mornings when the mist burned off the face of the water and gulls floated aimlessly, Chris struck out from Greenwood, looking for some quiet place to stretch out in the sun, and he caught his first glimpse of his neighbors, the Meadowses.

The woman was walking slowly, the man leaning heavily on her arm, and behind them came another man, dressed somberly, trailing them like a watchdog. They didn't see Chris, who, knowing their reputation for unfriendliness, decided not to approach them. They went on, talking quietly — perhaps the woman was scolding the man, he couldn't be sure. The old man's silvery white hair shone in the sun, but he seemed frail and unwell. Chris wondered just who they really were and why they had come to live on

Windswept Island.

"Chris —"

He turned about to find Alison, with Old Duggan beside her. She stood with her back to the sun, tall and slender with her dark silky hair in wisps about her face and an impatient way of standing, as if she might take flight at any moment.

"Salt wants you," she said. "Something about the generator."

"I was afraid of that," he said. "It's been on its last legs now for some time."

"Can you fix it?"

"Maybe. It's about time my electrical engineering degree was put to the test."

She came to sit down beside him. Dressed in yellow, she reminded him of a long-stemmed daisy, regal head lifted. Her hair was tied back with a scarf and her eyes seemed to reflect the blue of the lake.

"I keep learnings things about you, Chris. If you're an engineer, what are you doing here?"

She nodded toward the inn that despite all its problems was still an impressive sight. Looking at it, his heart told him that he had done the right thing in buying it, even if his head didn't.

""I'm not sure, Alison. I just wanted to come here. Like you, I was compelled."

"There's something you're not telling me, Chris. I heard Reba mention a girl — Amy, wasn't it?"

Chris looked away, the unexpected sound of Amy's name making him wince. Would this never stop? Would she always haunt him?

"I'm sorry," Alison said, putting a hand on his sleeve. "I didn't mean to make you unhappy. I should learn to keep my mouth shut."

He put his fingers over hers. "It's all right, Alison. Thanks for bringing me the message. I should get back and see what I can do to help Salt."

"But you don't want to go?"

Chris laughed. "No, I don't. I haven't had much time to relax, and this morning I somehow just had to get away from all the problems down there. How did you find me?"

"I've been all over the island on my hikes and I thought of the most remote spot I knew and was sure I'd find you here."

"How is it that you read me so well?"

She gave him a smile that was enticing, a little dimple showing at one corner of her mouth. "A woman's intuition."

He would have liked to linger with her, but he knew the generator would not fix itself.

"Could I have a rain check on this moment?" he asked.

"Yes."

He got to his feet and held out his hand. "Would you walk back with me?"

"Sorry. I can't. Bob's expecting me."

He tried to keep from scowling but couldn't. He just didn't like Bob and he disliked even more the thought of Alison being with him.

"Something cooking?" he asked roughly.

"He's going to show me some of his film. I'm very anxious to see it."

Chris held back the curt words that came rushing to his lips and walked away from Alison, determined to focus his attention on the balky generator that they could not afford to lose.

There were phone lines but no power lines to the island. Everyone had their own generator for electricity, and the one at Greenwood had seen better days five years earlier.

In the dingy basement Chris found Salt sprawled on the floor, a streak of grease on his face, a wrench in his hand, and a few rough seafaring words in his mouth.

"Ease up, Salt," Chris said. "Let me have a look, will you?"

"It will take a genius to fix that blasted thing," Salt said.

He relinquished the tool to Chris and paced about the basement, muttering to himself.

"It's not like the engine on *The Maiden*. I can fix that in the dark!" Salt said.

"It always sounds to me like your beloved boat could use some repairs," Chris said.

"Needs a complete overhaul, but Reba never had the money for it, and since it's the only boat we have —"

The wrench slipped and Chris skinned

his knuckles. But he kept working and finally got to the heart of the problem. It would require a new part.

"Call the mainland and see if you can locate what we need."

"That thing's so old, no one will have any parts in stock," Salt said. "You're going to have to buy a whole new generator."

"I can't," Chris said in despair. "I just can't swing it now, Salt. We have to fix this one!"

The calls Salt made bore no fruit. When Reba heard about the predicament, she suggested that Chris go over to the Meadowses.

"Talk to Stone. They have a generator like this one, and I'm sure he keeps extra parts —"

"The Meadowses?" Chris asked, wiping his hands on an old rag. "I don't think they'd appreciate being asked a favor like that."

"You have no choice, Chris."

"True," he admitted. "I suppose it won't hurt to ask."

By the time he had made himself

presentable, the morning was nearly gone. It was imperative that they get the generator going soon or they would have a freezer full of spoiled food, a house full of candlelight, and no water.

Chris walked the short distance to the Meadowses' house, which lay in a straight line from the east wing of Greenwood. Alison's windows must look directly at the house, he thought.

There was a fence and a firmly latched door. He unfastened it and went up the stone walk to the front door. He lifted the old brass knocker and let it thud heavily against the striker plate. The sound of it was startingly loud and somehow out of place.

No one came, so he knocked again, and at last the tall, unfriendly man he knew to be Stone opened the door.

"Yes?" he said in a voice that would have frightened some people away.

"I'm Chris Dumont, the new owner of Greenwood. I have generator trouble and there are no available parts in Donnerville. Someone suggested you might have what I need."

"We're not in the habit of lending —"

"I understand," Chris said quickly. "But it's an emergency. I can't tell you how much it would mean."

"What is it?" a feminine voice called out.

"I'll handle it," Stone said to the woman, tossing the words over his shoulder.

Chris saw his chance and brushed past Stone into the hallway, where he encountered Irene Meadows. She was a tiny wisp of a woman with gray mixed in her brown hair. She reminded him of a faded rose. He gave her his best smile and explained who he was and what he wanted. She in turn gave Stone an angry look.

"Of course, we'll be glad to loan you what you need if we have it! Stone —"

Stone gave Chris an angry look that he ignored and instead began telling him in detail the exact part he needed.

"Yes, I understand," Stone said. "I'll go and fetch it, if we have it."

This left Chris standing in the hallway with Irene Meadows, and he was aware of the house, simply furnished with a touch of elegance that was surely her doing. She seemed a little uneasy, and when he caught a glimpse of her husband, David, she rushed to him as if to hurry him out of the room.

But David would have no part of it. He came to Chris with an extended hand.

"Hello there, young man. You're from the inn."

"Yes. And you must be David Meadows. It's nice to meet my neighbors at last," Chris said.

David Meadows was very thin. He was rather nattily dressed and wore a tie heavily knotted at the throat. He leaned on a cane. Could it be that he had a touch of palsy?

"It's lovely weather we're having," Chris said.

David nodded. "Beautiful. Like it used to be years ago —"

"David, dear, it's time for your rest. You must come now," Irene interrupted.

"I don't want to go!" David said, his voice changing from the gentle tones Chris had just heard to a kind of stubborn, irate voice like that of a child ready to throw a tantrum. The change was so quick and abrupt that it took Chris entirely by surprise.

Irene was flustered and embarrassed. She took David by the arm, but he shook her off and beat his cane against the floor.

"Stop treating me like a child!"

"I'm just looking after you, dear, taking good care of you. Come along, darling —"

Irene apparently knew the way to coax him back into a good mood, for the old man relaxed and gave Chris another gentle, if rather vague smile. He said good-bye and permitted Irene to lead him out of the room.

Stone was back, the necessary part wrapped in a newspaper. He thrust it into Chris's hand with a quick, impatient motion.

"Thank you. You've no idea how much I appreciate this," Chris said.

Stone opened the door, and there was nothing for Chris to do but walk out of it.

"In the future, Mr. Dumont, please don't bother the Meadowses with things like this. Do I make myself clear?"

It was impossible not to get the message that was written on Stone's frozen face with its granite eyes.

"You do," Chris said. "I'm sorry I bothered you."

The door slammed behind him and he heard the lock turn. Chris looked back for a moment or two. The cottage seemed innocent, quaint, and very quiet. But the Meadowses were a strange couple, and he wondered why they were there. Wouldn't they be better off in a city where they could be near friends or family? There they were so alone, hidden like recluses behind locked doors. Chris moved along, the part he needed under his arm, and he decided then and there not to call again unless it was by invitation.

9

Like Chris, Alison's days at Greenwood
had not been as productive as she had
hoped. She had gone over her notes
numerous times, trying to make them all
come together, but still they eluded her.
She needed a focus and it wasn't there. As
she sorted her notes, rereading them and
putting them into some kind of order, she
kept waiting for something to leap out at
her and provide her with the starting point
she sought. She spent long hours walking
around the island, often with Old Duggan,
choosing the times when she knew Reba
would have Roy busy with various chores.
As she walked, Alison tried to imagine
what Leighton Thordsen had felt and
sensed about this place, but her attempts
to put herself in his shoes were without
success. When Joni suggested that she get

away from Windswept for a few hours, Alison was tempted.

"You've buried yourself in it. It's time to pull back and get a fresh perspective."

"Maybe you're right," Alison said. "But I *want* to steep myself in this place. I thought about going to the local library to see if there might be some material about Thordsen there."

"Excellent idea," Joni said. "If I had time, I'd go with you." Alison went to find Salt. She spied him down at the dock, hosing out his beloved boat.

"Ahoy!" she called.

He gave her a quick grin. "Ahoy yourself. What's up?"

"I was wondering if you would take me over to the mainland this afternoon and pick me up later."

Salt shrugged. "Sure thing. Just give me a few minutes to finish this —"

Alison found a place to sit down on the sun-baked dock and dangled her feet over the edge, watching her reflection in the water. Salt whistled while he worked, his red hair lifting in the breeze. She wondered how he had acquired the scar on his face and longed to ask, but she knew that a person simply didn't ask such questions of people like Salt.

"How long have you been around the island, Salt? Did you come when Reba took over the inn?"

He gave her a quick look. "No, long before that. I've lived in and around Windwept most of my life."

Alison straightened with surprise. "Then you must have known Leighton Thordsen!"

Salt shut off the hose and began coiling it into a neat circle. "Sure, I knew Leighton."

"Oh, tell me about him — all you can!"

"He was a strange fellow. Brilliant they say, but I wouldn't know about that, being next to tone-deaf myself. He was a bundle of nerves, as edgy as a black cat on Halloween." Salt ran a finger over the hard welt of his scar and nodded toward the boat. "Hop in and we'll be off."

"About Thordsen —"

"We didn't move in the same circles. I did some work around the place now and then and sometimes he'd hire me to take groups of his guests up the lake to the Grand Hotel."

"Ah, the place of ill repute that I've heard about!"

"Sometimes it was just Thordsen and his secretary."

The implication was unmistakable in his voice.

"You mean Miss Benson?" she asked quickly.

Salt nodded crisply. "Yes."

"I see! So Thordsen and Miss Benson *did* have a love affair!"

Salt brushed that aside to talk more about Thordsen. "He never gave a man much warning. He did things on the spur of the moment and he had a temper like a buzz saw."

"Do you realize that you're only the second person I've found who actually knew the man and talked with him. All this time, I never dreamed that you had any connection with him at all!"

Salt tugged the stained captain's cap down snugly onto his red hair as he turned the boat into the wind and nosed her toward Donnerville.

"I understand you've put him down in history as a big man. But he could be damned mean and small too if he wanted."

With that, Salt turned his attention to *The Maiden* and Alison sensed that the subject was closed, at least for then. She knew she would hammer Salt with more questions another time. But she sensed too that Salt was not going to be a very cooperative source.

The boat ride was always exhilarating, and Salt could put *The Maiden* through paces that surely must have strained her. They put in to dock and Salt helped Alison ashore.

"What time do you want to come back?"

"Would four-thirty be okay?"

"Sure," Salt said.

Then, without another word, he revved the motor and turned the boat back to the lake and Greenwood. Alison walked into town, enjoying the activity she found there. When all was said and done, the island was awfully quiet, and it seemed almost good to hear automobiles and trucks jockeying their way through the traffic and to see people walking on sidewalks and darting in and out of busy shops.

She had no idea where the library was but asked directions, and after a short walk she found a new brick building with a great deal of glass and landscaping. She went in to find a collection of books that any library would be proud to own.

The librarian gave her a smile. "May I help you?"

"I'm researching the composer Leighton Thordsen. Are they any books about him that I might read?"

"I'll show you what we have — which is precious little. He's one celebrity that just wasn't written about very much."

"How well I know!" Alison sighed.

The librarian pulled down three books from the shelves and put them on the table for her.

"That's it," she said. "I wish I had more."

One of the books Alison had already read and the second she went through quickly. It was a very thin volume and covered basically what was in the other. She gained only a note or two from it. But the third was a find. It was poorly bound, having been printed by a local printer and apparently at the cost of the author. From it she learned two things. Thordsen had lived in another house on the island and, from what she could gather, it was the place the Meadowses now occupied. And, Thordsen had never liked Venice. How strange that he should go there during his last days and how ironic that he should die there.

Closing the book, Alison carried it to the desk.

"Could you tell me anything about the author of this book?" she asked. "I take it he's a local person . . ."

"Clifton lived here for a few years at about the same time that Thorsden was on the island, but he's been away from this area for several years."

"And you have no idea where he is now?"

"None. I heard he'd gone to California, then I heard another time that he was in New York. I'm sorry, I can't be of much help."

"Thanks anyway."

Alison stayed in the library a while longer, mostly because she loved the very look, feel, and smell of books. She couldn't begin to count the hours she had spent in such places or the deep sense of contentment she found in them.

After a quick browse in some of the shops she hurried down to the dock, knowing that Salt did not like to be kept waiting.

The Maiden was tied up at the dock, but Salt was nowhere about. Alison paced up and down, waiting, and was surprised to see Chris walking toward her with his long stride.

"I had some business in town," he said. "I have Salt busy at Greenwood. How did things go at the library?"

"Not too well."

Chris looked at his watch. "It's early, but how about dinner here for a change? Frankly, I could use a breather away from the inn. There are some nice places here."

She looked at Chris—his dark hair, gray

eyes, the lines of fatigue around his mouth. He had been working very hard for several days. He needed a change of pace much more than he knew.

"All right."

"Good!" he said with a smile.

He took her arm and they walked a few blocks to a small restaurant.

"So, your trip was disappointing," Chris said once they were seated.

"I learned very little that was new. Only that Thorsden lived once in the Meadowses' house. I suspect it was while he waited for his house to be built."

"Sounds logical," Chris said.

He leaned back from the table, and she was aware that he was studying her. They had been alone together only a few times, and each time it had been under unusual circumstances. She remembered the night she heard the strange noises and she had gone running from her room in search of someone. Then, too, there was the night they had walked home from the beach picnic, the way they had fallen into each other's arms. She wondered if he was thinking about that now.

The waitress came back with their food, and as they ate, Chris talked about Greenwood and the work he was doing.

"You never told me very much about Chicago."

A shadow went across his face. "There were serious problems in the business and I decided I wanted out. I had liked the inn, I wanted to come back. I think it had been in the back of my mind for a long time to buy the place, to try my hand at being an innkeeper. Maybe you're like Bob and think I won't make it."

"I'm sure if you decide you can, you will."

"Thanks for the vote of confidence. God knows, I need it these days."

"It's a different world here."

"Different from Chicago," he admitted.

"Sometime you must tell me about Amy."

He looked at her for a moment and he seemed to want to say something, but he shook his head slightly.

"Touchy subject?" she asked softly.

"Very."

"Sorry."

"It's okay. But what about you, Alison? There is someone in your past too, isn't there — or is it the present as well?"

She flushed. Had she been wearing her heart on her sleeve? She hadn't thought about Regan that day, but he was always there just below the surface.

"Past, present — perhaps the future, I don't know," she said.

"I see," he said, arching his dark brows. "Then tell me something about yourself. Where are you from? Where have you been, and where do you want to go?"

"My home base is Mitchell Grove in Kansas, I've been nearly everywhere, and I don't know where I'm going. Right now this Thordsen thing has me totally stumped."

Chris reached out and took her hand. His fingers were warm and hard. "You'll whip it, Alison. I have a feeling that once you set your mind to a thing —"

"I can be very stubborn," she nodded in agreement.

"Sometimes you have to be to survive."

"But how did you survive a prisoner-of-war camp?''

The unhappiness came to his face again, and she regretted her question. He tightened his grip around her fingers. ''I don't really know. I think because of Billy. He kept more than one of us going. It's rotten that he should have died as he did. We were freed two weeks later . . . poor Billy.''

''Poor Chris,'' she said gently.

His eyes flickered. ''Someday I'll tell you all about it, Alison. I think I'd like to get rid of it all. I've never been able to with anyone else.''

''I'll be flattered.''

''But let's talk about more pleasant things. Your book for one, the island —''

''I think I'll visit the Meadowses' house, just to see it.''

''The Meadowses aren't very friendly — at least Stone isn't. I had to go there for the generator problem and I won't go again. There's something very strange about those people.''

''Well,'' Alison said with a cheerful grin, ''I never was one to let a little thing like that stop me.''

Chris laughed, and the sound of it was rich and true. Alison realized she had never heard him laugh out loud before. It did her heart good.

The time spent in the cafe was pleasant, but Chris had to get back to Greenwood, so it was just sundown when they climbed aboard *The Maiden* and made their way across the water. Walking back to the inn, Chris took her hand and they said very little, but there was a comradeship between them, a feeling of trust, and when they reached the inn Chris paused for a moment.

"The first time — it was awkward and shy and I felt a little like a high school boy. This time —"

His arms came around her. He held her hard and tight against him for a moment and then his lips found hers, and there with the soft lights of the inn around their feet and the sound of the water far away she gave him back his kiss.

"Better?" he asked.

"Much," she replied softly.

"Something brought us both here at the same time. If I believed in fate . . ."

The moment hung between them, sweet and golden, a promise that might disappear if examined too closely. Then he said good-night and turned away. Alison was reluctant to go inside and decided to go down to the Meadowses' despite Chris's warning. Surely they would understand her interest in the house and perhaps even let her tour it. Or was that asking too much? Nothing ventured, nothing gained she decided, and she set out toward the house. It was only a few steps away, and she had looked at it often from the window of her room.

There was a fence, an iron gate, and roses grew at the front door. She lifted the heavy knocker. It was some time before Stone came to the door. Looking into his cold eyes, she began to wish she had telephoned first.

"Hello, I'm Alison Blair. Do you remember me? We met once on *The Maiden*. As you may have heard, I'm doing a book on Leighton Thordsen —"

Stone gave her a calculating look and began to close the door. She stopped him.

"Please hear me out. I understand

Thordsen lived in this very house once. Could I speak to the owners about it?"

""Sorry, they aren't at home. If you'll excuse me —"

She didn't believe the Meadowses were out because she knew they seldom left the house. More than that, she was certain that someone was hovering just out of sight, listening.

"Stone, I want to speak with one of the Meadowses. This is very important to me," she insisted.

"Miss Blair —"

"It's all right, Stone," a woman's voice said. "I'm sorry, Miss Blair, but we don't normally encourage visitors of any kind. My husband is not well, you know . . ."

Irene Meadows was not what Alison had expected. She was younger, for one thing, and really quite lovely. But there was a determination in her slender shoulders that made Alison decide it was best not to push her luck. Perhaps another time . . .

"I'm sorry I've bothered you. Truly sorry," Alison said.

Irene gave her a winsome smile. "Thank you, Miss Blair."

"Who is it?" someone called out. "Who's at the door?"

David Meadows emerged, a frail, white-haired man who paused on the threshold as frightened and uncertain as a captured sparrow. There was something familiar about him that tugged at Alison's memory, but she could not place it. Did he look like her own grandfather, who was just a snapshot in an old album? Or did he resemble someone she had read about?

But the notion was instantly gone, for Irene gave her a look that could only have been one of dismissal. Alison quickly said good-evening and turned to go.

"She was talking about Thordsen, I heard her!" David said. "Irene, I want to know what she said."

"Never mind, dear. Come along. It's time for your medicine."

The door closed and the Meadowses were shut out of sight, but as Alison walked back to the inn she found herself thinking about them. Irene was the backbone of that family, it was plain to see, but David touched her heart. He seemed like a sweet old man, childish perhaps, curious and eager to talk. Why had Irene whisked him away like that?

Late that evening, with the Meadowses still in her mind and her desire to study the house at closer range all the more persistent, Alison sat down to play the piano in the music room. With Thordsen so much in her thoughts, it seemed natural to turn to his music.

The inn was quiet and the music poured out. Alison was so engrossed that she played for more than an hour. Suddenly, abruptly, she knew someone was watching her. She spun around to the doorway, but no one was there. Then she caught a glimpse of a face at the window. She screamed.

Chris came running. He took one look at her pale face and reached out to her.

"What is it? For God's sake, Alison, what is it this time?"

She couldn't look at the window again, but she pointed, burying her face against his shoulder.

"I'll go and look. Probably just Roy —"

But she was sure it hadn't been Roy. She waited at the piano, trembling, and it seemed that Chris was gone an eternity. Then he came back, shaking his head slowly.

"No one, Alison. Not a trace of anyone even being there."

"But he was there! Chris, I'm not imagining things. Someone *was* there."

10

Alison had never believed in haunts of any kind. It was hard for anyone with the kind of common sense she possessed even to consider anything supernatural. But so many things had happened since she had come to Greenwood that she was considerably more shaken than she liked to admit.

Chris saw how upset she was and put his hand against her cheek.

"Take it easy, Alison. There has to be some explanation."

"I've been trying to tell myself that, but it doesn't seem to work."

"We'll get to the bottom of it. I promise."

"Maybe there are such things as ghosts. Maybe Leighton Thordsen doesn't like having me dig around in his past. And he *has* a past. I've heard repeatedly how much he liked women and that he may have had an affair with his secretary."

"Any man who writes such vibrant music must have had some pretty hot blood in his veins," Chris pointed out with a smile.

She managed a laugh. "I suppose so. And it does make him more interesting, doesn't it? Sometimes you forget the real man behind a name — that he had problems just like the rest of us."

"Will you be all right now?" Chris asked.

She nodded. "I'm sorry to keep bothering you —"

"I rather like the bother," he said warmly. Then he kissed her forehead and she sighed. The first time he had tried to comfort her she had been uneasy with him, but now she was thankful for his arms around her, his very presence.

"Tomorrow I think I'll start doing some work in here," he said.

"I'm going to be uprooted?"

"It will be a little messy, but I'll try to keep it to a minimum."

"What will you do with this room?" she asked anxiously. "I like it as it is."

"Not much," he promised. "There are some leaks around the window, and that one wall will have to come out and be replaced. If I find any missing manuscripts that belonged to Thordsen, I'll be sure and turn them over to you," he teased.

"You don't think there is a missing manuscript, do you?"

Chris gave her a studied look. "I don't know enough about it, Alison. But it's obvious that you do. I'm sorry I haven't had time to take you on a search in the attic or the basement, but I'll get to it soon."

"I can't really hope to find anything. I just want to satisfy my curiosity. I have to make a very *thorough* search."

"Why would he have left it behind?" Chris asked.

"Why did he go to Venice in the first place — and apparently on short notice? He didn't like Venice — in fact, he hated the place."

"But he died there?"

"Yes. I'm sure he would have much preferred to spend his last days here. He loved this island."

"I have a feeling you'll find the answers eventually, Alison."

"Maybe."

She knew he was deliberately trying to get her mind off the strange face at the window.

"I'm all right now, Chris."

"Does that mean I have to take my arms away?"

"I think I'll go to my room now."

He let her go, and she picked up her music and hurried away to her room. It was very quiet and she strained to hear unusual noises. There was nothing but the normal sounds of the inn. Could it be Thordsen's music that lured these strange things into being? The night she had played the tapes of his music she had heard the sobbing voice, and this evening at the piano, when she had been engrossed again in Thordsen's compositions, something peculiar had happened. If ghosts did exist, then it was surely Thordsen's who was haunting her!

True to his word, the next morning Chris moved his tools into the music room. Thordsen's piano was covered with canvas, and by the time Joni arrived, Chris had begun to remove the old wall, with dirt and plaster dust flying.

"How will you decorate this room," Chris?" Joni wanted to know.

"Paneling probably. Something suitable that will match the rest of the room."

"It'll stick out like a sore thumb."

Chris frowned. "I don't think so. They have some very beautiful materials, and you can get almost any design you want."

"I don't agree with that idea at all."

"Why not wallpaper?" Alison suggested. "Maybe even flocked wallpaper —"

"Plaster," Joni said. "Done in a rough texture. Leave it the natural color, no paint."

Chris brushed a bit of plaster out of his black hair and looked at Allison. "You know what Thordsen was like better than anyone. What would he choose if he were standing right here beside us now?"

Alison weighed that question for a

moment. "Judging from what was here first, I'd stick with the wallpaper."

"Then wallpaper it will be," Chris said. "This room ought to be a kind of memorial to Thordsen."

"Even I have to go along with that," Joni said.

"It's a wonderful idea, Chris. And it should be a drawing card for your inn," Alison pointed out.

Chris grinned. "That also crossed my mind."

Chris went back to work and Joni and Alison were sitting in the lobby discussing ideas for the room when Bob Beale arrived, camera bag slung over his shoulder.

"What's all the racket? Where's Chris working now?" he asked.

"The music room."

"I'd better hustle in there and take a few pictures."

"I thought you'd already covered the place, Bob," Joni said.

He shrugged. "I have, but a few pictures of the work in progress might be interesting too."

"Have you got a travel magazine interested in your article yet?" Alison asked.

"Just a couple of nibbles," he said. "But I'm not worried. This type of thing is usually popular."

He disappeared for a few minutes, and when he came back, there was a frown on his face and a dusting of plaster on his shoulder. Alison sensed immediately that he and Chris had exchanged unfriendly words again, but she said nothing.

Bob sat down beside Alison and stretched out his legs with a sigh. "It's a great day. We should go boating, Alison. Or take a long walk. How can you stand all the noise and confusion around here?"

"I haven't much choice," she said. "I came here for the summer and I intend to stick it out, even if they tear the place down around my head."

"The other day, when you came to see my film, we hadn't gotten very far when the projector broke down," Bob said. "Why don't you try again this afternoon? I have it repaired now."

"Maybe I *will* walk up that way," she said.

"I'll expect you," Bob replied as he got up and left them.

Joni had been listening to all of this and making no comment, but Alison knew that she didn't approve. For a girl who boasted of no roots or ties, she seemed more than a little possessive of Bob.

"Bob's restless," Joni said.

"His heart is in Hollywood," Alison replied. "He needs a break and I hope he gets it soon. What little I saw of his film was fantastic. He has a way with a camera, that's for certain."

"He's had some bad luck," Joni said. "But things will swing his way again, I'm sure."

"What does he do when he goes to Donnerville?"

"Who knows? He doesn't talk much about it. There are two sides to Bob and I don't always understand him."

Joni went to check on Chris's progress, and Alison made herself go to her room and sit for an hour at her typewriter. She made several false starts and managed finally to get a few pages out, but they didn't really suit her. Surely things would fall into place soon. The summer was slipping away. Already, she had wasted far too much time. She felt close to Thordsen here: she looked at the same view he had looked at, pondered the same expanse of water, felt the same soft breeze against her face — why couldn't she put herself completely in his shoes? Why did everything conspire to hold her back?

She was glad by the time lunch had come and gone to put the cover on the typewriter, close all her file folders and stack them neatly on the card table, and leave Greenwood behind.

Bob had returned from the mainland and was expecting her when she arrived at his cottage. He sat on the porch, watching the path for the first glimpse of her. He was sun-tanned, relaxed and casually dressed. Bob's place was comfortable and had originally been built by a doctor who wanted a place to escape to on weekends and holidays. It was not fancy, but there was a cozy fireplace for cool autumn evenings and a window that faced the lake. The furnishings were handsome and masculine, and Bob had converted some of the rooms into a darkroom and workshop. The place was filled with photographs pinned on the wall, propped against chairs, and even overflowing into the kitchen.

Bob pressed a cool drink into her hand when they went inside, out of the brilliant sunlight. The house had a fresh smell and the windows were open to all the lake breezes.

"I've set up the projector in the darkroom," he said. "Too much light out here. I have some slides I'll show you first, and then I'll run the movies."

Alison's breath was taken away by what she saw. Bob was a marvelous photographer. He had captured the island at its best and at its worst.

"Now this will be movies of other places on Thunder Lake. Places you've yet to see, Alison."

He had amusing footage of fishermen, children splashing in the water, rustic cottages nestled in the trees. Then there was one of a very large, rather rundown building that still clung to a certain faded grandeur, a curtain flapping at an open window.

"What is that place?"

"The Grand Hotel," Bob said.

"So that's what it looks like!" she said. "I can imagine what it must have been like once."

"Quite risqué," Bob laughed. "At least in those times. I understand your dear Leighton Thorsden was a frequent visitor there. Was he a gambler?"

"If he was, I've never come across that bit of information."

"Perhaps a secret drinker?"

"Not likely; word would have leaked out. He didn't care much for liquor."

"Then the only other vice the Grand Hotel was noted for was women —"

"Leighton's weakness," Alison nodded. "He was supposedly in love with his secretary, Miss Benson, but I don't know if it was true or if they ever went there."

"Very probable," Bob replied.

"I'd like to see that old hotel."

"I'll take you," Bob offered. "We'll

make it an all-day outing. We'll go up the lake and poke around among the islands and we'll stop at the Grand Hotel. How about tomorrow?"

"I'd love to, Bob."

"I'll pick you up at about ten o'clock. There's a quaint little place we could visit on the Canadian side, and we could have lunch at the old hotel."

They finished looking at the rest of his film. Bob shut off the projector and turned on the lights.

"So now you've seen what makes me tick. What did you think? Be honest."

"I like your work, Bob. Especially the photos of the island."

"I hope to splice it all together in an interesting short film, one that will make all the filmmakers sit up and take notice."

There was an angry, bitter note in his voice.

"They will, Bob."

"Sorry, I shouldn't air my grudges like that, should I?"

"What are friends for?"

Bob followed her out to the living room

to mix another drink.

"Sometimes I think I should do something else. Sell insurance or take a job in an office. But, hell, Alison, I'm a photographer. I can't be anything else."

She understood his plight. She wanted to write. There was nothing else in the world that gave her as much trouble on the one hand but on the other satisfied a deep inner need. Putting one word after another on paper seemed to be the essence of her life.

For the rest of the afternoon they talked about their problems and their needs. Bob grew more relaxed, and when he came to sit beside her, he put his arm around her and kissed her warmly.

"You're good for me, Alison Blair. Did you know that?"

"I hope things break for you soon, Bob."

"They will," he said through clenched teeth. "They just have to!"

Old Duggan barked and Bob straightened with a frown.

"Someone must be out there. I can't think who, though. No one comes here but Joni . . .''

He went to investigate and Alison heard voices. She peered out the screen door, and when she saw Roy Zeller her muscles tightened. Had he followed her there? This was getting ridiculous and she didn't like it one little bit. Perhaps she should speak to Reba about it. She hated to stir up trouble, though.

Bob was being curt with Roy, and Roy in turn was being surly.

"I've told you, Roy, I don't have any work for you. I thought you were helping Chris at the inn."

"Not always busy down there," Roy said.

Bob finally persuaded him to go and at last he shuffled away, staring intently at the house before he left. Instinctively Alison shrunk out of sight.

Bob came back inside, annoyed at the interruption.

"He followed me," Alison said with a shiver. "He's been hanging around, watching me, it gives me the creeps."

"He said he wanted work."

"Roy is mentally retarded, but in some

areas he seems clever. Strange, isn't it?''

"If he is bothering you, I'll talk to Chris and tell him to get him off the island,'' Bob said angrily.

"No, please don't do that!''

"There is something spooky about the man. He just materializes out of thin air. How can he walk so quietly when he's such a big man?''

She thought of the face at the window — there one moment, gone the next. Maybe it had been Roy after all.

"Now, where were we?'' Bob asked, coming to sit down beside her again.

"I was in the middle of thinking about going back to Greenwood.''

"Too early,'' Bob said.

"I should work.''

"So should I,'' Bob said. "But this is more pleasant.''

"We'll both become very lazy if we —''

He stopped her words with a kiss. It was pleasant and nerve-tingling. Bob was a personable man, a little demanding perhaps, but very easy to like.

"I don't know why we haven't been doing this more often,'' he said.

She pulled away from him and got to her feet.

"I must go —"

She moved to the door and called to Old Duggan, who came padding faithfully toward her, his tongue lolling out of his mouth. A butterfly flitted for a moment around her head and fluttered against the door before soaring away.

"Please stay," Bob said, his voice very tender.

She turned away, not ready for this. Regan was still very close, and yesterday only a heartbeat away.

"Tomorrow," Bob called after her. "Don't forget about tomorrow . . ."

11

Bob watched Alison and the dog walk away, and he was both amused and annoyed. Amused because Alison had flown like some frightened bird, annoyed because now he was alone with time hanging heavily on his hands. He had shot every foot of the island that showed any promise and had scrounged out all the interesting places in Donnerville until there was none left. The truth of the matter was, he was running out of subject matter. When that happened, there were only two choices left open to him. One was to move on, the other was simply to sit back and let the world pass him by. But even that took a certain amount of monetary resource. The rent wouldn't pay itself, and he had this strange habit of liking to eat. The boat took gas and oil, the garage for his car took rental money, and California was a good many miles away. To get from here to there would take a few bills as well. He was between the devil and the deep blue sea, and at this point it was hard to tell which was going to win out.

The logical thing to do was to sack out in the old hammock for a while and watch the sky, for it had its own kind of pictures that he never tired of studying. If he lived to be a hundred and had every type of film and camera available, he could never equal Mother Nature's colors and he knew it. Who, in truth, could duplicate the blue of the sky or that pink blush of sunset or the green of the lake? Only God could do that — it was something he had learned at the tender age of ten when he was already an old hand at photography. He had started when he was eight years old; when he was eighty, he knew he would still be chasing sunsets or shapely women or the craggy face of a seaman if they were photogenic. It was in his blood.

"Damn!" he muttered aloud. "Why did everything have to blow up in my face —

right when things were going good?"

It had happened to other people, and he had made sympathetic noises and pulled a long face and patted them reassuringly on the back and that was all. He had been so darned egotistical. He thought it could never happen to him. But it had. Lady Luck had turned her back on him, and there were no signs of things changing for the better.

He tried to nap in the hammock, but he couldn't drift off. He smoked too many cigarettes, went inside to peer at his photographs with a magnifying glass, tossing some away and retrieving others from the wastebasket. By the time dusk grew near, he was gnawing at a fingernail and knowing he couldn't stay in the place another minute.

He took off around the island as he often did and, as a precaution, he took a camera with him. For Bob to go walking without one was like going out without shoes in the dead of winter. The camera was simply an extension of himself.

He took a few random shots, not especially happy with what he got, but the click of the shutter offered some degree of satisfaction.

He wandered down to the water on the left side of Greenwood and followed a path there. Several worn trails led down to fishing spots, and he was startled to see Stone perched on the sandy bank, a pole in hand and his line in the water. It was an unexpected sight indeed, for Bob had never seen the man relax before. Could Stone actually be made of blood and bones like anyone else after all? Somehow the sight gave Bob a lift. If Stone was truly human, there had to be hope.

He walked on, and as he neared the Meadowses' house he swung around to the rear of it, wanting to avoid the unfriendly people who lived there and the inn in particular. One encounter a day with Chris Dumont was enough.

There was a garden toward the back of the Meadowses' place, where a small vegetable patch was tended by Stone. There were flowers too, for it seemed Irene Meadows was addicted to roses. A stone bench leaned against an oak tree, and a birdbath drew sparrows who chased away robins, while the blue jay reigned supreme over all.

David Meadows was there! Bob was so surprised to see him that for a moment he could only stare. Then, without another thought as to why, he lifted his camera, brought the man within range of his zoom lens, and clicked away. David saw him, and Bob waited for the man's reaction.

"Hello," he said in a low, gentle voice.

Bob walked toward him. In all the weeks since early spring that he'd been on the island, this was only the second or third time he had come face to face with David Meadows.

"Do you remember me?" Bob asked.

"You're the photographer. Working on a film," David replied with a sweet smile. "Of course I remember."

"How are you, David?" Bob asked.

David lifted frail shoulders and ran a slightly trembling hand over his chin, a nervous habit he seemed to have, and for a moment his eyes went vacant and there was a lost look about him.

"I'm not well, you know. My darling worries about me. Bless her soul."

"Irene is a fine woman. A beauty."

"A rose. I tell her she's a fine thoroughbred rose, like those that grow in her garden. I'm glad you happened by, Mr. Beale. I get lonely sometimes."

"The island is a very quiet place to live," Bob pointed out.

"But a nice place. I remember —"

Then David broke off abruptly and pointed to Bob's camera. "You shouldn't photograph me, you know."

"Why not?"

"I'm a terrible subject. I was handsome once though, would you believe it?" Then, with a sad smile, he shook his head. "It's wrong that we must all grow old."

"You've a good face, David. Interesting," Bob said.

"Take something else."

"Well, I'd like to film your house."

"My house? What on earth for?" David asked curiously.

"I'm making a film about the island. I have pictures of every place, even yours at a distance, but I'd like some close-ups, maybe even inside shots."

"No. Irene doesn't like strangers about,

and Stone —"

David looked uneasy. Bob decided to press his luck. This was a golden opportunity, one that might not happen again.

"Just a few shots. Perhaps of you and your garden," Bob said.

"Well, I suppose . . ."

"I won't take long," Bob said. He began to adjust the camera to the dwindling light, though he was afraid that it was already too dark, even with high-speed film.

"To be truthful, David, I want the pictures for Alison Blair. She's staying at the inn and she's interested in your house."

"Why would she care about it?"

"She's writing a book about Leighton Thordsen," Bob explained. "He lived here once, you know."

David nodded slowly and sat down on the bench. He seemed tired at once, and it was easy to see that he was short of strength.

"Alison Blair. She's the girl at the piano."

"That's the one," Bob said. "A very nice young woman. You'd like her. Perhaps you'll agree to see her sometime."

"No," he said slowly. "I don't think so. Now, I must go in. Sorry —"

The old man got to his feet in a rush and went shuffling away, moving rapidly. Bob didn't know what had set him off, but he was as skittish as a high-strung racehorse at the sound of the bell. In another moment he saw Irene coming to meet David. She gave Bob an inquisitive look, and he suddenly felt that he should explain his presence.

"I was just out strolling," he said. "I saw your lovely roses and thought I'd photograph them. I hope you don't mind."

"It's a private garden, Mr. Beale."

Bob straightened, surprised by the steel he detected in her quiet voice. By sight one would take Irene Meadows for a gentle soul, but there was evidently more to her than that.

"I'm sorry, I didn't mean to intrude."

"Mr. Meadows is not well. Strangers confuse him. I hope you understand."

Bob clamped his lips shut. David had not seemed confused to him; he had remembered his name, knew who Alison was, seemed pathetically eager to talk to someone until something abruptly had frightened him off. Perhaps he had sensed Irene was coming for him.

"The night air is not good for him," Irene said, her voice softening a little. "It is quite damp, isn't it?"

"Yes."

"Good evening, Mr. Beale."

Bob stood there for a moment, wondering at the strange mortals who walked the earth, and then, feeling like a schoolboy who has been dismissed by his teacher, he hurried away.

His luck was indeed at the end of its string. He couldn't even get a few pictures for Alison's sake. She had told him about her endeavors to see the Meadowses' house and how she had been turned away. Well, privacy was privacy and many sought it to the nth degree. Apparently the Meadowses fell into that category.

He was too restless to go home, so he went to Joni's. Joni always welcomed him and moved over to make room for him by her fire. There was something about her silky blond hair hanging long and loose on her shoulders, the limpid blue of her eyes, that sent a ripple along his nerves.

When he reached the tiny cottage that Joni called home she wasn't there. So he sat down to wait, wondering what was keeping her so long at Greenwood. But then he knew the answer to that one too! Chris Dumont was keeping her. Thinking of Chris, Bob felt annoyed and angry and wasn't sure just why. Chris rubbed him the wrong way. There was something about his steady gray eyes, the way he knuckled down to even the menial jobs at the inn, the straight way he walked as if he dared the world to get in his way, that set Bob's teeth on edge.

"Hey, who's sitting there on my step?" Joni called out.

He looked up to find her coming at last, dressed in her old jeans.

"Just your friendly pest," he said. "You're late."

Joni lifted a thin shoulder in a shrug. "Time got away."

"I missed you."

"Oh, sure," Joni said, making a face. "You were just dying of loneliness."

"That's not far from the truth."

"You were with Alison earlier, weren't you?"

"Alison's not you," he said.

"One thing about you, Bob, you're *always* gallant."

"You're calling me a liar politely, is that it?"

"I've seen how you are around her. You're sweet on her."

"Come here and say that," he said. He reached out and pulled her close, but she put up her fists and pushed hard against his chest.

"Stop it, Bob."

He shrugged. "You're not all sweetness and light tonight. Anything go wrong today?"

"Nothing."

"I don't believe that. Look, Alison and I are just friends, like you and me. Didn't we agree that our relationship should be kept open and easy? Flexible?"

Joni brushed back a lock of hair.

"Yes, we agreed."

"Only you don't like the arrangement now, is that it?"

"I didn't say that."

"Hell, Joni, you can't have it both ways!" Bob said angrily.

Joni went inside and let the door slam behind her. Bob sat still for a moment, cursing silently to himself, wondering why he had picked the fight. With a sigh, he got up and went inside. Joni was poking at the dead ashes on the open hearth and snapping small twigs in her hand. In a moment she had held a match to them and the flames licked upward. He could have taken the same twigs, the same match, and never have gotten it started.

"How do you do that anyway?" he asked.

She turned about with a quick laugh, her anger gone as quickly as it had come. He began to feel better.

"Fires burn for me, I don't know why. Let's say I have the magic touch."

"How did the work at Greenwood go today?"

"Slowly, but we're making progress.

The music room will be a knockout when Chris gets done with it."

"The wonder boy is bound to make good, is that it?" Bob asked crossly.

Joni added a few more branches to the fire as she squatted before it on her heels, ignoring his last remark.

"Why do you go down there and work all the time? Is he paying you that well? I thought you wanted to be free to do what you wanted when you wanted. Now you're going down there as regularly as if you were punching a time clock!"

"He needs help."

"He has Roy and Salt."

"They don't get along. Salt gets impatient with Roy."

"Salt doesn't hit it off with very many people, does he?"

Joni brushed off the knees of her jeans and went to the tiny cupboard to peer inside. "Now that I think about it, he doesn't. He keeps to himself. He's a strange man. I never see him go anywhere on the island except to the Meadowses once in a while."

Bob lifted his brows. "You're kidding.

You mean he goes over there and they let him in?"

"Once they did. I saw it happen. It rather surprised me, but what surprised me even more was that when I mentioned it to Salt the next day he denied it."

"Salt lied about it? Why would he do that?"

"I suspect he just wanted me to mind my own business."

Bob nodded. "Everyone on this island seems to be that way. But the place isn't big enough for all of us to be recluses."

Joni laughed at that. Her mood seemed to be getting lighter by the minute. Bob took heart. He helped her put together a simple meal, and it was all rather rustic and cozy.

"How about a swim later?" he asked.

"Maybe," Joni said.

"I'm all pent up," he told her. "I have to work off some steam."

"No news from California?"

"Bills in the mail, nothing else. No phone calls."

"How soon will you put all the film together and ship it off?"

"As soon as I have my contacts lined up," he said. "I've sent several letters asking old friends to look at it. Funny how fast they can forget you."

"You'll make it, Bob."

He met her clear blue eyes and smiled. "Maybe. If you think so, that helps."

"I do. Chris is going to make it too."

Bob set his coffee cup aside and felt the anger boil up inside him again. "Why do you keep comparing me to Chris?"

"I *wasn't* comparing —"

"He's the golden boy around here, isn't he? He always does the right thing. He emanates success — he reeks of it. Well, it hasn't happened yet."

"Shut up, Bob, you sound like a jealous child."

Bob set his jaw. "Thanks a lot."

Joni came to touch his arm, her fingers cool and soothing.

"You'll make it again, Bob. And even if you don't, there are other things in life besides film."

"Like what?" he asked miserably.

"Chris turned his back on a profitable business. He had the courage to take a gamble and do something else, something that he wanted to do. Can't you do that, too?"

"The hell of it is, there's nothing else I care about," he said. "Oh, once I thought maybe I'd like to work around a yacht basin, maybe run charters for people, but I'd probably get seasick the first time out."

"You'll make it, Bob Beale, I'll bet my life on it."

"Your life's not needed," Bob said. "But I could sure use a little comforting about now . . ."

She put her arms around his neck and he pulled her close.

"That's more like it," he said.

"But you'd like Alison's arms better," she replied with hard bitterness in her voice.

"Just shut up and kiss me," he said.

But as he closed his eyes and sought Joni's mouth with his own, he wondered what it would be like to hold Alison like this, to have her willing and tender in his arms instead of surprised and hesitant. Then he blocked her out, as he blocked out the empty days with no phone calls, the film that would not promise to do anything spectacular, the sound of the water at the shore, the thud of his own weary heart.

12

Alison was primed for the day, eager to see this famed Grand Hotel that had held many a secret in its most shining hour. There was something romantic about the notion of seing the renowned hideaway where Leighton Thordsen had spent many weekends. Her one hope was to locate someone in that vicinity who remembered Thordsen, who might give her some fresh insight into the man.

She went down to the dock to wait for Bob. Salt was there, and when she told him where she was bound, he pushed his cap to the back of his head and looked at her with surprise.

"Why would you want to go there?"

"I'm curious. You told me that Thordsen used to go there with his secretary."

Salt scowled. "Yeah, I did, didn't I? Sure, they went. Sometimes he used to take his guests up there too. They thought it was a real lark."

By then Bob was coming. He docked and then leaped out to give her a hand inside his flashy boat. In a moment they were off, speeding away from the island and the inn that sat perched on it like a lonely sentinel.

"Don't look back," Bob shouted over the roar of the motor. "It's bad luck."

"Who says?"

Bob smiled and tapped his chest. "Me."

So she turned her face into the wind and watched Bob maneuver the boat up the lake, steadily putting miles between them and Windswept Island. She saw other patches of land, many uninhabited, a few sprouting motels and cottages for the tireless vacationing fishermen and others that were obviously lavish weekend homes. Always there was the lake itself, sprawling between Minnesota and the reaches of Canada. Thunder Lake was entirely a different matter than on the map and Alison began to think they never would reach the island that held the Grand Hotel.

"How much farther?" she shouted.

Bob held up two fingers. "We're nearly there."

The two miles vanished behind them in the boat's foaming wake.

Then a blurry line of trees began to take shape, and she could see a dock and the spindly masts of sailboats at anchor.

"There it is." Bob pointed ahead of them.

The Grand Hotel sat nearly on the water's edge, weathered by wind and sun to a slate gray that shone almost like silver in the sunlight. The many windows seemed like so many eyes staring out at them, and across the front was a large, almost southern veranda. It came as a surprise this far north.

"Shades of magnolia blossoms and mint juleps, Bob laughed. "A southern gentleman originally built the place. Perhaps that explains the architecture."

Bob docked the boat, fastened the mooring ropes, and then helped Alison out.

"Do you know anyone here?" she asked.

"No one except Jake Winthrop. He runs that little store and the gas pump over there. He's been around for ages.

"I'd like to talk with him."

"Let's see if we can find him."

But Jake Winthrop was busy. It was the height of the tourist season, and his place was stacked three deep with customers wanting this or that. Bob took her arm.

"Let's go over and look at the old hotel. They'll let you have a peek upstairs. They've restored it after a fashion. The ground floor is used by the restaurant and as living quarters for the present owners."

It was apparent that little had been done to change the appearance of the hotel. The floors were warped and needed varnish. A kind of lobby had been kept intact with furniture that had seen better days. Even the old desk had been retained, with its ledger open for visitors to sign. Alison signed her name and wondered if Leighton Thordsen had once stood in that very same spot. Had Miss Benson been with him or some other lady she did not even know about? Or could he have come alone, contrary to all the gossip and rumors that he was a ladykiller? A composer, just as a writer or a photographer, had to have time alone to contemplate, to churn up all the talent that was harbored in his soul.

"You're far away," Bob said.

She nodded. "Thinking of Thordsen."

"You do a great deal of that."

"That's why I've come here," she said simply.

"Such dedication," he teased, but she knew that he understood. He too had the same dedication to his own work.

They climbed the wide stairway with its worn treads and walked down the long upper hall. There were eight rooms on either side and a few of them were open for viewing. The furniture seemed terribly old-fashioned and must have been so even when Thordsen had come there. How many years ago would it have been? By quick calculations she estimated no more than seventeen years, when she was still a schoolgirl. From the few photographs she had seen, she knew

Thordsen had been a handsome man with a high forehead, intelligent eyes, a hard chin, and a mouth that was notably sensuous. A small man by physical standards but big in his own world.

"The old place still has a feel of its own, doesn't it?" Bob said.

"Yes. I understand why people came here to get away from it all and have a little fun."

"And to escape the little woman's bossy ways?"

She laughed. "We won't get into that angle. I was thinking of the hotel, rather grand — like its name — the atmosphere, this feeling of remoteness — gone now though because of airplanes and speedboats."

They finished touring the hotel, and since it was too early for lunch, they went again to find Jake Winthrop. A young boy had taken his place behind the counter, and he pointed to a shady place behind the store where an old bench leaned on rickety legs.

"Grandpa's out there, taking the air, as he calls it."

They went out the back way, the screen door slamming behind them, and they picked their way through empty cardboard boxes and old gasoline cans to find Jake Winthrop.

"Hello, folks," he said.

"Jake, this is Alison Blair, a guest at the Greenwood Inn. She'd like to talk to you," Bob said.

Jake smiled, showing a few missing teeth, and motioned for Alison to sit down.

"Anytime a pretty young woman wants to talk to me, I certainly have the time."

Alison sat down in the old lawn chair and explained what she wanted and why.

"Leighton Thordsen," Jake mused. "Lots of folks have been curious about him and asked me questions. What do you want to know?"

"Anything and everything you can remember."

"Big order," Jake said. "Well, I'll tell you, Thordsen was a ladies' man and a gentleman who appreciated good food and a glass of wine at dinnertime. But there was one thing sorely wrong with him."

"Yes?"

Jake grinned. "He didn't like to fish. Now there's something wrong with a man that doesn't like to fish!"

Alison laughed. "By your standards, I see there is. But Thordsen wasn't the type."

"Nope, he wasn't. But I liked him. Nice man. He always had a polite word for me, never looked down his nose like some of the others. I was just a handyman around the hotel in those days. Sometimes I carried the luggage to the rooms and sometimes I scrubbed the floors or hauled supplies from Donnerville in my boat. But Thordsen always treated me like a gentleman. I appreciated that."

"Did you talk to him very much?"

"Never had much occasion. But now and then I did him favors and he was generous with his tips."

"What about his secretary, Miss Benson. Do you remember her?"

"Any man would!" Jake said, lifting his brows. "She was such a pretty young thing. Bright as a button. They were in love, you know."

Alison leaned back. "You're positive of this?"

"Been around some, Miss Blair, and I know when two people have got something going between them. And they did."

"But they never married. That's strange, isn't it?"

"He wasn't the marrying kind. Would have tied him down too much. He was a temperamental man. I've seen him throw a tantrum that would frighten the best of us. Then again, he could be as gentle as a lamb. With her, he was always gentle. I never seen him cross her, but there was some talk . . ."

"I'm listening," Alison said with a laugh. "Keep talking, Jake."

"There was another man in her life, but I don't know who. Just heard talk. This was probably a problem between them and maybe it's why they never got married. Who can say?"

"The plot thickens," Bob said. "What about his work, Jake? Did you know anything about that?"

"Once I saw him out walking, long after everyone else had turned in for the night. It must have been four o'clock in the morning. I was up, believe it or not, because work in the hotel started then. Thordsen had never been to bed — said he was trying to work out part of a composition in his head and he was having a bad time of it."

"The last piece he worked on was called 'The Rains of Spring.' I don't suppose he ever mentioned that to you," Alison said.

Jake nodded. "Yep, he did. Said he had started it, didn't know if he'd ever get it finished. It was the one that was troubling him so much."

Alison drew a quivering breath. She could no longer doubt that such a composition existed, at least in part.

"Is there anything else?" she asked.

"No, afraid not. I didn't know the man that well. Just liked him, that's all. Different than most. He had a special quality that made him stand out in a crowd. A pity he died over there in the old country. I think he would have liked to have spent his last days on Windswept Island. He loved it there."

Jake's grandson called to him just then, asking about locating a spare part for a broken motor, and he excused himself and hurried away.

Bob reached out and took Alison's hand. "Did it help?"

"Yes. I get a different picture every time I talk to someone. There were so many sides to Thordsen's personality. But there's one thing that keeps bothering me. Why did he leave? What could have taken him away so abruptly, and what on earth did he do with that last composition?"

Bob shook his head. "Alison, you could sit here till doomsday contemplating that. Let's go and see if we can't have an early lunch. There's a great deal more I want to show you."

The food at the Grand Hotel was only mediocre, but it was fun to eat there and to imagine what it must have been like when Thordsen was there.

When they had finished lunch, Bob took her for a long, meandering boat ride, and it seemed that they were very far away from Greenwood. They docked on the Canadian side and bought souvenirs and a box of English toffee. Heading back, Alison felt pleasantly relaxed, and when they buzzed by the Grand Hotel once again she gave it a long, wistful look. If only its walls could talk.

The boat ride home seemed to go faster than the trip over, and before too long she saw the outline of the inn standing on the cliff, the sun setting squarely behind it. Where had the day gone?

Alison felt windblown and sunburned, but the day would always stand out in her memory with its own special glow. When Bob put the boat in at the inn's dock, she saw that *The Maiden* was gone. Salt must have been called to the mainland to bring guests. Considering the hour, it could be little else.

Bob walked with her up the path to the inn, and by now, the sun had dropped lower toward the horizon, bathing the island in a rosy light that glanced off windows and brushed pink along the white walls of the buildings.

"Thanks for a lovely day, Bob."

"It doesn't have to end just yet," he pointed out.

"I think it had better."

"If you say so."

She paused at the door to the lobby and

turned to him.

"I'll never forget the Grand Hotel as long as I live."

"Forget the hotel, but remember me."

Then he kissed her, and when she broke away he was smiling. With a wave, he hurried down the path toward his boat. As Alison turned to step inside the lobby she saw Chris. He stood very straight, his shoulders rigid. A roll of plans was in his hand; his black hair was mussed and he looked tired. Or was it anger?

"Hi," she said.

"Hello," he said gruffly. "So you're back."

"It was a wonderful day."

"With a wonderful finish?"

She knew then that he had seen Bob kissing her and she realized that it was anger she heard in his voice.

"How did your day go?" she countered.

"I've had better ones," he admitted.

"Oh?"

"Did you get the information you wanted?"

"Yes, some. I'm always anxious for more."

His jaw was set and his eyes burned. He tossed the plans aside with an abrupt gesture.

"I didn't realize you and Bob were so chummy."

"We're friends."

"It looked like more than that to me!"

"Did it?"

"You know it did," he said. Then, with a sigh, he ran a hand through his hair and shook his head. "I'm sorry. I had no right to say any of that. It's just that all day long I thought of you out with him and I . . ."

He turned away and Alison stared after him. Was it possible that Chris had begun to care for her, really care? But what about Amy? She was so sure that Chris was still carrying a torch for her.

"Chris . . ."

He paused for a moment, and when he faced her again, she saw that he was bewildered and uncertain.

"I'm sorry your day went so badly," she said.

He smiled tiredly. "So am I. The next time *I'll* take you to the Grand Hotel or wherever you want."

"I rather think you could use a day of rest. You've been going at it full throttle ever since you took over."

"Would you spend that day with me?"

"Maybe."

He smiled in earnest then. "Thanks. Alison . . ."

He reached out his arms and she moved into them. With a happy sigh, she dropped her head to his shoulder and he pressed his lips to her hair.

"I think you and I have just broken down a few barriers," he said.

"It would seem so."

"And I have other news," he said. "Salt went to the mainland. It seems you have visitors."

"Visitors! Who?" She gasped. "Regan — is it Regan? Chris, who is it?"

13

"I don't know who it is," Chris told Alison. "I just know we had a phone call from someone saying that they wanted to see you and asking us to pick them up. They also asked for a room for the night."

"How long has Salt been gone?"

"He should be coming back very shortly," Chris said. "Why don't you come and see what I've accomplished in the music room."

She really didn't want to see the room in a state of repair and disarray, but Chris had cleared out all the old debris of the wall. While it still looked raw and unfinished, she could at least see what he was trying to accomplish.

"It will be nice, Chris."

"I'm sorry to say I found no manuscript or any strange little caches anywhere. I know you're anxious for me to get down in the cellar, but I just haven't had time."

"Are you teasing me?"

"Maybe." He grinned. "But then, who knows, something *could* be here. I wouldn't know why a famous man would want to hide his work, but many a genius has been a little eccentric."

"Thordsen was a complex person. I learn that more every day I try to write about him."

She peered anxiously out the window for the sight of Salt coming back with *The Maiden,* but it seemed to be taking a very long time. When she heard the boat at last, she was tempted to go down to the dock to meet it, but she held back. Instead she went to her room and freshened up. If it *was* Regan, what would they have to say to each other? If he had come, what did it mean?

Her heart was thudding by the time she heard Salt's voice outside the lobby door. It swung open, and Alison was more than a little startled to find her parents.

"Mother! Dad!" she cried.

With a laugh, they hugged one another

and everybody tried to talk at once. Salt had put their luggage aside and disappeared to have a quick drink at the bar. Chris stood in the doorway for a moment, watching the reunion, and then he too disappeared.

"What a wonderful surprise," Alison said. "But why didn't you give me some warning?"

"There wasn't time," her father explained. "All of this is on the spur of the moment. We're actually on our way to Europe. I've got some business for my bank, and while we're there, we're going to take a little vacation and see some of the sights. We thought if you'd go along we'd add Venice to the list."

"Venice!"

"Thordsen died there and is buried there too, isn't he?" her father asked.

"It's a temptation," Alison sighed. "A real temptation, but I'm not sure . . ."

"We'd love to have you, pet," Mr. Blair said. "But it's for you to say."

Mrs. Blair squeezed her hand. "We'll be honest. There is another reason. Regan has hinted that he might join us. He wouldn't say for certain."

Alison blushed and she looked at her parents with surprise. "Regan? He's been in touch with you?"

Her father cleared his throat. "Actually, it was my idea. He's often said he would like to tour Europe and he had some unexpected free time this summer, so it seemed —"

"Did he actually say he would join us?" Alison asked.

"Nothing definite."

Alison swallowed hard, trying to imagine what it would be like to be in Venice with Regan. It could be good and beautiful, but on the other side of the coin, she knew very well that the old quarrels could surface again, making every second miserable. It would be a terrible shame to spoil a trip to Venice or even to risk that happening.

"I don't think I'll go," she said. "But I really appreciate the invitation."

Her parents exchanged glances, and she saw that they were disappointed but understanding.

"It's all right, dear. Under the

circumstances, I expect you made the right decision. Regan should have been in touch with you about it himself. We don't want to be meddlers."

"You could never meddle if you tried for a hundred years," Alison said warmly. "Now, come and let me show you the inn."

The next morning, Alison and her parents breakfasted together and she walked them down to the dock, where Salt waited to take them back to Donnerville.

"Have a wonderful time in Europe, and if you do go to Venice, leave a rose at Thordsen's grave for me."

"I'll take care of it," her mother promised.

Then, with hugs and kisses and shouts of good-bye, they were off. All too quickly the lake seemed to swallow them up and the sound of *The Maiden* faded away.

Alison felt a little lonely and empty after they'd gone. Goodbyes were not her strong suit. Going back to the inn, she heard Chris pounding away in the music room, and she went to peer inside for a moment.

"Did they get off okay?" he asked.

"Yes."

"Nice people. I hope they'll come back for another visit sometime when the inn is really in good shape."

"I think they will."

"I was surprised that you turned down a chance to see Venice and to visit Thordsen's last haunts," he said. "How come?"

It wasn't only Regan, she knew. He might have been a part of it, but the other part . . . She sighed. She wasn't sure.

"I guess I just wanted to stay here. I can't ignore the feeling inside that everything I want is here, in this house. Even if it doesn't make good sense, that's the way it is."

"Sometimes our instincts are our best guides, Alison. Selfishly, I'm glad you're staying."

He gave her a long, tender look with his gray eyes, and she felt an answering warmth come from her own. Then Reba called, shattering the moment.

Chris's days were filled with such interruptions, and he was beginning to wonder if he would ever be able to do as much work over the summer as he had hoped. It didn't look promising. There was just too much work, and he would have to spend the next year doing more of the same. But if he could just complete a large share of it, he wouldn't feel so badly.

In the course of the morning, he sent Salt to Donnerville for lumber. He was trying to reuse all he could, but it wasn't practical, and it seemed he never had what he needed. Work in the music room was held up until Salt would return, so Chris decided to look at the basement. He had been wanting to see exactly what was there and, remembering his promise to Alison, he kept his eyes open for anything unusual.

The place was so cluttered that he called Roy down to help him move away some of the heavier things that had rusted away — an old furnace, old bathroom fixtures, boxes of junk.

"If you see anything that might be valuable, show it to me, Roy," Chris said.

Roy nodded dumbly and kept shoving

things around, grunting with the effort. Roy wasn't the world's best helper and often simply disappeared when he grew tired or bored.

Chris, on the other hand, attacked the work with vigor and kept a close eye on his half-witted helper. Salt returned, but Chris decided to continue in the basement and put Salt to work at something else. Two in the basement were enough.

It was shortly after noon when he discovered the small trunk. The mice had nibbled at one corner and then had given up. The dampness had warped the wood and damaged the leather straps. The lock that held it shut was rusted beyond use. But as he wiped off the dust, he was startled to see the initials L. T. Leighton Thordsen!

"Roy, go and find Alison and tell her to please come down here."

Roy straightened with a surprised smile. Then, with a quick nod of his head, he rushed away. While Chris waited for her, he took a hammer and a chisel and worked away at the rusted lock. It was stronger than he had anticipated, but just as he heard Roy and Alison on the stairs, the lock broke and fell off.

"What is it?" Alison asked. "Did you find something? Roy mentioned a chest."

"I don't suppose it's really anything of importance, but I think it may have belonged to Thordsen. I just now got the lock off. You can have the honor of opening it."

Roy had become very attentive and pressed close like a curious child, eager to see what was inside.

"If there is anything in there, it'll be ruined," Alison worried.

"Maybe not," Chris said. "The trunk seems tight, and some of these trunks were designed to keep things dry. This one was probably one of the best to be had in those days."

Alison reached out with trembling hands to raise the lid. Chris saw the excitement in her eyes, the color that had come to her cheeks. Roy was impatient.

"Open it up, hurry!" he said.

Chris prayed that Alison wasn't in for a disappointment. Perhaps he should have looked inside before she came. She lifted the lid. The interior was surprisingly dry, thanks to its leather and silk lining. The papers inside were slightly damp, a little moldy around the edges but legible.

"Concert programs," she said. "A few books, souvenirs, and travel folders. Nothing new. At least not at first glance."

She was disappointed and he put his arm around her shoulder. "I'm sorry. I was hoping this would really be something important for you."

"Could I have the trunk? Would you carry it up to my room? I'd like to go over every inch of it, although I don't really expect to find anything."

"Sure, I'll take it up for you. Let me clean it up a little. At least you have something that belonged to Thordsen. That should count for something."

Alison ran her hand over the trunk and looked pensive. "He surely must have gone away in a tremendous hurry to have left a trunk full of souvenirs behind."

Chris carefully dusted off the old trunk and prepared to carry it upstairs. Alison went ahead to open doors for him and he took the trunk into her room and put it in the spot she indicated.

"I'll sort through everything," she said.

"Maybe you'll get lucky."

"I don't really think so. It's nothing more than a box of sentimental souvenirs."

She was obviously very disappointed. He felt a tug at his heart and wanted to do something to lift her spirits.

"How would you like to go to the mainland on Sunday, Alison? I think we could both use some time away from Greenwood and all our problems."

She gave him a quick smile. "I could certainly use a good time about now!"

"Then count on it," he said.

He left her to the trunk and walked down the hall. Roy was on the phone, a rather surprising sight, for he had never known Roy to use the phone before. When he saw Chris, he hung up hurriedly. Chris was about to ask him about it when Salt appeared, anxious to get back to work, so Chris turned his attention once again to the music room.

There was satisfaction in hearing the buzz of the saw, feeling the jar of the hammer as he drove the nails in. With the sunlight brilliant on the water beyond the windows and with Sunday a sweet promise in his heart, he could only feel joyful.

Even Reba noticed it. Chris often ate in the kitchen with her, enjoying the comfort and happy confusion there. Reba could turn out meals that would please anyone's palate, and he was glad that she had agreed to stay on with him.

"What makes you so happy today?" she asked.

He sampled her excellent Swiss steak and shrugged. "Just optimistic — no good reason. Don't you have days like that, Reba?"

"If I do, something always happens to spoil them. Usually it's Roy."

"Where is he? He's always hungry as a bear and here well before I am."

"I already fed him. You've been good to him, Chris, and I appreciate that."

"He's developed a crush on Alison."

"I know. I've told him to leave her alone, but I'm afraid he doesn't pay much attention to me sometimes. I've looked after him all my life. There's no one else to do it, and what worries me is, what if something should happen to me? What would become of Roy then?"

"You really shouldn't think that far ahead. Where is he now?"

"Sulking down on the dock. We had a quarrel. I try not to get angry with him, but sometimes my patience runs out."

"I'll have Salt tell him to come up and help me again this afternoon. I'm sure he can be of some use."

"Bless you, Chris. You're a sweetheart."

He ate a second helping of Reba's cooking and wished there was time simply to go and sit lazily on the patio in the sun. But that day was far in the future. He had to keep hustling to do what he could before the summer ended.

Roy didn't come to help, but it was probably just as well. Sometimes he was more trouble than he was worth. Salt was off on other errands, so Chris worked alone. It was the middle of the afternoon when he heard a speedboat put in at the dock and he wondered who it was. Most of their guests used Salt for transportation.

When the man came into the lobby, Chris recognized him at once as Ed Reeves, the piano tuner's son.

"Hello," Chris said.

"I'm looking for Alison," Ed said.

"She's probably in her room. I can go and call her —"

"Just tell me where it is, I'll find it," Ed said.

Chris gave him directions, wondering why he wanted to see Alison. But it was none of his business; it probably had something to do with Thordsen's piano. He tried to put it out of his mind.

Roy suddenly reappeared and Chris put him to work. Before long he saw Alison on the patio with Ed, leaning on the railing, talking intently. Chris tried to keep his attention on his work, but he hit his thumb with a hammer and swore to himself. He made an error in measuring a length of wood and had to cut another. His concentration was a shambles. All he could seem to think about was Alison standing there with the wind blowing through her dark hair, laughing with Ed Reeves.

Roy grew tired of his work and, true to form, he simply put his things down and walked off. Chris struggled on alone, but it was slow going. Finally, agitated, he tossed his tools aside and stalked out of the room. He found Reba in the lobby. She took one look at him and lifted her brows.

"What did Roy do now?"

"Nothing more than usual," he said with an edge to his voice.

"Then what's bothering you, Chris?"

Without meaning to, he glanced out the window toward Alison and Ed Reeves, but Reba didn't miss it. She smiled slowly.

"Oh, so that's how it is."

"What do you mean?" he demanded.

"It's Alison."

Chris swallowed hard. He hadn't really let himself think about it, but the feeling was always there, a kind of warm glow, an awakening. Even when he deliberately made himself think of Amy, it wouldn't go away. The truth was that he had fallen in love with Alison, and he was jealous of any other man who came near her, including Bob Beale and Ed Reeves. He was jealous of Regan too, a man he had never laid eyes on. This whole situation was making a wreck out of his emotions.

"She's a nice girl, Chris," Reba said in her gentle, motherly way. "And you're a red-blooded man. You shouldn't go through life alone."

"But the summer will end and she'll go away. I may never see her again."

"Then do something about it, Chris. Don't stand there like a bump on a log."

Well, there was Sunday ahead. Alison was going out with him and maybe then . . .

14

Alison was surprised to open her door and find Ed Reeves.

"Hello, Alison," he said.

He gave her a smile, and the eyes behind his glasses were bright and quick.

"What on earth brings you back here?" she asked.

He smiled at that and would have stepped farther into the room, but she barred the way. The table she used for a desk was a mess, but more than that, the old trunk stood wide open on the floor.

"How about letting me tell you? Is there a coffee shop or something here?" he asked.

"We could go out to the patio. It's very pleasant there."

"Good."

She closed the door firmly behind her

and Ed talked pleasantly about casual things. He asked if his father had done satisfactory work on Thordsen's piano.

"Yes. Very," she said. "I didn't have much hope that he could restore it, but he did."

"Well, I guess Dad's had lots of practice, and he takes pride in what he does."

The patio was sunny, but a fresh breeze kept it from being hot. Ed complained that it was humid.

"Tell me, how's the book going?" he asked.

"Not too well," she admitted.

"You mean you've made no great discoveries since coming here?"

She gave him a sharp look. Had he seen the trunk in her room and guessed that it had been found in the basement? No, that wasn't possible. He was only making conversation.

"No. Not yet."

"Does that mean you might decide to stay around here longer?"

"Who knows?" she asked with a sigh. "I really thought I'd have the book well on its way by now and I don't. Chris intends to close Greenwood when winter comes and that means I couldn't stay here."

"Lots of nice places in Donnerville," Ed said as he leaned toward her with his handsome smile. "I'd be glad to help you find something."

"That's sweet of you. I'll have to think about it and see how things stand when the summer is over."

Ed reached into his pocket for a cigarette and extended the pack to her, but she shook her head. He lighted one and smoked for a moment, leaning on the railing, staring intently out at the lake. She sensed that he had some particular reason for coming to see her so unexpectedly.

"What do you think of Dad's pet theory?"

"Theory?" Alison asked.

"That Thordsen's last composition still exists, could possibly be hidden here. You have searched for it, haven't you?"

"Not personally, but Chris hasn't found anything."

"Nothing?" Ed asked, giving her

a quick look.

"Nothing," she said flatly. "Ed, I can't believe that Thordsen would have left something so valuable behind."

"It could be an extra copy, something like that."

"Frankly, I'm beginning to have my doubts that the composition even exists."

Ed lifted his brow. "No, I think it exists all right. It may be lost, but lost things can be found. Dad firmly believes — well, why speculate? Let's talk about the future, not the past. How would you like to go out to dinner sometime, Alison. Could we make it Sunday?"

"I'm sorry, but I have other plans."

"Just my luck. Well, then, sometime next week."

"Ed, I'm very busy and —"

He turned to face her, and she met his eyes with a lift of her chin.

"Actually, I had a special reason for asking you out, Alison. I've located someone that knew Thordsen personally. If you'd like to visit with him —"

"Someone in Donnerville?"

"Yes."

"Why didn't you tell me before? That's wonderful news! Thordsen knew so few local people."

"I could set up a meeting if you like. How about next Tuesday afternoon?"

"But you have the store to run and you must be busy. If you'd just give me the man's name, I can contact him."

"I'd really like to do this for you, Alison," Ed said.

He made it hard to refuse and her curiosity was keen. She was always hoping to find people who could tell her something new and different about Thordsen, and the temptation was too great.

"All right. Thank you, Ed. I really do appreciate this."

"My pleasure. I'll pick you up in my boat at about four or so. We'll see this man and then we can have dinner."

On Sunday, Chris came knocking on Alison's door and invited her to have a late breakfast with him.

"Then we'll have Salt take us to Donnerville and we'll see what we can find there."

Reba served them at a table next to the window, and they watched the usual busy Sunday activity on the lake. But the inn and the island itself were quiet on Sundays, and Alison was rather glad.

Chris wore a shirt open at the neck, casual slacks, and sneakers. The sun had turned him a golden brown, and she liked the clean, hard look of his hands.

"I take it you didn't find anything in the old trunk of any real worth or I would have heard about it."

"Just souvenirs. Interesting, of course, but no sign of even a fragment of the missing manuscript."

"Salt hasn't unearthed anything more either. I had him search thoroughly through the rest of the basement. There's still the attic, but from the one quick peek I took, I don't think anything was ever stored there."

"It's gone, like the man himself," she said with a sigh. "And what a pity! It would be such a tremendously important discovery."

Chris reached out and covered her hand with his. "My mother used to say it was always the darkest before the light. Maybe it will be that way with you."

"You've never told me very much about your family."

"My parents live in Texas now. Dad's retired, and being an active man, he likes to keep busy. He runs a little hobby shop. He likes to make things out of wood, and when he began to sell a few of his items, he had so many orders he could scarcely keep up. Mother suggested turning it into a small business, so they did. They're very busy and very happy."

"Brothers and sisters?"

"One brother in New York. He's a lawyer and a good one. He has a nice family — three kids, two girls and a boy. I'd been hoping they'd have time to come for a visit, but Paul's always up to his ears in work. Maybe next year . . ."

"I'd really like to ask about Amy," Alison said.

Chris drew his hand away, and she saw a flash of pain cross his face.

"I think I should tell you about her, Alison. Amy and I were in love with each other, or I thought we were, when I went into the service. It was during the last days of the Vietnam War, and before it was over I was taken prisoner. I was one of the last to be released, long after the shooting had stopped. I came home and Amy was still waiting for me. I thought we'd pick up where we'd left off. We came to Greenwood to get reacquainted, to make plans for our future. But things went sour shortly after that. We broke off and Amy married someone else. It seems she had been seeing him for some time before I came home.''

There was a hollowness in his voice and she knew he had been deeply hurt.

''I'm sorry. It hardly seems fair —''

''It happens,'' he said simply. ''I just didn't think it would happen to me.''

''But why did you come here? You said you had a good business going in Chicago —''

''Another sour note,'' Chris said. ''My partner did something I didn't like, something slightly dishonest, and I pulled out. George was my friend and he betrayed me. Amy betrayed me too. If I seem distrustful at times, perhaps now you'll understand why."

They grew quiet as they ate Reba's breakfast, and Alison realized that Chris had suffered much more than she had imagined. He was not a man to take either incident lightly, and she had to admire the way he had boldly taken his fate into his hands. Too many people would have let such things turn them bitter and miserable, with an angry outlook on life. Chris had done a good job of pulling himself together and going on.

The day she had gone to Donnerville with Bob Beale, they had looked at the art on display, had supper in a fancy club, and went speeding down the highways, the wind in their faces. Going with Chris was entirely different.

They explored the countryside, driving up and down little byroads and enjoying the simple sights. It was rather nice to be out of the sight of water for a change. They walked hand in hand in a small park nestled between the trees and sat down in the tall grass, leaning against the trunk of a large tree. There they talked of when they had been children, what they had done and what their dreams had been.

"You were a serious little boy, weren't you?"

"Most of the time," Chris said with a smile. "Paul was the daredevil. I was always more cautious. I still am, I suppose. Coming here and taking on the inn was contrary to my nature. It's the first real gamble I've ever taken."

"And you'll make it pay off."

He stretched out and put his head in her lap. She plucked a bit of bark from his dark hair.

"Even if the inn is a flop, I'm glad I came," he said. "How else would I have met you, Alison?"

His gray eyes flickered, and then he reached up and put a hand behind her head, pulling her down until their lips met. The kiss was long and sweet, and when he dropped his head to her lap again he kept her hand against his cheek.

"You've never told me about Regan."

She drew her hand away and thought about the man she had left behind. There hadn't been a single phone call, letter —

nothing — to let her know that he still thought of her or perhaps missed her or was sorry it had come to this between them. She would bet her last dollar that he had not gone to Venice.

"Regan was an intense kind of man, a teacher of science. He wanted things cut and dried, black or white, right or wrong. There was never any in between with him, and life just doesn't stack up that way. I couldn't either."

"Is it over? Truly over?"

She didn't answer. She wasn't sure, but she thought so. Right now she was in a kind of limbo, suspended, letting the summer run its course, and she had put all her concentration on her work, Windswept Island and Leighton Thordsen.

"I hope it is," Chris said. "Because I'm falling in love with you."

She stared at him and tightness came to her throat. "Oh, Chris —"

"I didn't think it could be like this. I didn't know how to handle it when it started to happen. But I can't run away from the truth anymore. I love you, Alison."

Then he folded her deep into his arms, and there with the sky drifting overhead, the grass waving in the breeze, he held her close and hard against him and his mouth found hers again and again.

"I think we'd better walk on," she said.

"I've shocked you, I've handled this badly."

"You make my head spin," she laughed. "I'll agree to that. Come on. Let's go back to the car."

They walked back, hand in hand, and ate lunch in some small town whose name she couldn't remember later. They wandered into a movie theater where they sat in the dark and saw little of what was on the screen.

All too soon it was time to be back at the dock at Donnerville. Alison hated to see the day end. Chris had stirred her heart, and while it upset her, it excited her too. She was tingling with emotions, filled with warmth, and when Salt came tearing toward them in *The Maiden,* she was almost sorry to get aboard.

Back at Greenwood, Chris saw her to

her room. When she stepped inside, she froze.

"Someone's been in my room!"

"What?"

He came in behind her and looked around. Everything looked perfectly normal, in place, untouched.

"Why do you say that?" he asked. "It looks okay to me."

"Someone's been in here," she replied anxiously.

"Where's the old trunk?" he asked.

She groped in her purse for the key and went to unlock the closet near the bath. With a sigh of relief, she saw that it was there, safe and sound.

"You locked it up?" Chris asked with surprise.

"It's valuable to me. The other closet has no lock, so I put it in here. I didn't want anything to happen to it. I don't know, it just strikes me as being odd that the trunk was left behind. I've gone through its contents a dozen times, but I can't shake this feeling that maybe there *is* something important about it."

Chris went to peer out the window for a

moment and then excused himself, saying, "I'll be back in a moment."

Alison opened the trunk and satisfied herself that nothing inside had been disturbed. Then she closed and locked the closet door. In a few minutes she heard Chris coming down the hall with quick steps.

"I was talking with Reba," he explained. "I asked her if anyone had been here to see you or if she saw anyone lurking around your door."

"And the answer was no," Alison said. "You think I'm crazy, don't you?"

"I never said that, Alison. But I want to know why you think someone was here."

"The fragrance on the air. Didn't you notice it? It's a man's cologne. But not yours or Bob Beale's or even Ed Reeves's. This is a different scent."

"Could it have been a woman's cologne?"

"Possibly, but this seems to be more of a manly scent."

"I don't know what's going on around here, Alison, but I'd like to get to the bottom of it," he said.

"No more than I would."

"Are you afraid here? Would you like to move to another room?"

"You're just across the hall," she said. "And I like the room."

"I wish I had the answer."

She put a hand on his sleeve and shook her head. "I'm sorry to bother you, truly."

He smiled at that and pulled her close. "Darling, bother me all you want. I like it —"

He kissed her for a moment and then let her go. "Reba has something to discuss with me. I suppose there's another problem to be solved. I have to get back to the kitchen."

"Poor Chris, no rest —"

He was gone, closing the door behind him, and she stood very still for a moment, sniffing the air, wishing she didn't have such a good sense of smell. But she did, and she knew someone had been there. It did nothing at all for her peace of mind.

Could someone have come looking for the old trunk? Was it possible there was something in it that she had overlooked?

She pulled it from the closet again, raised the lid, and took all the contents out. Once she'd read a story about a trunk with a false bottom, but she had already looked for one with no success. Still, she might look again . . .

She thumped the sides of the trunk, feeling for concealed hinges or buttons, but found nothing. The bottom sounded hollow and that worried her a little. She kept thumping, ears keen for the difference in tones, and then she saw it. There was a worn place between the side and the bottom. Reaching for a nail file, she thrust it into the spot and, with a hard twist, lifted it. The bottom moved! It took a few minutes to free it, but she soon had it out. Lying snugly on the real floor of the trunk, hidden all these years, was a notebook.

It was something like a diary for the years that Thordsen had lived at Greenwood and was written in what she believed was Thordsen's hand. Several random musical notes had been scrawled on each page. They seemed to mean nothing but a kind of doodling.

With shaking hands, Alison carried the notebook to her table and turned on a light. Some of the writing was hard to read because of its poorly, perhaps hurried, scrawl, but she read it through in less than an hour.

There was nothing of significance — just notes about the weather, a few names she recognized as being Thordsen's friends, news of concerts and bookings, and an occasional mention of his health, which seemed to worry him.

With a dismal sigh, she slapped the notebook shut. She seemed plagued by dead ends. What should have been a tremendous find and of great value had proved to be banal, uninteresting, and almost dull. She laid the notebook back inside the trunk and put it away in the closet.

When she saw Chris down by the dock later, he took one look at her face and knew something was wrong.

"What is it?" he asked.

She told him about the diary and her disappointment that it contained nothing of importance.

"That's a tough break," Chris said.

"I had such high hopes . . ."

Chris put his arms around her for a moment, and with a sigh, she dropped her head to his shoulder.

"Don't give up, sweetheart," Chris said. "Keep looking, keep hoping . . ."

She closed her eyes. She did not easily give in to tears but they burned against her lids. Chris lifted her chin and bent down to kiss them away.

Then with a start he stiffened, and Alison saw that Roy Zeller had appeared in his quiet, mysterious way and was staring at them.

"How long has he been there?" Alison asked.

"I don't know," Chris said.

She moved out of his arms, and when Chris took a step toward Roy, he turned and hurried away.

"I suppose I should pity him instead of being angry," Chris said. "I think he's fallen in love with you too."

15

By morning Alison had shaken off her despair, and she began to feel that there was something special about the diary. Why else would it have been so cleverly hidden? But what it was escaped her. She spent the next day rereading it, making a few notes, trying to put it all together, but there was simply nothing there!

By the time Ed Reeves came for her on Tuesday evening, she was all keyed up. If this trip with Ed proved to be another false lead . . . She sighed heavily. She was beginning to wish she had gone to Venice with her parents.

From the music room she saw Ed's boat coming and went down to the dock to meet him. He was informally dressed, and instead of getting out of the boat, he simply gave her a hand and helped her aboard.

"You look lovely, Alison."

"Thank you. You never told me the name of this person that knew Thordsen," she said.

"Larry Hames. He uses a cottage up the lake that belongs to a friend of mine and he's always there this time of year. We'll buzz up and have a chat with him."

"How did he figure in Thordsen's life?"

Ed shrugged. "I don't really know, except that they were acquaintances."

Ed revved the motor and soon they left the dock behind. Once again she found herself surrounded by the huge lake, the air rushing against her face. Ed gave her a fast ride, and when he began to slow the boat, she saw another island just ahead. He turned to the left and began to circle it. Only a few cottages were visible, and he put in at the dock in front of one of them and tied up the boat.

"We'll find Larry and see what he can tell us," he said.

"It looks awfully quiet."

"I have a key. We can go inside and wait. I'm sure he won't be away long."

They walked up to the cottage, Ed taking her arm. He was being very charming, and there was no question in Alison's mind that he was attractive. He rapped sharply at the door, and called out Larry's name, but there was no reply.

"I noticed that his boat was gone. He must have gone out for a spin. Let's go inside and wait."

"Should we do that?" she asked.

"Sure," Ed said easily. "Larry only uses the place now and then. He doesn't own it. As a matter of fact, I come here quite a lot myself. It's a very nice cottage if you don't mind roughing it a bit."

Ed unlocked the door and they stepped inside. The place was very neat, rather sparsely furnished but comfortable, and from the living room window they had a lovely view. Ed gave her his handsome smile.

"Cozy," he said.

"What does Larry Hames do?"

"Larry does as little as possible. He's retired now and pretty much just lives it up. Originally, he was an attorney."

"Perhaps Thordsen went to him for

legal advice?''

Ed came over to her and put a hand on her shoulder. It felt very warm and heavy there. "My dear, don't you ever get Thordsen out of your mind?''

"It's why we came here, isn't it?''

"Sure, but Larry's not here, and until he comes . . .''

He let the sentence hang in the air, and there was something about the tone of his voice that caught her attention. His smile was very slow and his eyes lingered for a long moment on her face.

"There are some records if I remember right. Want to put on a stack? We could probably find something to drink in the refrigerator.''

"Don't you have any idea how long Larry will be away?''

"There are no phones out here, so I can't call him,'' Ed explained. "I assumed he would be here. He always is.''

"I really don't think we should stay.''

"Oh, come on,'' Ed said. "Relax. It's a lovely place and we could get to know each other. I'd *like* to know you, Alison.''

"That's very flattering, but —''

He came and put an arm around her shoulder. "If you don't want to stay here, let's take a walk. There are some paths on the island and it *is* a nice day."

She moved deftly out of his grasp. There was a terrible suspicion in the back of her mind that Ed Reeves had plenty of ideas, and none of them had to do with her interviewing Larry Hames.

"I'd like to leave, Ed."

"Compromise," he urged. "We'll take a walk and when we come back, if Larry hasn't returned, we'll go somewhere and have dinner. I'll set up an interview with Larry for another time. Okay?"

It seemed fair enough, and she did want to see this man if at all possible. So she consented to the walk, and they began following a path that had been worn by other restless people. The island was heavily wooded but overgrown with brush, and it did not have the appeal of Windswept. She began to wish that she hadn't come at all. Ed tried to put everything on a personal basis and she was having a little trouble keeping out of his reach.

When they returned to the cottage, Larry Hames still wasn't there, and no boat had put in at the dock. Ed made himself a drink while Alison paced restlessly.

"Why don't you sit down?" Ed said.

"I think I'd like to go back to Greenwood, Ed."

His eyes looked blank for a moment. "We haven't had dinner yet."

"But it's late and I have so much work to do. I really don't think this trip is going to be of much help."

"How's the book going now?"

"Not much better."

"And still no missing composition?"

Alison looked at him sharply. "Why are you so interested in that?"

Ed gave her a cool smile. "My dear, any fool with half a brain can figure it out. It's worth a fortune!"

"Oh?"

"Listen, I've been thinking. If by some chance you *did* find it —" He held up his hand when he saw the look on her face. "Now bear with me, Alison. It *could* happen. I doubt anyone else has really gone after it, mostly because I think the majority of people don't think it exists. But we know better. You know, with a little maneuvering we could really make it pay off."

"We?" she asked with a wry smile.

"You'd need some help, Alison, in a deal like this, and while I may seem a two-bit music store owner to you, I do have connections. I could get the best possible price for it. Let me help you with it and have a share of the profits. You'll be ahead, I'll be ahead —"

Alison couldn't help but laugh aloud. "Ed, you're amazing! You really can stand there and try to make a deal for a manuscript that hasn't even been found?"

Ed gave her another cool look. "If you haven't found it."

She flushed. "I resent that!"

"Okay, okay, don't get angry. I'm just trying to be hardheaded about this. You're so damned sentimental about Thordsen, you're apt to find it and rush out and *give* it to the world. I favor turning a dime every chance I get."

"I think you've made yourself perfectly clear, Ed."

"Well?" he asked anxiously. "It's something to think about, isn't it?"

"Of course," she said, trying hard to hold back her anger.

"It would be nice, being partners with you. Why don't we do something about that right now?"

He stepped around the bar toward her and with a rush pulled her into his arms and tried to kiss her. She pushed him away firmly.

"I have a strange suspicion that you *knew* Larry Hames wasn't going to be here."

He gave her another slow smile. "It's very cozy here, remote. We could —"

"Let's go home now, Ed," she cut in decisively.

"What about dinner?"

"I'd like to go back to the inn."

He saw that she was determined and, without a word, he poured the rest of his drink down the drain and went to hold the door open for her. She walked through it, her head up, trying her best to hang on to her temper. She began to wonder if there was a Larry Hames, and if so, has he really known Thordsen? Or was all of this just a clever maneuver on Ed's part?

He was still angry and said very little as they climbed into the boat and headed back toward Greenwood. For Alison, their little expedition was the crowning blow. Her spirits were sagging badly again, and she wished there was something she could do to buoy them up. Ed's flimsy proposition had made her miserable. It even flitted through her mind that it might be better to leave Windswept and go home to do her writing.

Ed was pushing the boat hard and fast, and when they reached the dock at the inn, he gave her a questioning look.

"You will think about what I said, won't you, Alison?"

"Forget it, Ed. I'm not interested."

She got out of the boat unassisted. Ed was in a rage but knew better than to argue. He revved the motor, turned the boat around, and was gone.

"You're back early."

She turned around to find Salt winding

line on a fishing reel.

"Salt, do you know Larry Hames?"

"Hames?" Salt asked, finishing with his line. "No."

"Don't you know most of the people around here? He was a lawyer."

"I don't think there was ever a lawyer here by that name."

"Just as I thought," she said.

Her head ached with anger and her heart with dissatisfaction.

"Something wrong?" Salt asked.

"I was had," she said with a frown. "And I don't like it one bit."

"Ed Reeves always was a slicker," Salt said.

"Thanks for telling me — *now*," she replied wryly.

Salt got to his feet. "I haven't had any supper, and I take it you haven't either. Let's go up and see what Reba has to give us."

He fell in step beside her, talking about his old sailing days and the fish he had caught or lost.

Reba was surprised to see Alison but asked no questions and served up one of her delicious meals. At Alison's invitation Salt joined her, and from their table they watched the last of the color disappear out of the sky.

"You told me you often took Thordsen to the mainland when he lived here," she said.

Salt nodded. "Yes."

"What did he do there, do you know?"

Salt lighted a cigarette and shook out the match, running a finger over the rim of his coffee cup, a pensive look on his face.

"Sometimes I knew. Other times we made some rather secret trips over and back."

"Secret?"

"Usually late at night. In those days, I kept a car over on the mainland and I used to take him around. He tipped well, I'll have to say that for him."

"Where did he go?" she asked.

"There was a certain house that he visited. I don't know much more than that. I'd take him there and wait for him. He'd go inside, maybe be gone an hour or more. Maybe only a few minutes. It was hard to tell."

"Who lived there?"

Salt squirmed in his chair. "I'm not sure."

"Salt, you're not telling me everything!"

"I could only guess," he said. "A doctor lived there. I suspect he was romancing the man's wife."

Alison drew a deep breath. "I see. Well, that jibes with what Herman Reeves told me. He thinks Thordsen left hurriedly because a scandal was about to break concerning the wife of a prominent man. A doctor's wife would fit, wouldn't it?"

"That could be wrong," Salt pointed out. "Reeves is guessing."

"It seems Thordsen was a very amorous man."

"Yeah," Salt said with a trace of irony in his voice. "So they say!"

"Is that house still there? Do the same people live there?"

"Don't know. Been ages since I was on that street."

"Sometime soon, would you show me where it is?"

Salt lifted his shoulders in a shrug. "Why not?"

"Bless you! So far, you've been the best thing that's happened to me today."

Salt raised his coffee cup at that, and she looked into his blue eyes and tried to read the expression there. But Salt did not reveal himself very often and he didn't then. She wondered how he had cut his face to leave such a scar, but she didn't ask and knew she probably never would.

The next day, despite all her setbacks, Alison tackled the work at hand again. She barely stopped for lunch. Joni looked in at her door once, saw that she was busy, and went away with a wave of her hand. Chris was still working in the music room, and Salt had gone to the mainland to take Irene Meadows on some errand.

It was about three o'clock when she heard a commotion in the lobby and went out to investigate.

She was as surprised as everyone else to find Irene Meadows standing there. She was a wisp of a woman, very straight, with a trembling chin and tears on her eyelashes.

"It's David. He's disappeared and I can't find him. He must be wandering around the island. He's not a bit well, you know. We must find him. Would you help me, please, all of you?"

"How long has he been gone?" Chris asked.

"I don't really know. I went to the mainland and was away a couple of hours. Stone isn't feeling well and was in his room. David must have slipped out without his hearing, and God knows where he is —"

"Take it easy," Chris said. "We'll find him. I'll take the east side, Salt, you take the north ridge, Joni can go up the middle, and Alison, if you could take the south path —"

"Oh, thank you," Irene said. "You can't know what this means. I'm so afraid he may have fallen and hurt himself —"

They left the inn, fanning out in all directions as Chris had planned, and Irene told them she would wait for them at the house just in case he returned there.

Alison followed the familiar path that led south and wondered where David could have gone. Putting herself in his shoes, she felt he might have climbed to the highest part of the island for the view. But on the other hand he was frail, a climb like that would probably be too much for him.

She looked carefully as she went, and now and then she stopped to call his name. But there was only the quiet stirring of leaves in the trees, the ripple of water at the shore. She hoped the others were having better luck for there were no clues at all that he might have come her way.

She was about to return to Greenwood when she caught sight of something blue, a bit of cloth, and retrieved it from the bush that had snagged it. It was a piece of expensive linen.

Alison raised her eyes. Just a short distance away, perched precariously on some rocks that looked out to the lake, she saw him. He sat with his knees drawn up, his arms wrapped around them, and he looked frightened.

"David," she called gently.

He started and looked about. "Oh, you found me," he said. "Thank goodness, you found me. I, I was lost . . .''

From there she could easily see the outline of the inn, but she realized that perhaps the poor old soul didn't recognize it, perhaps in his frightened state he hadn't even seen it.

"I'll help you down," she said. "I'll take you home, David."

"I don't want to go home," he said stubbornly.

"But you must. Irene is so worried about you."

"Afraid of what I'll do, what I'll say. She watches me night and day . . .''

"She wants to take care of you, David," Alison explained.

The old man seemed bewildered and confused. She took his arm to help him down from the rocks and was shocked at how thin he was.

"You're the girl at the piano," he said. "I've heard you play."

"You have? When?" she asked.

"I was walking by one time," he answered. But his eyes shifted away from her and he coughed nervously. "You play very well."

"You must come and visit me sometime and I'll give you a real concert. All I need is a little encouragement." She laughed.

David smiled. It was a sweet, childish smile and there was something wistful about his face, something maddeningly familiar. She wished she could pinpoint what it was that nagged at her memory. Where had she seen this man before?

"I'd like to come," he said. "But I can't. Irene wouldn't permit it."

"I'm sure if you told her I'd invited you —"

"No," he said, and there was bitterness in his voice. "I can't come. I'm a prisoner, you know. I only got out today because Stone was asleep and Irene was gone."

She stared at him, wondering if he was rambling or if he could be telling her the truth. Then he began to talk in a way that told her he was badly mixed up. He was totally disoriented and argued with her about the way to go, showing a temper that startled her. Then he became docile and meek as a lamb again. She tightened her grip on his arm and took him toward his house. The poor old fellow. No wonder Irene had been so frantic when she found him missing. It was apparent that he was not responsible and needed watching. But it was pathetic too, for she often saw snatches of the kind of man he must have been once.

"You're almost home, David," Alison reassured him.

"Yes," he murmured, a vacant look in his eyes. "Almost there."

But he was so confused that he was staring at Greenwood instead of his own house.

16

Bob Beale had been spending long hours in his projection room, putting together all the bits and pieces of his film, splicing and resplicing, changing his mind dozens of times about the proper sequence. He had stared at the film so long he was becoming bleary-eyed. It was only in the evenings that he finally allowed himself a break. Often he walked down to Joni's, where they ate a simple meal together and she told him about the progress at the inn. It was from her that he heard about David Meadows's disappearance a few days earlier and their search for him.

"Well, no harm was done. He was found," Bob said.

"It was luck. He could have fallen from that perch where Alison discovered him and really hurt himself. He seems so sweet, Bob, so dear —"

Bob leaned toward her. "Do you think I'll turn into a sweet old man when my time comes?"

"I wouldn't bet on it," she said saucily. "I think you'll be just as temperamental as you are now."

"I have things on my mind," he retorted.

"I know," she said.

There had been a couple of responses to the inquiries he'd sent out to old friends and acquaintances in Hollywood. One of them had sounded favorable, at least he had promised to give his film a really good look. It was because of that that he had been working such long hours to finish it. Just that morning he had taken one last look at the completed film and, satisfied that it was right at last, he boxed it up and took the boat to the mainland to put it in the mail, sending it special delivery.

From then on he had to play the waiting game and try not to go crazy while he waited. Restlessness had come to live in his bones, and it robbed him of sleep and threatened his appetite. Joni was sensitive to his moods and tried to help him pass the time by asking him to help her with some of her craft work.

"Aren't you going to Greenwood tomorrow?"

"No. I've about done all I can to help Chris. And he said he couldn't afford to pay me any longer."

"That old devil — money!" Bob said. "Well, I'm glad you'll be here. I never liked the idea of you being up there with Dumont anyway."

"Chris is all right, Bob, and I'm not going to get in a fight with you about him."

"I'll come up sometime and see what's going on."

"You mean you want to go and visit Alison," Joni retorted. "Let's call it like it is."

He didn't deny it. Why should he? He owed Joni nothing and from the beginning they had agreed on that. And Alison *did* interest him. He had often wondered how she was coming with her book on Thordsen and hoped she'd had better luck than he.

He soon became bored with Joni's craft work and broke away to take long walks; more often than not, he found himself up at the inn, looking for Alison.

Chris was still working in the music room, hanging the last piece of wallpaper, when Bob looked in one morning.

"Where's Alison?" Bob asked.

Chris looked up for a moment and shook his head. "I don't know."

"Probably in her room, working away," Bob said.

Chris turned back to his task and Bob set his jaw. The guy could be so damned arrogant when he wanted. Bob had decided some time ago to drop the idea of the "then" and "now" photographs of the old inn. Chris just hadn't been very cooperative, and Bob thought that maybe the idea hadn't been such a hot one anyway.

He was about to go when Roy Zeller appeared. Roy had sawdust on his clothes and a hammer swung from his hand. He was acting very important. Bob knew that Chris allowed him to help out with the work, and to Bob's way of thinking, this was more proof that Chris was into something he knew nothing about. Roy Zeller could turn out to be one really big headache.

"Chris, there's something funny about that basement wall," Roy said.

Chris gave him a quick look. "Why do you say that?"

"One corner of the cellar has a big, thick foundation different from the rest."

"They used native stones. Maybe there was some reason for constructing it that way."

"Well, I can't do what you told me because of it."

Chris nodded patiently. "Okay, Roy. You can help me in here."

Bob walked away and left them to their remodeling problems. Behind Alison's door he could hear the sound of a typewriter. He rapped sharply and the typing stopped. In a moment Alison appeared.

"Oh, Bob —"

"Hi," he said with a smile. "I know I'm interrupting, but I wanted to talk to you.

Could you take a break for a few minutes?"

"I'm right in the middle of something, Bob."

"Why don't we take a boat ride or go over to Donnerville?"

"I can't, Bob. Truly."

Around her he could see the fruits of her labor. Papers were strewn all over the room, and from the little lines in her forehead, he sensed that she wasn't having a very easy time of it. He knew the feeling, and he knew too that getting away from it might help.

"You'll work better when you come back if you'll take time out to get some fresh air and sunlight right now."

She paused for a moment and then with a laugh agreed. "You're right. I have a way of forgetting that. I just want to stay here and battle away at it."

She closed the door behind her and they stepped outside onto one of the paths that led to a glen thick with trees and wild flowers. It was one of Bob's favorite spots, and they sat down in a patch of sunlight.

"I take it you haven't any news," she said.

"Too soon yet. But I keep hoping for a phone call just the same."

"One day soon it will come, and then you'll be flying off to Hollywood again and we'll all brag about having known you," Alison said.

"You're mighty good for a man's ego," Bob replied. "I hope it happens, but there are days I know it won't. I can feel it like some dark despair in me."

"You have to think positively," Alison said.

"Do you?"

She stared at him for a moment and then shook her dark head slowly. "No. I can't seem to home in on the target, Bob. I'm writing all around it. I have some good material and I have the feel of this place, but it all ought to be better than it is. I'm missing something, and it bothers me no end."

"Thordsen can't be an easy personality to capture on paper."

"He's as elusive as a moth. Just when I see what I think holds him together it's gone, like a dream you can't quite remember the next morning."

"You'll get it."

"There's one angle I haven't followed through on yet and I think I will. Maybe this time something will show up that I can use."

"What's that?"

"I'd rather not say until I've checked it out."

"Good heavens, Alison, Leighton Thordsen has been dead — how many years?"

"Seventeen," she replied. "Just the same, I feel a kind of integrity where he's concerned. I want no facts in my book that aren't checked and double-checked."

"Who would sue?" he asked with a grin. "Thordsen had no heirs as I understand it."

"No, no family at all."

"Funny, a man who was so crazy over women never got married."

Allison laughed. "Many a man likes to play the field and then, suddenly, it's too late. They're old and settled in their ways and no one wants them."

"And this happened to Thordsen?"

"I don't really know. But it's sad in a way. In some areas I think his life was very empty. He had only his music, but it was the one thing he could count on. Without it, he would have preferred to be dead."

Bob knew that once Alison started talking about Thordsen, she might not want to talk of anything else, and he had other things in mind. He was not only restless but bored. His gaze swung to Alison and he took her all in, from the top of her dark, glossy head to her long legs and slender feet. She was a beautiful young woman and he felt a stirring inside.

"Alison, when I leave here, why don't you come with me?"

She was startled. "You're kidding!"

"I'm not. We operate pretty much on the same wavelength. I think we could have a whirl together. We might even work together. You write the script, I'll film it."

"And where do we get the players?" she wondered.

"They're all around us!" he said

excitedly. "We could use real people and put together film stories of their lives. We could travel all over the country."

"And what do we use for money? People don't live on daydreams, Bob."

He sighed and stretched out in the grass, putting his hands under his head. "Did you have to burst my balloon quite so fast?"

She laughed. "Oh, Bob, you're a dreamer. But that's good. In your line of work, you need it. You have one of the best imaginations I've ever come up against, and you have a keen eye for what looks good on film. I think you'll make it and make it big."

"And then you'll wish you'd come along for the ride?"

"Maybe," she said.

There was a lonely note in her voice, and he looked at her for a long time, studying her.

"What is it, Alison?"

"Nothing."

"I know better."

"Affairs of the heart are not easily cured," she said.

"No, they're not. Who is it? Chris Dumont?"

He couldn't keep the edge out of his voice. He sat up and plucked a few blades of grass, ripping them into shreds. Chris was just the sort that would make a success of Greenwood. He was hardheaded and practical, and his determination would see him through. Bob knew this was one of the reasons he disliked him. Chris had his feet solidly on the ground, and no matter how he tried, Bob knew he would never be as settled. Whatever it was that drove him would not let it happen.

"Chris says he loves me," Alison said.

Bob tossed away the bit of grass in his hands and reached out to her. He shook her gently. "Give me a chance and I'll love you too. Maybe I already do. It's a hell of a way to say it, but it's true. My world has been upside down for so long —"

He bent his head and kissed her, surprised when she didn't resist. Instead, her arms went around him for a moment, and with a sigh, he pulled her closer and closer. When the kiss ended, she dropped her head to his shoulder.

"See what it could be like, Alison."

"Yes," she murmured.

"It would never be dull between us. There would always be this spark, this excitement."

"Are you sure?"

"Yes," he nodded, "I am."

She smiled and reached out to trace the shape of his mouth with a fingertip. "Every time I'm with you, Bob, you mix me up. You get my head all out of kilter."

He laughed. "That's good."

"Maybe," she admitted. "But right now I'm going back to Greenwood and the sanity of my room and my work."

"Don't go. Stay."

She shook her head again. "No. I can't."

There was nothing he could do. He wanted to walk with her, but she shook her head.

"Relax, Bob. Look at the sky or study the lake. I know how tense you really are."

Then she blew him a kiss and was gone. He did as she suggested and he must have fallen asleep, remembering her kiss on his lips, for he awakened only when he heard *The Maiden* heading out for Donnerville. He sat up and took a look. He could make out Salt at the wheel and Alison standing beside him, her dark hair whipping in the breeze. They were off to the mainland, but he wondered why. She hadn't mentioned going there today. Or did this have something to do with the secret lead she had mentioned? He decided he was too tired to contemplate or argue with himself.

He took a moment to scan the island, an old habit, for he never knew when he'd see something for his camera. It was then he saw David Meadows — alone!

He waited for a moment, certain that either Stone or Irene would appear, but after a few minutes he knew that David had managed to slip away. Was the old gentleman going to wander off and get lost again?

Bob got up and decided he had better investigate, or at least keep the old boy in sight.

David seemed to be wandering

haphazardly until he reached one of the higher elevations on the island. From there, he looked out to the lake and seemed to be searching for something. Was he watching for someone to come or for someone to leave? It was impossible to guess. Bob only knew that David abruptly turned about and quickly began to make his way toward home. Bob was surprised at how swiftly the old man could move, even with a cane.

Out of curiosity, and because he had nothing better to do, Bob continued to follow him. David was making for his own house, and Bob turned away for a moment to glance at a bright-winged bird. When he looked back, the old man was gone. A sense of alarm gripped him and he began to walk faster. David must have taken a fall.

But there was no sign of him, and just as Bob was about to shout his name, he saw the outside cellar door ajar at the Meadowses' house. David must have gone in there for something. When he didn't come back in a moment or two, Bob went to investigate.

"Hey, David, are you down there? Are you all right?"

There was no answer, only the echo of his words, the damp air against his face. He went down the rickety steps. He had never known them to use this entrance before, and if it was like most places on the island, the cellar was also connected by stairs to the upper part of the house.

There was no sound inside the cellar, and feeling a little foolish and something like a trespasser, Bob decided that David simply had gone elsewhere or had gone upstairs to the inside entrance.

The cellar was depressing and dark and Bob wasted no time in leaving. He left the outside door open as he had found it, thinking it was none of his business.

But he knew something was odd. It bothered him all afternoon, but when he mentioned it to Joni that evening she shrugged it off.

"David's senile, out of it. God knows what he does or thinks or where he goes! Or why! So don't worry about him. If he had a little adventure out from under the thumb of Stone or Irene, more power to him!"

"But it was as if he disappeared into thin air!"

"I rather doubt that."

With a laugh, Bob reached out and twirled a finger around a lock of Joni's hair.

"Okay, if you say so."

She reached up and took his hand away with a quick motion.

"You went to see Alison today, didn't you?"

"So?"

Joni had built a fire on her open hearth and had started some food cooking in the blackened pot that hung there. She turned her back to him as she stood before it.

"Are you in love with her?"

Bob thought for a long moment about that. "I think I am. It's funny — I don't believe I truly knew that until this very moment."

Joni stabbed at the fire with a poker and every line of her body froze.

"Look, Joni, you're a free spirit. You don't want to be tied down. For a little while I didn't either. But things are going to break for me. You wait and see. I'm going to become a very respectable citizen and I'm going to settle down. But I don't want to do that alone."

She tossed the poker aside. She was in control again, and if her eyes were a little too bright, he pretended to ignore it.

"Sure, I understand. Great!"

17

Alison had persuaded Salt to take her to the mainland and show her the house where he had taken Thordsen secretly, usually late at night.

"I'm not sure that house is even there anymore," Salt said.

"I have to find out," replied Alison.

"Okay." Salt shrugged his shoulders.

Once they reached Donnerville, they hired a taxi, and following Salt's directions, the driver turned into an area that had once been one of the better parts of town but that had deteriorated in the recent past. Several of the houses had been razed for the new four-lane highway that came in from the west, and it was there that Salt said the house had once stood.

"I was afraid of that," Salt said. "But I

wasn't sure."

"And what was their name, Salt? You must have known their name."

Salt set his lips and shook his head. "Driver, take us back to the dock."

Alison was frustrated. Just when she thought she was getting close to something pertinent about Thordsen, it disappeared into thin air. Salt was being stubborn and she couldn't imagine why. What possible difference could it make to him?

"Salt, please tell me the name of the people who lived there. You said you thought it was a doctor's home. What kind of doctor? A dentist, an M.D., a vet? A professor?"

"Look, Alison, I think you should just drop it. What can it matter anyway? You wouldn't put that in your book, would you? What do you want to do, tarnish the man's name?"

"I just want the truth about him," she said. "That's all!"

"Okay, okay, if you'll rest any easier. As far as I remember, the doctor's name was Willows. Ben Willows. He was an

M.D. and that's all I know about him.''

"Even when you've lived around here all your life?''

"That's right.''

"What happened to them? Where are they now?''

"I swear to God I don't know!'' Salt said. "Now I have to get back to Greenwood. I promised Chris I'd help him this afternoon, and here I am fooling around on a wild goose chase!''

Alison decided it was best to drop the whole business just then, but there had to be a way to find out more about Ben Willows, and she vowed she would, whether Salt liked it or not.

When they returned to the inn, Salt disappeared without a word and Alison went back to work. She leafed through what she had written, but it left a bad taste in her mouth. It was dull and lifeless and read more like an encyclopedia of facts than a biography. Somehow or other, she had to pump real breath and blood into it!

All that week Alison made herself stay in her room and work. Reba asked for

Sunday off, and since there were no other guests and no reservations for anyone else, Chris was glad to let her go.

"God knows you deserve it," he said. "Have a good time."

So when Alison awakened on Sunday morning, it was to the sound of *The Maiden* taking Roy and Reba over to the mainland. And when someone knocked on her door, she knew who it was.

"Breakfast is served in ten minutes," Chris said. "Okay?"

"Who's doing the cooking?"

She heard his low, pleasant laugh. "Me. Eat at your own risk."

She dressed hurriedly and went out to the dining room to find Chris with a towel tied around his middle, putting plates of scrambled eggs and bacon on the table.

"You can pour the coffee," he said.

"Have you noticed how quiet it is?" she asked. "I'm rather glad we have the place to ourselves. At least Roy isn't around spying on me. And I never realized until now how noisy Reba is."

"She loves the sound of pots and pans clattering around. Frankly, I'm glad she and Roy have gone too. I gave Salt the day off as well. I think he intends to stay in Donnerville until he brings Reba and Roy back late tonight."

"I see."

Chris's gray eyes studied her for a moment as he sat down opposite her. "We can have a long, peaceful day together. Will you mind being alone with me?"

"No."

He reached out to take her hand in his for a moment. "I'd like to start every day out like this, just you and me —"

""Chris —"

"I know. You don't want me to say things like that. But I can't seem to help myself. By the way, later I have a surprise for you."

"Tell me?"

"Later," he said with a shake of his head, his eyes laughing.

Breakfast was delicious, and they took their time. Looking out over the lake, Alison was alarmed to notice a touch of autumn color coming to some of the leaves.

"It's later than I think."

"For all of us," Chris said. "But autumn comes early here. We're so far north. We've still a lot of nice days left. But I wish I could have gotten more work done. Some of it will have to wait now until next spring."

"You won't winter here?"

"I haven't really decided. I may. I could keep plugging away inside, redo some of the guest rooms. It would occupy my time, and then next spring I could concentrate on the outside work. I know it makes sense. Maybe if I knew what your plans were, it would help me decide."

"I haven't anything to do with it," she said.

He shook his head. "But you do, Alison. You have *everything* to do with it. I can't imagine this place without you. Don't you know that?"

"Oh, Chris —"

"It's true. When I came here, I was an empty man. In more ways than one. I'm not empty anymore because I've found you and because I have this place I love. I have my work, my dreams, my hopes — but they'd mean very little if I didn't have you, Alison."

"I only came for the summer."

"You could work here. While I fixed up the inn, you could do your writing. We would be shut away from everything, locked in for the whole winter. Could you stand that?"

"I don't know."

"Think about it."

They finished their breakfast, and then Chris took her to see the surprise. The music room was completely finished. He opened the doors with a flourish, and she saw that the room had been put in order. A few pieces of furniture salvaged from the basement had been added, the new wall was elegant and rich-looking, and the piano stood in the center of the room, commanding all the attention.

"It's lovely, Chris!"

"I think it's a fitting memorial to Thordsen, don't you?"

She nodded and linked her arm through his. "I like it very much. I should have known that you wouldn't spoil it."

"Play for me," he said.

She sat down at the piano and put her

hands on the cool keys. It seemed natural and right that she should play some of Thordsen's music. She played it gently, with a kind of deep love and understanding, and the notes came out pure and true, filling all the corners of the room, drifting out the open window toward the Meadowses' house and up the hill to the trees.

When she stopped at last, Chris came to take her hands and pulled her to her feet. Then he kissed her, a long, passionate kiss, and she found it as beautiful as she had found Thordsen's music only moments earlier.

"Darling, I love you," Chris whispered.

"But before you came here . . ."

He broke away, a shadow across his face. "I know. I still thought I cared about Amy. I was a desperately unhappy man. But now I've found what I want here and you're part of it, Alison."

"Let's go outside. Let's not waste all this sunshine."

"All right."

He knew she had put him off, but he went along with it and she was glad. It was such a perfect day; it would have been wrong to spoil it in any way.

They walked past the Meadowses' and along the opposite side of the island, where Alison had not been very often. She found the other side more attractive, but it was quieter and there was less chance of seeing anyone. She sensed that that was why Chris had come this way.

"You haven't told me about your book lately."

"It still isn't going well."

"And the old diary still hasn't yielded anything?"

"I've studied it by the hour, Chris, and there's just nothing there."

"Nothing else in the trunk —"

"Useless souvenirs. I should give them to you for the music room and let you put them on display. The public might find them interesting."

"That's a good idea. I have thought about trying to gather some memorabilia, concert programs, old news clippings, snapshots —"

"Thordsen was rather camera-shy, you know. There aren't a great many pictures of him. He gave only a few concerts; most of his work was in composing. But making the music room a kind of memorial to him is a good idea."

"Maybe you'd like to take on the task. You're the logical one."

"When I've finished my book, I could turn over some of the things I've gathered. They belong there."

They walked on, and when Chris put his arm around her, she didn't mind at all. Later, sitting under the trees, he held her hand and they talked of many things — their youth, their dreams and ambitions, their family stories, their better days.

"Tell me about Regan." Chris said. "Please tell me about him."

"It's over," Alison replied. "I haven't heard from him since I came here and I don't think I will."

"But you want to?"

"I'd like to know that he's well and happy, that he's forgiven me, that we're still friends."

"And that's all?"

She lifted her chin and swallowed hard. "Yes. I think so."

"But you're still not sure."

"No."

"Thank you for being honest."

"I'm not good for you, Chris."

He laughed at that. "Don't be silly. You're the best thing that ever happened in my life. Think about that sometime, will you?"

They walked on, wandering here and there, and had a relaxed, happy time. They seemed to shake off all their past uneasiness, their unhappiness, and their fears and frustrations. They romped and frolicked like children, and when they went back to the inn at last, they feasted on the contents of Reba's refrigerator.

That afternoon they argued about politics and challenged each other to a swimming race. Alison won easily, but she suspected that Chris had let her.

At sunset there was no sign of *The Maiden,* and they knew that Reba and Roy would not be returning until much later. When the phone rang, Chris was tempted not to answer it.

"Someone wants to come over to dinner and I'll have to turn them down," he said.

"It might be a reservation for another night," she pointed out.

Chris answered the phone, and Alison heard him say Salt's name. He talked for a few minutes and then hung up.

"Well, what do you know."

"Something wrong?" she asked.

"That was Salt. It seems that Reba tracked him down at a friend's house and told him that she and Roy were going to stay overnight and come back early in the morning. Salt's staying on the mainland too."

"Oh!"

Chris's gray eyes held hers. "That means we're here alone — for the night."

"Yes."

Chris went to turn on a few lights against the growing dusk. The inn seemed very quiet. Alison imagined that she could hear its old timbers creaking, and now and then the wind brought the sound of the water slapping against the shore, hitting away at the rocks below the patio. Alison stood at the railing, counting the stars as they came out. Chris came up behind her and put his arms around her. He held her against him, his lips against her hair, and with a little cry she turned around and put her arms around him. She found his lips with hers and their kiss was fire and ice. When she pulled free of his arms, his eyes were gentle and filled with tenderness.

"You *do* love me."

"I don't know," she said. "Please, Chris — I don't know, I can't say anything now."

"Let it happen."

"I wish it was that simple."

They stood at the railing for a long time, the night air against their faces. Chris filled and lighted his pipe. Later, they dined outside on red wine and a plate of fruit and cheese.

A wind came up suddenly as it did sometimes on the island, and the swift drop in temperature forced them inside. Alison sank to the comfortable couch before the old fireplace where the musket hung and listened to Chris's footsteps as he went from room to room, making sure all was tightly sealed against the impending storm. By then the rain had started to fall in sweeping gusts, the huge drops sounding almost like hail against the windows.

"Just as well Salt wasn't planning to come across tonight. He'd have been caught in this, and *The Maiden* isn't all that seaworthy anymore," Chris said.

The room had grown so chilly that Chris decided to build a small fire on the hearth. Soon kindling was crackling and the flames were a cheery sight. He sat down beside Alison, stretching out his long legs. He had grown pensive, thoughtful, far away. She knew he was thinking of Amy. Had they sat here once, before such a fire, on such a night? She wanted to ask but didn't.

She was very much aware of the big house, the rain outside, the fact that they were completely alone. Chris stirred and looked at her, and the moment grew between them like a tangible thing.

"Darling —"

"I think I'll say good-night now, Chris."

"It's early."

"I'm very tired."

"You're frightened," he said.

"Of you?" she asked with a smile.

"Yes."

"Never in a million years. You're a kind, gentle, sweet man. And you're not the sort that beats down women's doors."

"True," he admitted. "I'd much rather they were opened for me, willingly . . ."

She flushed, said good-night again, and hurried away. Once in her room, she closed the door tightly behind her and stood there for a long moment. Not much later, she heard Chris go to his room across the hall.

Outside, the storm abated and the wind died away. The stars soon came out and the lake was calm once again. Alison wished she felt as calm. She knew she couldn't sleep, for her heart was in a turmoil, her thoughts tripping all over themselves, and she was very much aware of Chris just a few steps away across the hall.

She must have dozed after all, for she awakened to hear a strange, sobbing sound. She was instantly wide-eyed, remembering the other times she'd heard strainge noises. Had Thordsen come to haunt her again?

She was out of bed in a flash, anxious to discover the source of the sounds and determined not to be frightened away. Then she realized that the sounds were not in her room but outside.

She pulled open the door and again heard the cries, louder and more painful now. They were coming from Chris's room! Without another thought, she ran across the hall and wrenched open his door.

It was Chris! He was crying out in his sleep, calling out to Billy not to go, not to run, not to die.

"Chris," she said gently, trying to awaken him. "Chris, wake up. You're having a nightmare. Chris darling —" She held him in her arms and he clung to her, perspiring and exhausted. In a moment he grew calmer. She smoothed back his hair and touched his face.

"It's all right, Chris. It's just a nightmare, darling."

"Yes," he murmured, clinging to her. "Yes, a nightmare."

"Will you be all right now?"

"Yes, but I wish you'd stay."

"No."

"You called me darling," he said, a touch of awe in his voice. "Did you know you called me darling?"

She left him and moved to the door. "Good-night."

And she closed the door behind her.

18

In the morning Salt brought Roy and Reba back along with a pouch of mail. He sorted it out and knocked on Alison's door.

"Mail," he said.

"Thanks, Salt."

There was a letter from her parents postmarked Venice. Quickly she slit it open and read it. They'd had a fabulous time in Europe and their last stopping place was Venice.

"Sorry, dear," her mother wrote. "We went to visit Thordsen's grave, but he is buried in a private vault and the caretaker wouldn't let us through the iron fence that surrounds it. So I left the rose with him and he promised to take it in. I wish you had been with us. Perhaps you would have been more persuasive."

There was more about the sights they'd

seen and the people they'd met. The postscript was very brief: "Regan did not join us."

She read and reread that short line several times. It told her a great deal. Regan had not gone because he was sure she would not miss an opportunity to visit the place where Thordsen had spent his last days. It could only mean that he definitely did not want to see her again and had no desire to pick up the pieces.

She was surprised at how much it bothered her and wrecked her concentration. She left her desk and went out to find someone to talk to. Chris was nowhere in sight — she hadn't seen him all morning — but Reba was back in the kitchen, happily at work.

"Did you have a nice time yesterday?" Alison asked.

"Yes. We hadn't expected to stay over, but Chris didn't seem to mind."

Reba was making fresh bread for lunch, and Alison watched her supple hands as they worked the dough.

"You're so efficient, Reba."

She laughed heartily at that. "I've made

bread all my life. My mother taught me, and everyone that eats it says it's good.''

"It's delicious.''

"You have something on your mind,'' Reba said. "I can tell.''

"Yes, I do. Reba, do you remember a Dr. Ben Willows who lived in Donnerville?''

Reba puckered her brow for a moment. "Vaguely. But he's not there anymore.''

"Do you know anything about him or where he might have gone?''

Reba began shaping the dough into small individual loaves and topped them with butter.

"He's been away from here for about ten years, and it seems to me that he moved to California.''

"Oh, no!''

"Why do you want to know about him?''

"Do you know if he had any family in Donnerville that might still be there?''

"I couldn't tell you,'' Reba said. "You might check the phone book.''

"I already have. There are no Willowses listed, but a married daughter would have another name or they could have unlisted numbers."

"Try the city directory. At the library."

"I'll do that," Alison decided.

She made arrangements to go to the mainland with Salt later in the day when he had to go for Chris's building materials.

"I'll be in town an hour," Salt said. "Will that be long enough for you?"

"With luck, no. Without luck, yes."

He gave her a quick look and probably suspected that she was still on the trail of Dr. Willows, but he said nothing. They parted at the dock, and once again Alison found herself on the way to the library.

With the city directory in front of her, she scanned the names quickly but found no one by the name of Willows. She asked the librarian, but she was a young girl and didn't even remember the doctor.

Her next stop was the courthouse, where she ran into more dead ends. Ben Willows did not own property in town anymore, and the clerk could tell her nothing about the family.

Alison thanked the woman and left. She walked back to the dock and found Salt waiting for her. He took one look at her face and decided to say nothing.

Alison's mood was still glum by the time they got back to Greenwood. When she saw Chris she paused for a moment, and he came toward her, a thoughtful expression in his eyes.

"Could I talk to you for a little while, Alison?"

"Sure."

"I just want to apologize for last night. Crying out like that, waking you up — I haven't had a nightmare like that in ages. I'm truly sorry I bothered you."

"It's all right."

"Alison, another thing about last night . . ."

She met his clear eyes and felt a tingling sensation along her nerves.

"I'm glad you were there," he said quietly. "I won't ever forget how gentle you were, how you erased all the nightmare away, how you —"

She smiled. "I hope it doesn't happen again."

"So do I. Was your trip to the mainland successful?"

"No."

"And you're disappointed," he said with sympathy in his voice."

"Something *has* to break pretty soon," she said.

He put his hand against her face and smiled into her eyes. "It will. You're anxious to get back to work. How about lunch?"

"All right."

Then she moved away and hurried back to her room. Sitting down at her desk, she saw a white envelope lying on the floor in a place that made her think it might have been pushed under her door. Curious, she got up to retrieve it and saw her name written on it in a shaky hand. She opened it and unfolded the single piece of paper inside. Her eyes widened with surprise. It was from David Meadows, of all people!

"Please, Miss Blair, do me the honor of meeting me secretly tonight at midnight. Come alone. This is of the utmost importance."

There were specific instructions as to where he would be. Why on earth would David Meadows want to see her at such an outrageous hour and why must it be kept secret? Could it really be possible that he was virtually a prisoner in his own home? But if it was true, it was surely for his own good.

Alison didn't know what to make of it. She was sorely tempted to go and talk with Chris, but David had stressed that it be a secret between them.

All day long she debated with herself whether or not she would go. It wasn't her idea of fun to go poking around the island at midnight to meet some daft old man. But she remembered his sweet smile and childish laugh, and her heart was touched. It seemed best to humor him — although if he didn't come, she wouldn't be a bit surprised. By evening he might forget he had ever written the note.

Alison had a quick lunch with Chris, and she asked in a very casual way if David Meadows had ever visited Greenwood since he had taken over.

"Not to my knowledge," he replied. "Irene has been here only once. They're not exactly the neighborly type."

"No. Strange about them, isn't it?

They're such odd, remote people."

"But the island suits them. They're not forced to meet or contend with others. If they want to hide away, this seems to be the perfect place."

So Chris hadn't seen David at the inn that morning. She put the same question to Reba later and got the same answer. How could David Meadows slip in and out of the inn and go to her room without anyone knowing it? She recalled another time when she thought someone had been in her room and no one had been seen. Perhaps everyone was so busy they just hadn't noticed.

Alison argued with herself far into the evening about whether or not she should keep the rendezvous. She considered phoning Irene about the note, but somehow she couldn't bring herself to betray David's trust.

When the inn settled down for the night, it was past eleven o'clock, and Alison had not yet dressed for bed. But she had put out her light and pretended to be asleep. She heard Chris go to his room and close his door. Several times she looked at her clock, watching the time tick away. It would take her about ten minutes to walk to where David would be waiting. It was a quarter of twelve when she slipped out of her room, a flashlight in her pocket, and crept quietly down the hall and out to the lobby.

Old Duggan was asleep in front of the fireplace and, awakening, twitched his ears when he saw Alison. He wanted to go with her, but she motioned for him to stay, and with a switch of his tail he lay back down and put his nose sleepily between his paws.

Soon she wished she'd taken the dog with her, for it wasn't a clear night. Only a very few stars were showing and there was no moon. But she knew the path well enough. She walked carefully, conscious of the deep quiet around her and the dark shapes of the trees. She began to wonder if she had lost her mind. What was she doing out there, wandering around at midnight to meet a crazy old man?

She found the huge oak that David had mentioned in his note and called out his name.

"David —"

There was no reply. She sat down to wait, hunching her knees up under her chin. The air was cool, almost brisk, and she wished she'd brought a sweater. Straining for the least little sound, she heard all kinds of imaginary noises, and she felt sure she had been waiting for more than ten minutes. If David was coming, he was late.

The sound of footsteps brought her quickly to her feet. She shrank back out of sight. It couldn't be David — he walked with a cane and moved slowly! These footsteps were heavy, almost thunderous, and they came with purpose.

"You'd better get out of here!" she told herself. "Fast!"

She tried to slip away unnoticed, but a twig broke underfoot. She heard a muttered oath and a man turned in her direction. She sped away, running like she had never run before in her life. Somehow she managed to keep from falling down. She was cut off from the path and she fought through the brush, slipping on pine needles, rushing on, only to find herself caught in a thorny bush. Her blouse ripped as she tore away, and she felt scratched and bruised. Behind her, the man was pursuing hotly, nearly on her heels. She expected to be caught any second.

But she got a break! The man fell and she made one last desperate effort to push on. She knew she was headed in the general direction of the inn. Just steps away she could see the yawning doors of the cellar that connected with the Meadowses' place.

It looked like her best bet and she dashed for it, stumbling down the steps into dank darkness. It was like a dungeon inside, and ignoring the risk, she flashed her light about with a shaking hand. She was gasping for breath, her legs were about to give out, and she had to find a safe place to hide.

He was coming! She heard the footsteps behind her and darted for a corner of the cellar. There was a jog in the wall and she squatted there, hidden behind a large packing case.

The man had a light too and began darting it around.

In a moment it was going to come in her direction. Filled with terror, she pressed hard against the wall at her back. It began to move, swinging open noiselessly, and she found herself tumbling into another room. Behind her the door swung back but did not completely close.

She lay very still, afraid to look, even to breathe. When she heard the man on the other side of the wall stamping about and swearing to himself, she knew that she was safe. He had not heard or seen the door open, and in a few minutes he gave up his search. After listening for a long time, she knew he had gone.

She risked a light only long enough to see if the strange door would open from her side. It did, but only because it was ajar, for there was no handle. She pried it open, breaking a fingernail, and then stepped back into the cellar. Behind the door she had been vaguely aware of a narrow passageway, very low and very dark. She hadn't wanted to look or even contemplate where it went. All she wanted to do was to get back to Greenwood and the safety of her room.

She eased up the steps to the outside, pausing to look and listen. Then she ran, hoping and praying that there would be no footsteps behind her.

The inn had never looked as beloved to her as it did now. She dashed to the door and let herself in. A dim light burned in the lobby and Old Duggan was still there. He growled in surprise until he saw who it was.

"Sh!" she said. "It's all right."

She collapsed for a moment on the couch, exhausted, and Old Duggan put his nose against her hand. She stroked his head and put her cheek against his fur.

"I wish I'd had you with me," she said.

He pressed closer as she tried to put the nightmare in proper perspective. Had the note been a fake? Had someone lured her out there deliberately? But why? For what possible purpose? She was just an ordinary person, a writer trying hard to write a book. But she had been doing a lot of nosing around, asking a lot of questions about Thordsen. Could she have rubbed someone the wrong way?

19

Alison slept very little that night — or what was left of it. She found herself listening for strange sounds, and when she did drop off, she dreamed of those footsteps pounding after her in the dark.

In the cold light of day it all seemed like a dream, but she knew that it had happened, that it *was* real. From her window she could see the Meadowses' house, but the cellar was not visible from that angle. Where had the hidden corridor led and why had it been built?

Alison decided that she had to tell someone about her escapade. Chris was the logical candidate, but he was busy with Salt, and she didn't want to interrupt. Then too, Roy came bumbling in on her heels and was anxious to hear everything she said.

She didn't want to talk to anyone but Chris and realized that she would have to wait for the right time. She couldn't seem to settle down so she paced about the patio, then spent a few minutes at the piano in the music room. She couldn't get the secret door in the Meadowses' cellar out of her mind. Finally, taking Old Duggan with her, she went down to the basement of the inn and looked about. Feeling a little foolish, she tapped on the walls and searched for concealed doors, but there was nothing. If there was anything strange about Chris's basement, she certainly couldn't see it. She wished that she had examined the door at the Meadowses' cellar more closely the night before, but her one thought had been to get out of there as fast as possible.

"Hello —"

She turned about with a start but was relieved to find that it was Chris.

"I'm sorry. I frightened you, didn't I?"

"I'm glad you came down here, Chris. I have to talk to you. I have to tell you what happened last night."

He listened while she explained, and a

range of emotions crossed his face.

"You shouldn't have gone wandering around alone like that in the middle of the night!"

"I know that now," she said. "But David stressed that I should come alone and I didn't want to betray him — he's such a sweet old man, Chris."

"It's possible that David didn't write the note," Chris pointed out. "Have you thought of that?"

"Yes. But somehow I think he did. There's something very strange about the Meadows couple, Chris."

"Granted. I just want you to promise that you'll never do anything like that again."

"I won't," she said.

"Why did you come down here?"

"I had some crazy notion that maybe the tunnel I stumbled into last night led here. I've been looking, but haven't found a thing."

"I've been all over this cellar," Chris said. "And I haven't found anything unusual either, but if you want me to look some more . . ."

"Yes, please!"

Chris went to find a flashlight. The two naked bulbs hanging from the ceiling cast a dim light over the cellar. Together they poked and probed and looked for hidden doors or walls that opened, but there was nothing odd about the moldy stone foundation. They found only cobwebs, dirt, and despair.

"Nothing," Alison said with a sigh, near tears again. "I just don't understand any of this, Chris! I feel it's all right under my nose but I'm missing it!"

"Hey, take it easy," Chris said gently. "If there's anything here, I promise you, we'll find it. But right now, I can't see anything strange."

"Let's go back up," she said. "It's depressing down here . . ."

Chris knew how upset she was, and when his words of encouragement didn't seem to lift her up, he had another idea.

"Let's throw a party. Here at the inn. Before long the season will be over and everyone will scatter. I've been so busy all summer, I really haven't had time for much fun. Why don't we ask Bob and Joni and even those strange Meadowses?"

"Do you think they'll come?"

"We can ask them. If they do, you'll get a chance to talk to David and find out if he remembers leaving you a note."

Alison began to feel more enthusiastic about the party, and once Chris had decided on it, he swung into action, conferring with Reba about the food and asking Salt to check the stock at the bar. Then he phoned Bob to invite him and Joni. The Meadowses were asked by written invitation, delivered by Salt. When he came back, Chris asked him for their reaction.

"I gave the note to Stone, who promised to give it to them, but I wouldn't plan on them," Salt said.

Still, Chris went ahead with the plans with a kind of boyish enthusiasm. It would be a small affair but a pleasant one, and Alison knew he was eager to show off his progress at the inn.

The party was set for the next evening, and even Salt seemed pleased about it. He came wearing his best clothes and looked so different that Alison blinked. In his day, Salt must have been rather handsome.

"Why hasn't some woman captured you?" she teased.

Salt gave her an unexpectedly serious answer. "There was only one woman I ever cared anything about." He rubbed a finger nervously along the scar on his jaw. "When that fell through, I decided to go through life a happy bachelor."

"But you're not so happy," she said.

And this idea surprised her too. Until then, she hadn't really thought much about Salt and what he felt or thought. He was always just there, a bit cranky at times, but dependable and willing enough to do his job.

Bob and Joni arrived early. Joni's long blond hair streamed to her shoulders and her clear eyes seemed restless and unhappy. Bob gave Alison a kiss for everyone to see, including Chris, who tightened his grip on his glass and turned away.

"I thought you'd left the island, Alison," Bob teased. "I've seen so little of you the last few days."

"Just busy," she replied.

"Or you're avoiding me."

"Has there been any word from Hollywood?"

"Not a hint, no call, nothing. Things like this take time."

"Sure they do."

"Too *much* time," he said despairingly. "What about your book?"

"I'm struggling through it, but I'm still not satisfied."

He nodded. "I know exactly how you feel. That's one thing about us, Alison, we have a lot in common."

Joni had disappeared, and when Alison saw her again, she was huddled with Chris, talking avidly, reaching out now and then to touch him. Alison was sure that it was all for Bob's benefit. If it was, he was ignoring it.

"You've been avoiding me," Bob said. "You won't deny it, will you?"

"No."

"Why? For God's sake, Alison, I told you I loved you —"

She turned away, but he put a hand on her arm and kept her beside him.

"I don't want to talk about it now," she said.

"I've stayed away from you purposely, to give you some time to think. But I kept hoping I'd look up and see you coming up my path."

"I hope you hear from Hollywood soon."

"Don't change the subject, Alison. We have to talk about this sometime."

"I can't believe you're serious. There, I've said it!"

She saw the disbelief come to his eyes, and his handsome face grew cold as he said, "What am I supposed to do to convince you?"

He was angry and she didn't know what to say. Above all, she didn't want to spoil the party. Reba had worked so hard and Chris had been so enthusiastic preparing for it.

"Let's not worry about it tonight, Bob," she pleaded. "Can't we just have fun? It *is* a party, you know."

Bob looked at her for a long moment. There was a certain appeal about him. He was so different from both Regan and

Chris. She couldn't deny that she liked him more than just a little.

She moved away to go over to Chris.

"It doesn't look as if the Meadowses are going to come," she said.

Chris shook his head. "I was hoping they would. We got off to a bad start and I'd like to be friends. It's not my nature to be on bad terms with my neighbors."

"You shouldn't feel badly about it," Joni said. "The Meadowses never looked twice at me when I first came here, and they barely speak when they do see me. They're just an odd couple."

At that, Old Duggan began barking, and Chris left the group to go and see what was wrong. In a moment, Alison heard voices, and she was surprised to see Chris returning with Irene Meadows on his arm.

Irene was primly dressed, her hair waved naturally and brushed back from her face. Bob Beale was taking her in with eyes that were almost like the shutters on his camera. There wasn't a soul in the room that wasn't surprised to see her, but Salt probably reacted the most. He promptly dropped a glass behind the bar and it shattered into a dozen pieces.

"It was very nice of you to invite us over, Mr. Dumont," Irene was saying. "I'm terribly sorry that David wasn't able to come along. He's not well, you know, and in a crowd he only becomes more confused."

"Yes, I understand," Chris said graciously. "But I'm so happy you were able to come. Please give David my regards and tell him how sorry I am that he couldn't join us."

He motioned to the others. "I'm sure you know everyone here — Salt, of course, Bob Beale, Joni King, Alison Blair."

"Yes, yes, nice to see you," Irene said with a quick nod of her head, giving them all a glance.

"I was about to show everyone the music room," Chris said. "I've been doing it over."

"Oh?"

"Yes, the composer Leighton Thordsen lived here once, as I'm sure you know, and he worked in that room. Would anyone like to see it?"

Irene seemed to hesitate, as if she

wasn't really interested, and Salt came to stand behind her.

"It's quite nice now," he said to her.

Irene lifted her chin and followed the rest of them into the room. She paused in the doorway for a moment, a hand at her throat, looking a little pale. A mixture of emotions came over her face. Salt stayed beside her and said something to her again in a voice so low that Alison couldn't hear him.

Perhaps Irene had been an admirer of Thordsen, like Alison, and was as touched as she by the skillful way Chris had worked to preserve the room.

The piano commanded all one's attention, set as it was in the middle of the room with a small lamp burning on it. It was as if time had turned back and, any moment now, Leighton Thordsen would come walking in, a vital man, smiling, nodding to them, his rakish eyes dwelling a moment too long on the beautiful women present. Then he would sit down at the keyboard and put his hands on the keys, filling the room with his music, his talent, his overpowering personality.

Alison could feel that moment in her bones as if she had been there in those days, as if she had lived it herself. But her imagination had run away with itself.

"It's, it's very lovely," Irene said in a oddly choked voice. "You've done a marvelous job, Mr. Dumont."

"Thank you. I intend to make it a kind of memorial to Leighton Thordsen. Alison had promised to help me with it."

Irene Meadows gave Alison a swift smile. "How nice of you."

"My pleasure," Alison said.

Salt noisily cleared his throat. "Let's have a round of drinks. I'll fix them," he said. "Maybe we should move out to the patio . . ."

Chris agreed and everyone trooped out, Irene hesitating at the door to take one last look over her shoulder.

Once Salt had fixed the drinks and served them, the talk turned once again to Leighton Thordsen.

"They say he was working on a composition when he died," Bob said. "No one has ever found it. I wonder if it ever really existed or if that's a myth. Now our author here seems to think it *does* exist and is determined to find it."

Alison found all eyes turned toward her. Chris gave her a wink, and Irene asked a few questions.

"Do you really hope to find it?" she asked.

"Frankly, I should be ready to give up, but I'm the sort that keeps right on hoping. It would be such a tremendous find!"

"Yes," Irene said.

She still seemed pale, and her hand was trembling as she lifted her glass to her lips. Then the talk turned to other things, the weather, when Chris would officially close down Greenwood, Joni's craft projects, and Bob's hopes about his film.

Soon Irene rose anxiously to her feet.

"I really can't stay, Mr. Dumont. I don't like leaving David for long at a time."

"But isn't Stone there?"

"Yes, but Stone isn't too patient with him, I'm afraid. David relies so much on me. Thank you all again for having me."

"Please come again," Chris replied.

"It's very dark out tonight. Would you like me to walk you home?"

"That won't be necessary."

"I'll see the lady home," Salt said.

Irene protested, but Salt was firm and polite and took her arm. Calling goodnight, they left the room.

A silence came over them. Joni had moved to the railing and stood there, very still and quiet. Bob ignored her and turned his attention to Alison. Chris went to bring a plate of sandwiches from the kitchen.

"I suspect the Meadowses are having money problems," Bob said.

"Why do you say that?" Alison asked.

"I've seen a man that works for a collection agency over there."

"You always know it all," Joni said crossly. "Just because he went there doesn't mean he wanted money!"

"I'd bet on it," Bob replied.

"Well, I like Irene," Joni said. "She's sweet, and so is David."

"Then why do they act like they do?" Bob asked angrily.

"They think they're better than anyone else."

Chris reappeared at that moment.

"They have a right to live as they want," he said. "If they came to the island with the idea of being hermits, that's their privilege."

"They think they're too good for common, ordinary people."

"That's nonsense," Chris said. "You can't say that when you don't even know them."

"Are you such an authority?" Bob asked angrily.

The men stared at each other. Joni stiffened and gave Alison a look of alarm.

"Bob, I want to go home," she said.

"Well, you know the way."

"Bob!" Alison said with surprise. "How can you be so rude?"

Bob flushed. "Oh, hell, I don't know. Everything's upside down for me. I didn't mean to blow up. Okay, Joni, let's go. I think the party is over anyway!"

Bob took Joni by the arm and hustled her out of the room. Joni called good-night to them and thanked Chris for the party. Then they were gone.

Chris sat down tiredly and reached into

his pocket for his pipe. In a moment, he had filled and lighted it, and he clenched it tightly between his teeth.

"It didn't go too well, did it? I never was much at the social graces. I shouldn't even try, I guess."

"Bob's just anxious about his work. There's been no word from Hollywood and it's getting on his nerves. And poor Irene . . ."

"She's a sweet lady, no matter what Bob thinks."

"I agree. You were so nice to her, Chris."

"I don't know why exactly, but I feel sorry for her."

"I know. She was so interested in the music room. You really impressed her with what you did."

"I wonder if she was ever here before, when Thordsen lived here."

"What on earth makes you say that?"

"I don't know. A hunch. The way she acted, the way she seemed so entranced with the place. Wasn't that a bit odd?"

"So you noticed too! But then, I was entranced just as much."

Chris leaned toward her. "With just the music room?"

She smiled. "Oh, and maybe with the man that put it all back together."

Then Chris gathered her lovingly into his arms and held her close. "I'm glad everyone has gone. We'll have our own private little party, just you and me."

"Chris, please —"

She pulled away, and she saw a hurt look cross his face.

"Why not?" he asked.

"I can't go into it now."

"Maybe you don't have to," he said sadly. "I saw how you and Bob Beale got along!"

20

Chris watched the confusion come to Alison's face. Even though he wanted to force the issue, to demand an answer from her, he let it die. He was suddenly very tired, and when Alison said a quick good-night and hurried away, he sat very still and listened to her retreating footsteps. His head began to ache, and he went to fix himself another drink. He was not one to overindulge, but tonight he felt in need of it.

Old Duggan padded along behind him, and when he returned to the patio, the dog put his head in his lap and Chris rubbed his silky ears.

"You love her too, don't you?"

Old Duggan whined at that as if he understood. Chris drained his glass and set it aside. There was a closeness in the air, a mugginess that told him a change in the weather was probably due.

The summer was drifting by, would soon be gone, and exactly where was he? With that thought, he got up and went inside to a small room he had been using as an office. He had been meaning to do some paperwork for days and hadn't been able to find the time. As a result, things were in a jumble on his desk. Never in all the time he had worked with George had he let his books get so far behind.

He began sorting through the stacks of receipts, invoices, and bills and knew before he tallied it all up that he had spent nearly all his money. Working on the old inn was like pounding sand down a rathole — there was simply no end. There were times when he felt that it was not a good investment, that he would work himself to the bone and probably end up losing his shirt. Why had he decided to do it in the first place? Was it spite, a stubborn determination to show George he could do it?

He began putting figures in the ledger, and when midnight came he was still hard at it. By one o'clock he knew the sad truth. He was going in the red and fast. It would mean cutting back on some of the things he'd planned to do, and it also meant that he would probably have to find other work this winter.

He remembered some statements he hadn't paid that were in a jacket in his room and went to get them. As he walked quietly down the hall, he turned the corner to the corridor leading to his room to find Roy Zeller outside Alison's door.

"What the hell!" Chris said.

Roy straightened with a foolish grin on his face and tried to brush past him, but Chris stopped him.

"Hold up there, Roy! Just what were you doing outside Alison's door?"

Roy ran the tip of his tongue over his lips and shook his head. "Nothing! Honest, Chris, nothing!"

"What were you going to do, break in?"

"I was just listening to the music, that's all. Music —"

Chris glared at him, not certain if he was lying or telling the truth. Roy usually was straightforward, but there had been times when he had been devious too. In his own way, Roy could be very clever.

"I don't want you bothering Alison, is that clear?" Chris asked.

"Sure, sure."

Roy wrenched away. When he was angry, he was very strong. Even if Chris had wanted to detain him, he knew he probably wouldn't have been able to. Reba had warned him not to make Roy too angry, for he could react dangerously.

"Okay, clear out," Chris said.

Roy hurriedly shuffled away, casting a glance over his shoulder to see if Chris was still watching. When he had rounded the corner and disappeared out of sight, Chris moved on with a frown. As he pushed open his door, he heard the music coming from Alison's room. So Roy hadn't lied after all. He recognized it as more of Thordsen's music that Alison often played on her tape recorder. It seemed strange to him that Roy should enjoy the music, but he knew that Roy had often gone to the music room whenever Alison played Thordsen's compositions. Perhaps it was true that music could soothe the savage beast.

Chris got the papers he wanted, spent another half hour at his desk, and then tossed his pencil aside. Figures were swimming before his eyes. He felt tired and defeated, and his uneasiness over Bob Beale and Alison gnawed at him and wrecked his concentration.

He decided to call it a night and go to bed. The next day he was going to have to make some rather painful decisions. For one thing, he had overspent in the music room, a place that wouldn't net him a dime. He had let his sentiment rule his head, and that was death to a businessman.

As he went to his room, he paused once again outside Alison's door. He could imagine her inside, asleep breathing softly, her hair falling around her face. He ached to go in and gather her into his arms, to hold her hard and close against him, to kiss her until she surrendered her heart to him. But things had gone badly tonight. The moment Bob Beale appeared the party started to go sour. The memory of Bob kissing Alison drove nails into his heart and tore at his nerves. Bob had always rubbed him the wrong way, perhaps because from the start he had sensed he was interested in Alison, and perhaps from the very beginning, even as far back as the foggy night Salt had brought them both to the inn, Chris had cared about her too. The moment he had seen her sitting on her suitcase on the dock, waiting impatiently, he had sensed she was someone special who might touch his life. Though he had not admitted it before, he was admitting it just then. The last little flame of love he'd held for Amy had started to die that night.

The next morning, Chris had breakfast with Reba at the roomy kitchen table.

"What do you know about Bob Beale, Reba?"

Reba shrugged. "Not much. But he's a charmer."

"Yes," Chris sighed. "Isn't he though?"

"And he doesn't amount to much. I ask you, what does the man really do?"

Chris smiled at that. In Reba's book, Bob didn't measure up, but then, she didn't understand the artistic soul. He didn't doubt that Bob knew his way around with a camera or that he'd had a few tough breaks. Still, he couldn't like the man.

"You're worried about Alison, aren't you?" Reba asked.

"Does it show?" he asked.

Reba smoothed her starched apron and nodded. "It's hanging out all over. You'd better do something about it or it'll make mincemeat out of you."

"True," he admitted. "I'm not sure I can *do* anything, Reba."

"Alison's too smart to fall for a man like Bob Beale. Mark my words."

"I hope so."

But he wasn't convinced, and his dark mood lingered throughout the morning. It didn't help any when he saw an unfamiliar boat pull into the dock and he watched a man climb out and start up the hill to the inn. His old partner, George!

Chris took a deep breath and went out to meet him. George offered his hand and Chris took it. They had parted in deep anger, and he had not expected to see

George again, certainly not here.

George stood back and took a look at Greenwood. Suddenly, Chris was seeing it through his eyes.

"You've got to be kidding, Chris."

"I have a lot of work left to do," he said stiffly. "I'll get to it next summer."

"You can't make a place like this pay. No way."

"That's for you to say and me to prove you wrong," Chris said with an edge in his voice.

"Well, aren't you going to ask me in? I could use a cold glass of beer right now."

"Sure. I'll get you one."

As they stepped into the lobby, George looked around with quick eyes and said nothing. But he wasn't missing a thing, and Chris was trying in vain to hang on to his temper.

They took chairs on the patio, where a sweet breeze was blowing pleasantly. Autumn had been held back again, and Chris silently thanked whoever was responsible.

"What brings you here, George?"

"A couple of things," George said. "I'll

admit I was curious about this place you'd bought — and something has come up."

Chris waited, giving George plenty of time to explain his last statement. George drained his glass and lighted a cigarette. He seemed very calm, but it was deceptive with George. Chris had learned how to read him long before. He wanted something from him and he wanted it badly.

"I have a proposition to make, Chris. I want you to hear me out before you say no and start arguing with me. I'm going to put my cards on the table. I'm not really anxious to do so, but I will. It's like this. Since you left the business, things have gone downhill. The profits have taken a nosedive, I've had some personnel problems, and business is off. It takes two to tango, Chris. I've found that out. I want you back as a partner."

Chris shook his head. "I've left all that behind, George."

"For your information, I haven't taken one little misstep, I've played it straight. Right down the line. You taught me a dear lesson. We had a narrow squeak —"

Chris started to protest and George put up his hand. "Correction, *I* had a narrow squeak. I was the one that got us into trouble in the first place. But I've kept my nose clean and I'll never do it again, Chris. We work as a team. My good right arm was chopped off when you pulled out. I need you back."

Chris knew that George was telling the truth for a change, and the whole thing surprised him. George did not swallow his pride easily. Chris lighted his pipe and bit down on the stem, thinking. The inn was bleeding him dry. It would be a long, hard row to hoe, and even if he managed to hang on, to get the inn running as it should be, would he be successful? What did he really know about being an innkeeper?

"You came all the way up here just to tell me this?" Chris asked.

"Tell you, yes," George nodded. "But more than that. I came to ask you, *beg* you, to come back to Chicago and rejoin the firm."

"I'm doing what I want here."

"Are you? Or are you just kidding yourself, Chris?"

He didn't answer that. George's visit couldn't have come at a worse time. If only he hadn't faced a few facts last night when he did the books, if only he were sure of Alison, he might have been able to stand up to George more easily.

"You came here to get over Amy," George said. "It's really the only reason you came, whether you want to admit it or not. So maybe you've accomplished that, I don't know. I do know you look good, you seem fit, and you have too much sense to moon around over a woman forever."

Chris smiled at that. "I do feel fit and I have gotten Amy out of my system. But that doesn't mean I'm ready to give this up and go back to that madhouse in Chicago."

"Look, Chris," George said earnestly. "I need you, I hate to admit how *much* I need you. Don't just say no. Think it over. Carefully. Will you do that much?"

Chris nodded. "Sure. I'll think about it, but I'll make no promises and I don't want you to get your hopes up."

George got to his feet. "Okay. Good

enough. Now, are you going to give me a grand tour of this rattrap before I go back?"

Chris showed him what he had done and what was left to do, and he knew that George thought he'd lost his mind. When he left an hour or so later, he clasped Chris's hand tightly.

"We had a good thing going, Chris. We can have it again."

"So long, George. Have a safe trip back."

"Let me know?"

"Sure," Chris nodded.

George left with a wave of his hand, and for a crazy second Chris wanted to go with him. He had been on safe ground in Chicago, he had known what he was doing and where he was going. What did he know on Windswept?

He left Greenwood and walked aimlessly around the island, turning over George's proposition in his mind. George had made some good points, and he would be a fool not to reconsider. He had been a bit rash to throw in the towel as he had, pulling up stakes and leaving everything behind. But could he ever be happy in Chicago again?

He was near Bob Beale's place and began to walk in a wide swath around it. The last thing he needed was another encounter with Bob! But as he turned away, he saw something that made him freeze in his tracks. It was Alison in Bob Beale's arms, being very thoroughly kissed. Expertly, he might say. And Alison wasn't fighting back; she seemed to be enjoying it.

His heart flopped over. An ache came into his bones that reminded him of the cold he'd endured as a POW. A sickness came into his blood and fevered his brow. He turned his eyes away and hurried off in the opposite direction. By the time he reached Joni's cottage, he was breaking out in a cold sweat.

"Chris —"

Joni had seen him. He didn't want to stop and talk to her, but it was too late.

"Come and sit," Joni said.

Joni was on the step of her cottage, barefoot and wearing her usual faded jeans. He walked over and sat down beside her.

"It's unusual to see you out like this," she said.

"Yes," he said tonelessly.

"You came from Bob's place?"

"No. I just walked past."

"Alison's there."

Chris drew a deep breath. "I know."

"Isn't it a hell of a thing, Chris? I've always been so careful to stay detached from people, to drift my own way. I wanted no ties and now . . ."

He looked up to see two enormous tears sliding down Joni's cheeks. He reached up and rubbed them away.

"You love Bob?"

"That big brute, yes! Despite all his faults I love him, and I don't know what to do about it."

"I don't think there's much either of us can do, Joni."

"You love Alison as much as I love Bob?"

"More than I've ever loved anyone, including a girl I thought I'd die without only a year or so ago."

"Life certainly has its little surprises. I don't understand myself and it's tearing me apart. What can I do, Chris?"

He wished he could help her, but he couldn't. There was nothing to say, so they sat in companionable silence, each thinking his own thoughts, each bearing the ache in his heart.

Chris finally said good-bye and walked back to the inn. Salt was there, a scowl on his face.

"Have you heard the news?" he asked. "The Meadowses are going to leave."

"For the winter?"

"No. Permanently. They're selling out."

"But why?" Chris asked. "I thought they liked it here."

Salt shrugged and walked away. He seemed upset, although Chris couldn't imagine why. He went to confirm the news with Reba and learned it was true.

"Their place would make a nice addition to your property, Chris."

He gave her a wry smile. "Sure it would. But I'm not even sure *I'm* staying, Reba."

"If you're interested at all, you'd better get your bid in. Places like that are snapped up in a hurry."

"But Reba —"

"It won't hurt to ask how much," Reba insisted.

He turned that over in his mind for a little while. The house would serve perfectly as his own home or as an exclusive guest house. It was an intriguing idea, and as Reba said, it wouldn't hurt to ask.

So he found himself going to the Meadowses' house though he had promised himself never to go there again. He lifted the heavy knocker. The sound echoed through the house, and in a moment Stone came to open the door.

"I'd like to see Irene," Chris said. "It's an urgent business matter."

Stone stood very still, as if determined not to let him inside.

"If the house is for sale, Stone, I might want to buy it!" Chris said firmly. "Now if you don't mind —"

Irene came to investigate. She looked

pale, and her eyes were red-rimmed from crying.

"If I've come at a bad time . . ." Chris said.

"It's all right. I heard you tell Stone you might be interested in the house."

"Perhaps as my own living quarters or as a private guest house in connection with the inn."

"I suggest you contact the real estate agent, Stan Walker, about it. I'm not prepared to discuss this —"

With a smothered sob, she rushed from the room. Chris was startled and stood for a moment, wondering what to do. Then, turning on his heel, he started for the door.

"Psst," someone called. "Wait up —"

He turned about to find David Meadows coming on his cane, his face flushed, his eyes a little wild.

"Wait, I must talk to you. I have to tell someone. Wait, please —"

"David, how can I help you?" Chris asked.

But the old man had no opportunity to reply, for Stone materialized again and took him by the arm.

"Back to your room," Stone said severely. "Come now, don't give me any problem."

Chris started to protest Stone's abrupt manner, but Stone gave him a look tht said it was best he not interfere. But Chris felt sorry for the old man and for Irene too. He didn't know what was wrong in their house, but something was very much out of tune, and he felt uncomfortable and uneasy there.

Chris opened the door and stepped out into the fresh air and sunlight. The door closed softly behind him, but before he had taken more than two steps, he heard the steady click of a bolt being shot and a key turning solidly in the lock.

21

The news that the Meadowses were putting their place up for sale and leaving the island came as a real surprise to Alison. They seemed fanatical about privacy, and where better to get it than on Windswept? But by the same token they were strange people, and no one could second-guess their reasons for doing anything.

The next surprise came one morning when Joni came to Greenwood to see Alison. She knocked at the door and Alison let her in.

"I know you're busy," Joni said, looking at the clutter of papers on Alison's desk. "But I have to talk to you."

"I need a break anyway."

"How's it going?"

Alison shook her head. She didn't want

to admit it to anyone, least of all herself, how bad the whole thing was. It wasn't that she didn't have enough information or the talent to put it together, it simply lacked the punch she wanted it to have. She needed some spectacular twist to give it snap.

Joni had tied her hair back from her head and pulled a sweater over her blouse; the air was cool and the bright sunshine deceptive, for it didn't hold its usual warmth.

"I've decided to move on," Joni said.

"Oh!"

"It's time. The weather is going to change one of these days soon, and I don't want to winter here again as I did last year."

"What are your plans? Where are you going?"

Joni lifted her shoulders in a shrug. "I don't know. Wherever life takes me."

"Are you really happy just wandering around, Joni?"

Joni gnawed at her lower lip with her tiny white teeth and sighed. "I used to be."

"It's Bob, isn't it?"

Joni's eyes filled with tears. "I really don't think we should talk about him. I know how he feels about you, Alison."

Alison was at loss for words. She hated the entire situation. She had never wanted to hurt Joni. She was a likable person, and despite her different ideas, she had been a pleasant companion and they'd had good times together. Someday she might appear in one of Alison's books, under another name of course, but basically Joni King, the free spirit. Only now the free spirit seemed almost eager to be captured and tied down.

"Joni —"

"You don't have to say anything. I just wanted to tell you I was leaving."

"How soon?"

"In the next few days."

"But you can't just go!"

"Why not?"

"Well, at least we have to have a farewell party," Alison said, stumbling over her words, grasping for the right thing to say.

Joni laughed. "I'm always game for a party."

"I'll take care of it," Alison said. "And Joni —"

"Yes?"

"About Bob —"

"I don't want to talk about him. Okay?"

Alison saw the clear, steady light in Joni's eyes and heard the edge in her voice, and she knew she'd better let the subject drop. But she wondered if Bob had any idea how much Joni loved him.

When Joni had gone, Alison thought about Bob and the amorous way he had reacted to her the few times they had been together. The odd thing was that she was drawn to him too and couldn't seem to help herself. Did everyone have an experience like that? Bob said he loved her, and she didn't doubt him. But what did she feel for him? What did she feel for Chris? Perhaps what she really needed was to see Regan again. But Regan had written her out of his life and she couldn't blame him. In her own way, she was as mixed up and confused as Joni.

Alison went to find Chris. He was busy

in his office entering a row of figures on a sheet of paper. She had heard about his former partner coming to see him, and she sensed that there was some kind of business deal brewing.

"Are you too busy to talk to me for a few minutes?"

"I'm never too busy for you, Alison," Chris said, tossing his pencil aside.

"Joni came to see me. She's leaving."

Chris arched his brows at that. "Everyone's leaving the island, it seems. What are her plans?"

"That's just it, she has none."

Chris shook his head slowly. "Poor Joni. A lost soul."

"I want to give her a beach party. It would be more to Joni's liking than an indoor affair. I'll invite everyone on the island — even the Meadowses, although I'm sure they won't come."

"I wouldn't bother them just now," Chris said with a frown. "They seem to be in some kind of turmoil over there. I think the idea of selling the place is really bothering them. I wonder why they're doing that myself."

"Bob said that he had seen a man from a collection agency going there once. He thinks they're in bad financial straits."

"Like the rest of us," Chris murmured.

They talked about the party for a little while, and Alison went to see Reba about preparing the food.

"Sure," Reba said. "You just tell me what you want and I'll fix it. I like Joni. She's a sweet girl. I'll miss her."

"So will I," Alison said.

The next day the weather turned very warm and balmy, and it seemed to be the perfect time for the party. They picked the secluded spot on the beach just below Joni's cottage. Reba came with Roy in tow, and Alison was once again painfully aware of the man, for he watched her continually. She supposed she should have become used to this, but she hadn't.

Bob came armed with his camera, and he made it a point to act friendly toward Chris, who registered surprise but was able to respond in the same way. It was all for Joni's sake, and Alison silently thanked them both. Chris in turn was determined to make the affair a gala one and Bob fell in with his plans, but the effort was wasted on Joni, who seemed remote and out of it and sat staring into the fire.

Reba stuffed them with picnic food, some of it cooked over the open fire, and she had baked a special cake for Joni.

"I don't like good-byes," Reba said, dabbing at her eyes. "But I wish you luck, Joni."

Everyone began to feel a little sad. But Bob broke the spell by posing everyone for his camera, even coaxing a smile from Joni.

The food was delicious and most of it disappeared, although Joni ate little. Bob was being nice to her, even sweet, but Joni was paying no attention to him. Alison could tell that it was beginning to bother him a little.

Salt arrived late, and it took Alison only a few minutes to discover that something was wrong with him. Still, it came as a kind of shock to realize that he had been drinking and had had a little too much.

"Salt, how nice of you to come," Alison said.

He sat down in the sand and stretched out his legs, putting his hands on his knees. He stared out to the water, and when she spoke to him, he gave her a long look as if he barely recognized her.

"Joni's a good kid, thought I'd join the big send-off," he said.

"Yes. It seems everyone is leaving the island. I suppose soon it will be time for me to go too."

"Summer's over and the winter here is long and lonely."

"What will you do when the snow falls, Salt?"

"Wish I were dead," he said tonelessly.

He seemed so unhappy that she was touched. "What's wrong, old friend?"

For a moment she thought he was going to tell her, then his lips clamped shut. He ran his finger nervously over the scar on his face.

"How did you get that?" Alison asked. She had often wondered but had never before had the nerve to ask.

Salt laughed bitterly. "It was over a woman, naturally. Women always get you into trouble. They chew you up into little pieces and then spit you out.''

"You were in a fight over a woman?''

"Years ago,'' Salt replied.

"Oh, it was the woman you loved, and you will never love another?''

"How did you know about that?'' he demanded.

"You told me,'' she said.

"Yeah, well, there was a fight all right. I was always tough, always knew how to use my fists, and this guy was soft as putty, not the kind that knows how to defend himself. I thought it was going to be duck soup. Then he got cute and broke a bottle and came at me. He cut me and she screamed and got all upset and the fight was over. I got a slash in my face — and he got my woman.''

"Poor Salt.''

"Is there anything to drink at this party?''

"I suspect you've already had enough, Salt. Why don't I get you a cup of Reba's good coffee?''

He didn't reply. He was sunk in despair. Alison wondered who the woman in his past was and thought she must have been quite a lady to provoke such a fight and such undying love. It may all have happened years before, but she suspected that to Salt it was as fresh as the day just past.

The party began to pall. Maybe it was Joni's attitude, or Salt's mumbling to himself, or Roy's restless poking at the fire that got on everyone's nerves, but it seemed time to break it up.

"It was a great party," Joni said. "I'll never forget it — or any of you."

She flung her arms around Reba and embraced her. She kissed Salt and patted Roy on the back. Chris gave her a hug and then she looked at Bob.

"Good-bye, Bob."

"Just like that?" Bob asked, leaning down to kiss her cheek. "If you're ever in Hollywood, look me up. I'll be there."

Alison pressed a small gift into Joni's hand as the men began to stamp out the fire and cover it with sand. Joni put a cool cheek against hers.

"Thanks."

"I hope we'll stay friends, Joni. Please

keep in touch. You have my home address
—"

"Make him happy, Alison. Just tell me you'll make him happy."

"Joni, you're jumping to conclusions! I've never said that I love Bob, or that I'll be with him or —"

"You don't have to. Even if it doesn't work out with the two of you, Bob will find someone else. I just know it won't be me."

Then, with a sob, Joni rushed away. There was nothing to do but let her go. Bob looked angry and upset but didn't follow her. He paced about for a little while and then left too, calling good-night over his shoulder.

Then he walked off toward his house. Chris fell in step beside Alison as they returned to Greenwood. Reba and Roy had gone on ahead, carrying the picnic baskets. Salt still sat staring out to the sea, remorseful.

"What's wrong with him?" Alison asked.

"I don't know," Chris answered. "He's been awfully moody the last day or so, but

I don't dare ask. He's not the sort that confides in anyone. It's all bottled up inside him."

"What's to become of all of us?" Alison asked, suddenly full of despair herself. "For one summer we were all together, and now it's breaking up. What will happen, Chris?"

He put an arm around her shoulder. "Who knows, Alison? But I think, of us all, Salt will be the one who will stay."

"And you?"

"George wants me to come back to Chicago. Greenwood is costing a fortune and is far from being renovated. Much more work needs to be done. In black and white, it looks as if I should let it go and return to Chicago . . . I don't know. It depends on so many things."

They walked on in silence, and Alison knew that she too must think of leaving. In another week or so Chris would be closing the inn for the season and it would be time to give up her room. How could the summer have gone so fast?

Lights were burning in many of the rooms at the Meadowses' house, a rather unusual sight.

"They must be busy packing," Alison said. "Where are they going?"

"I don't know," Chris replied. "They don't say much and I didn't want to pry."

When they reached the inn, Alison hurried away to her room, barely saying good-night to Chris. She knew he was puzzled and perhaps hurt by her behavior, but she wanted no good-night kiss. Joni was in love with Bob and was leaving because she thought Alison loved him too. Alison couldn't deny that she liked Bob very much. They struck sparks when they were together. But when she thought of Chris, she felt a different, deeper warmth go through her bones. She had come to a crossroads in her life.

And where should she go? Home again to Mitchell Grove? Her parents would welcome her, and there was still work to be done on her book. Perhaps back in Kansas she could get a new perspective on things and decide what she felt and how deeply it went.

Sleep was elusive that night. Dozens of thoughts and ideas went through her head.

She wondered what the inn was like in the wintertime, with the lake frozen, the snow falling, the wind whipping against the windows. How cozy it would be there, with the roaring fire, Old Duggan asleep on the hearth, mugs of hot coffee to fight off the cold.

She turned over and closed her eyes. She would not think about that. Or about Chris being there alone — or perhaps selling the inn and leaving along with the rest of them. Chris belonged here. If ever she was certain of anything, it was that.

The sobbing sounds started just as she dropped off. They echoed into her room, rasping along her nerves, making her leap out of bed in fright. She snatched up her robe, forgetting her slippers, and went across the hall to Chris's door, where she rapped sharply and called out his name. When he didn't reply, she went in. He was sleeping soundly, and she had to shake him to wake him up.

"What is it?" he asked with alarm. "Alison —"

"The noises — I hear them again. Chris, I have to know where they're coming from or I'll go crazy —"

"If just once I could hear them myself —"

"Hurry —"

They dashed across the hall and paused to listen. Alison clutched Chris's arm as the sobbing and crying out of unintelligible words started again. Chris snapped on a light. The sounds continued, and he began walking around the room, listening, trying to determine their source.

"That's it!" he said. "It's coming through the heating system. Somehow the sound is getting into the furnace pipes. Let's go to the basement."

They took a portable lantern that Salt used to see passengers down to the dock. The basement was not Alison's favorite place at any time, and it was even worse now. Chris started at the furnace itself and traced the pipes to the ones that led to Alison's room. But as they listened and waited, there was only silence. The sounds had stopped.

"Wouldn't you know it!" Alison said with despair.

"I can't figure it out," Chris said. "These pipes all seem perfectly normal. How can the sounds be coming into your room? I'll make you a promise, though, Alison. I'm going to find out, even if I have to tear this entire system apart!"

22

The next morning Alison found Chris down in the basement early.

"Have you found anything?" she asked.

"No. Not yet. But I will."

He was working on the pipes directly beneath Alison's room.

"These run into your wall," he said. "This one to the east, this one to the north."

"But I have only one register, Chris. On the east."

He stared at her. "What?"

"It's true."

"But the pipes are here. Maybe they started to put them in and didn't finish for some reason. Let's go up to your room and have a look. If my calculations are right, this should be in the west corner."

"One of my closets is there."

"A closet! That may be the answer."

They went back upstairs, Chris quickly examined the large, older closet in Alison's room. "No signs of any heating pipes in here, but that doesn't mean they aren't inside the wall. At any rate, sounds could come from there and through your wall."

"Then the sounds are originating in the basement?"

Chris frowned. "That seems a little strange. I've never seen any sign of anyone being down there, although I'll admit the place is in such a state of confusion . . ."

He leaned for a moment against the wall of her closet, deep in thought. "Now that I think about it, this is where the basement wall has a jog in it! Alison, I think we're on to something."

They began tapping the wall, feeling for a secret button or a spring to release. Just when they had decided that there was nothing to be found, Alison pushed one last time and they heard a click.

"Move back," Chris said. "It's opening!"

The door was small and beyond it were dark steps. Chris reached into his pocket for a flashlight.

"Let's see where it goes."

He went down the steps first and gave Alison a hand. "Just a minute. We'd better wedge this door open. It might close and shut us off."

He fixed the door and took Alison's hand. They reached the bottom of the steps and found themselves in a narrow corridor. Chris flashed his light up to the ceiling.

"Well, there's your answer. There's an old heat register up there. They must have put a little heat in here in the wintertime. It looks like there used to be some electric wiring too, but that's been disconnected."

"Then the sounds were coming from here —"

"Into the heating pipes that connect with those in your room," Chris said. "It acted like a direct channel. The tunnel goes north toward the Meadowses' house."

"I bet it connects with their cellar!"

"We'll soon find out."

They walked cautiously, holding on to each other, the light bobbing up and down ahead of them. Alison's throat was tight with fear, and she was glad that Chris was leading the way.

Cobwebs brushed their faces, for the corridor was very narrow, barely wide enough for one person.

"I don't like this, Chris."

"Just a little farther. I estimate we've come about fifty feet already. The Meadowses' house can't be much farther if this really does lead there."

"Why would Thordsen want to build something like this?" Alison wondered aloud. *"Why?"*

"I don't know," Chris murmured. "Perhaps it was simply an easy way to get from one house to the other when the snow was deep."

"Thordsen was eccentric," Alison said with a shiver. "But this is the limit!"

They came abruptly to the end of the tunnel.

"Sealed off," Chris said. "And there's no latch on this side, but I bet there's a door here. Look, there are scratches, like it's been pried open —''

"This is where I stumbled through!'' Alison said. "I'll bet on it. Then that means the Meadowses' cellar is just beyond this wall.''

As Chris shone the light down toward the floor of the corridor, they saw footsteps in the dust.

"Someone has been in here besides you,'' Chris said. "Perhaps they got as far as your closet, maybe even into your room. That could explain a few things, couldn't it?''

Alison pressed closer to Chris. "You mean someone can get into my room whenever they want?''

"Not just anyone. Only the person who knows about this.''

"But who could that be? The Meadowses? I doubt they ever go into their cellar.''

"Let's go back now,'' Chris said. "I don't much like the looks of this.''

She was only too glad to retrace her steps, and when they returned to her room, she was relieved to close the secret door to her closet.

"Lock your closet," Chris said.

"I can't. The lock doesn't work."

Chris frowned. "That would make it *very* easy for someone to come into your room through the tunnel, into the unlocked closet, and from there —"

"But why would they want to do that?" Alison asked with a shiver. "What could possibly be here that anyone would want? And why the strange sobbing sounds? I don't understand it, Chris."

"I don't either. Who could we ask who would know anything about the construction of this house?"

"There's just one person, Chris. Salt. He's been around the island most of his life, and he knew Thordsen and was here when the place was built."

"But I don't really want to tell Salt too much about this," said Chris. "The fewer who know, the better."

"Let me talk to him, Chris. He'll think I'm just asking questions for my book."

"All right," Chris nodded. "See what you can find out and let me know."

Alison found Salt in the bar, badly hung

over and fixing himself a pick-me-up.

"Coffee might help more," Alison told him.

He looked up with bleary eyes. "I have what I need right here."

"Salt, were you around when Leighton Thordsen had this house built?"

Salt shrugged. "Yeah, I was on the island."

"Did you watch them build it?"

"Sure. It was quite the project, you know. Nobody else had ever built such a grand place."

"Who were the builders?"

"Nobody local. They weren't good enough for Thordsen," Salt said bitterly. "He had some outfit come in from New York to put up the place."

"Who?"

"Hell, I don't know. Why are you so interested in all this?"

"I just want all the information I can get," she said. "You didn't like Thordsen much, did you. Any particular reason?"

Salt downed the drink. "Don't care to remember, thank you."

"Whatever happened to Thordsen's

secretary, the one he was supposed to be having an affair with? Benson, wasn't that her name? What was her first name?"

Salt banged his glass down. "I don't remember," he said angrily.

Alison looked at him for a long moment. His eyes had gone cold, and the scar on his cheek stood out like an angry red welt. She knew he was lying to her, and he was more upset than he wanted to show. Suddenly something clicked in Alison's head.

"Of course, you knew Miss Benson," she gasped. "And you knew her well, didn't you?"

"I don't want to talk about it, I tell you!"

"Salt, was Miss Benson the woman in your life?"

"What a ridiculous idea. I was nobody, she was —"

"You can tell me, you know. I'd like to know what's troubling you," Alison said kindly.

She was trying to keep very calm. This could be the big break! No wonder Salt had been so cool and silent about all of this. He surely knew a great many things she wanted to know but had kept them to himself, anxious to protect his old love.

"Was she as lovely as I've been told?" Alison asked.

Salt's face softened and he downed his drink thirstily.

"A beauty," Salt murmured. "Never supposed she'd even look at the likes of me. But strange things happen between a man and a woman."

"She loved you?"

Salt fixed himself another drink and stirred it, tinkling the ice. "I thought so. But he won out. Thordsen had her wrapped around his little finger. She couldn't move unless he said she could. Do you know what he called her? His Little Mouse. I hated him every time I heard him call her that. He always called everything the opposite. If a woman was beautiful, he gave her an ugly name — Little Mouse!"

"And the scar on your face?"

"We had a showdown one night. I was going to take her away, but he wouldn't let her go. He got ugly and threatened her. He could turn on people, you know. Sometimes I think he was a little mad. He had a dual personality, and that night I saw the bad side of him. I lost my head, I acted like the old sailor I used to be. I was itching for a brawl. But Thordsen was stronger and quicker than I'd imagined. He slashed me with the bottle. And she changed on me, too. She decided it was Thordsen she really loved. She sent me away, and I went like a whipped dog. I left the island for a few days, and when I came back they were gone."

"And you never saw her again?"

Salt turned his glass around and around on the top of the bar, and his face looked flushed and unhappy. He seemed lost in another world.

"She dropped out of sight after Thordsen died," Alison pressed. "No one knows where she is, and she's never been heard from since. Salt, if you know anything about her —"

"Just go away and leave me alone, Alison. Go away! I've talked too much already."

He seemed so upset that she decided not to question him further. She left him there, feeling sorry that the wounds of his lost love were still so raw and painful.

Her head spun with this information. It put a new slant on everything. If Salt had not betrayed himself, she would never have guessed that he had played such an important part in Thordsen's life. Going to her room, she was startled to see Irene Meadows come into the lobby. She looked nervous and harried, and Alison sensed that the poor woman needed help of some kind. Was it David again?

"Where is Salt?" she asked anxiously. "I must see him."

"You'll find him in the bar," Alison answered.

"Thank you."

Alison went in search of Chris but could not find him. Passing the bar on her way to the music room, she noticed Irene talking earnestly with Salt.

"You have to help us again, Salt," Irene was saying. "I have no one else."

"I'll take you to Donnerville whenever you want to go but nothing more, Irene."

"Please —"

"No!" he said sternly. "Now go away and leave me alone!"

"Oh, Salt, I didn't think you'd come to this —"

It seemed a strange conversation for Irene Meadows to be having with Salt. There was something sad and almost personal in her voice, and Salt turned away. After a moment Irene lifted her chin and left the room with a haughty air.

Alison put it out of her mind and went to find Chris. When she told him what she had learned, he was equally surprised.

"Salt and Thordsen's secretary! Now that's a twist if ever I heard one."

"I'm beginning to believe the whole story about Thordsen is twisted. But I don't think Salt knows anything about the tunnel."

Alison returned to her room with a strange, uneasy feeling that something was there, just beyond her reach. Was she missing some signal?

She took the diary out of the old trunk again. Those notes on the pages, could they mean something? Taking a blank sheet of music paper, she began copying the notes just as they appeared in the diary. Then, carrying them to the piano in the music room, she began to play them, but it was only a jumble. They made no sense and sounded like a madman's work.

Still, there had to be some reason why the diary had been hidden. Nothing else was unusual about it, so it had to be notes. Could they be part of the last composition that Alison was looking for?

She made several attempts at breaking the code — if indeed it was a code! — but had no luck.

Then she remembered something! Thordsen had been superstitious about the number three. In fact, he had loathed it. Then again, Salt had said that he always put the opposite name to things. Could three be the codebreaker?

She gave it a try, beginning with the first note, picking up the fourth note, the seventh, and so on, copying them down on her music paper. Once through the diary she started again, picking up the second note, the fifth note, the eighth, and so on, until she had copied down every last note in the diary. She looked at what she had, and her head began to swim with excitement. Humming the notes, she was certain she had found "The Rains of Spring."

She snatched up the sheets of music paper along with her small tape recorder and went to the music room. It was empty, and it was just as well. Alison wanted to be alone, for if this was the prized lost composition, then it was an unheard-of dream come true! With an ache in her throat, her hands trembling in anticipation, she started her tape recorder, put the music on the rack, and placed her fingers on the cool ivory keys of Thordsen's piano.

By the time she played the first few bars she was certain of her discovery. Every note was true and pure with Thordsen's style and brilliance.

She was so deeply absorbed in the music that it was with a start that she realized she wasn't alone. She spun around on the bench to face Roy.

"Oh, Roy, go away!" she said with annoyance. "I'm busy."

"You're playing new music," he said. "I never heard that before."

"Roy, I want you to go."

He came toward her with purpose, his shoulders broad and hulking. He stared at the music she had written, and with a sweep of his big fist, he grabbed it from the rack.

"You found it, just like Ed said you would."

"Ed!" she gasped. "Ed Reeves? Roy, give me back the music!"

He shook his head dumbly. "No. Music is for Ed."

First Salt's involvement with Miss Benson and then Roy! Ed had plotted and planned to get his hands on the lost composition, should she find it, and he had done it in a way no one would suspect, for who had thought Roy would be smart enough to know?

"The music is not Ed's," Alison said quietly, but firmly. "Roy, you're my friend. I have to ask you to give it back to me."

"No," Roy said stubbornly. "I have to get this to Ed. He's going to give me a lot of money for it. Then I'm going away to a big city."

Alison dashed for the door, but Roy grabbed her arm and pulled her back. His grip was bruising her, and she gasped with pain.

"Let me go, Roy. You like me, don't you?"

Tears came to Roy's eyes. "Roy likes you a lot, Alison, but I have to do this for Ed. I took money. I have to do what he wants —"

Out of the corner of her eye Alison saw someone in the doorway. With a sigh of relief, she knew it was Salt.

"Salt!" she screamed. "Help me!"

Salt sprang forward quickly and agilely, like the sailor he had been, and dealt a blow to the back of Roy's neck that knocked him cold.

Alison pried the music out of his hands and smoothed the pages, looking up to give Salt a grateful smile.

"Oh, Salt, thanks for coming to my rescue."

"What was all that about?" he asked.

"Just Roy's amorous ideas, I think," she said.

Salt shook his head slowly. "More than that, Alison. I heard you playing too. That's why I came in from outside. I recognized it. I've heard the music before, Alison. You've found Thordsen's lost composition."

She shook her head. "Don't be silly, Salt. It is Thordsen's music, but not the lost composition."

Alison didn't want to tell anyone until the music was safely in the right hands.

"I know better, Alison," Salt said calmly. "I remembered it as soon as I heard it because I was around when he was working on it. You've found it, all right!"

"Ah, Salt, you're imagining things!"

"The hell I am!" Salt said with a sudden burst of rage that startled her.

Before she knew it, his hand came toward her, and she felt the blow of his palm against her face. She staggered back and he came after her.

"Salt, you can't do this, Salt —"

He wrenched the music from her hand

and ran for the door. She went after him, but he turned and gave her a rough shove that sent her reeling back into the room. By the time she picked herself up, Salt had escaped. She ran after him, dazed and struggling to understand the meaning of it all, but there was no time now to do anything but follow him.

If only she could call to Chris outside! Where was Salt going? She could hear his footsteps dashing down the hall and a door slamming behind him. Then silence. Where was he hiding?

With a tingling sensation along her scalp, she knew. The tunnel! Of course, he had made for the tunnel. She burst into her room to find the closet door standing open, and she knew that she had guessed right.

Alison got the secret door open and thudded down the steps into the depths of the pitch-black tunnel. She had no flashlight, but there was no time to go back. She couldn't let Salt escape, and she heard him running just ahead of her. He had to be near the end of the tunnel by now. Abruptly, there were no more sounds. Had he already pried open the door to the Meadowses' cellar and fled? Alison stopped, a clammy feeling in her heart. Maybe Salt had guessed that she was following him. Maybe he was waiting around the next bend. What should she do? Her heart thumped, and decision was like a slash of fear across it. She could turn back to go for help and risk Salt's escaping the island for good, or she could take her chances and plunge on.

23

Alison moved slowly, crouching against the wall of the tunnel, afraid to breathe. But the silence grew, and she heard the murmur of voices that seemed to come drifting down the tunnel toward her. Was it Salt, talking with Irene?

She decided to be brave and go a little farther. She groped her way to the far end of the corridor and saw that she was in luck. In his haste, Salt hadn't pulled the door shut, and she could see a crack of light. She pried anxiously with her fingers and the door opened into the Meadowses' cellar.

She spied the stairs that went up inside the Meadowses' house and climbed them as quietly as possible. She was within earshot of voices by then and heard Salt talking with Irene.

"Oh, Salt, can you imagine what it means to have this in my hands?"

"The thing to do is take it and get every penny for it that you can," Salt was saying. "God knows, you need the money, and the music belongs to you, doesn't it?"

"But what about Alison? I'm sure she'll tell someone about this. We're not going to be able to just take it and run."

"I'll take care of Miss Blair," a rough voice said, and Alison recognized it as belonging to Stone.

A new lump of fear began to rise in Alison's throat. If she had any sense at all, she'd clear out as fast as she could. Yet she was riveted to the spot, needing to hear everything she could.

"I'll make sure that even if Allison tells the story, no one will believe her," Salt said. "A few little lies here, a hint or two there, and no one will give her a second thought. Why should they? Who would ever have thought the music would turn up anyway?"

"Where did she get it? How did she find it?"

"I don't know. What does it matter? It's

in our hands — the biggest find of the century!''

"We must go, and quickly," Irene said anxiously.

"Are your things packed?"

"Yes, nearly everything."

"Hurry! The sooner we get out of here the better. Alison's probably trying to find Chris right now."

"We have to stop them!" Stone said. "Where is Alison?"

"I left her in the inn."

"You stupid fool!" Stone shouted.

"I've had about enough of you, Stone," Salt retorted. "Where would you be if it hadn't been for my help?"

"Yes, yes, that's true," Irene said. "Please, we mustn't quarrel now. We have to keep our wits about us and think what to do . . .''

Alison had heard enough. They were leaving the island and taking the music with them! They had to be stopped. She charged back down the steps, heading for the outside stairs and the inn, but in her haste she stumbled, narrowly escaping a very bad fall. But she had made too much noise, and in a moment she heard someone coming after her.

She screamed and started to run for the daylight of the open cellar door, but before she could reach it, someone had grabbed her from behind and a rough hand covered her mouth. She felt herself being half-dragged, half-carried, up into the Meadowses' house. It was useless to struggle — Stone was her captor. As he pushed her roughly into a chair, she looked around to find Salt and Irene hastily gathering their belongings and preparing to go.

"How can you do this, Salt?" Alison asked with despair and disbelief.

He gave her a cold smile. "Just shut up and stay out of this, Alison. You've already poked your nose around too often."

"I want the music back."

"You have no right to it!" Irene said stiffly.

Drawn by the angry sound of voices, David came wandering into the room and looked about in a dazed manner.

"What's going on?" he asked.

"Nothing, dear. We're just getting ready to leave," Irene explained.

"But where are we going?" he asked, bewildered.

"Away," Irene said. "Don't you remember, I explained it all to you last night, that we would be leaving here soon."

"I don't want to go," he said.

Then David saw Alison and his face broke into a smile. He came toward her, his hand outstretched. "Well, hello! It's the lovely girl at the piano —"

"Stay away from her," Stone said. "Come on, old man, I'll take you back to your room."

"I want to speak with her!" David said temperamentally. "I *will* speak to her. Take your hands off me. How dare you —"

But Stone was relentless, pulling him away, and before Alison's horrified eyes she saw David crumble and begin to cry. She recognized the sobs! It had been David she had heard crying and calling out! He must have been in the tunnel and his sobs had echoed in her room.

"What do we do with her?" Salt asked, staring at Alison.

"I don't know. I don't want to think about it," Irene said. "Oh dear, what a mess, what a terrible thing —"

"Stone will fix her," Salt said.

Alison knew that her fate was in Stone's hands. She looked to the door, the window, seeking a way of escape, but Salt was watching her. Salt, her old friend who had betrayed her. She still couldn't believe any of this was happening.

Then Stone was coming toward her with a white cloth in his hand. A sickeningly sweet smell filled the air. Chloroform! She tried to run, to escape, but Stone grabbed her once again and held her. The cloth came down on her face and she gagged and gasped, but the darkness came anyway.

Chris had been busy that morning working with Salt outside the inn, and he heard Alison playing the piano. He paused for a moment to listen, and Salt did too. The next thing Chris knew, Salt had disappeared, probably to get something to drink, Chris reasoned. Salt was in a bad way just then.

When he didn't return after a while, Chris grew angry and went to look for him. But Salt was nowhere to be found. Chris went to the music room to ask Alison where he might be. There he found Roy just coming to, holding the back of his head and groaning. Chris rushed to his side.

"Roy, what on earth happened?"

"Salt," he whispered. "Salt took the music. Alison followed him —"

His words struck terror in Chris's heart. Alison must have found the missing composition, but what could Salt have to do with it? He was so stunned for a moment that he couldn't think of what to do or where to turn.

Then he began to search the inn, shouting Alison's name, going first to her room. The door was ajar, and he heard Old Duggan whining and sniffing inside the closet. The tunnel! Alison must have followed Salt down there! Chris had the presence of mind to grab a flashlight from Alison's belongings before he went down into the dark corrider. Old Duggan sprang ahead of him, sniffing the way.

Chris followed, afraid of what he might find or see. When he heard Old Duggan begin to whine just ahead, he flashed his light to the floor of the tunnel.

"Alison!" he cried out.

She was out cold, and there was a sickening smell around her. Chris recognized the chloroform. He picked her up in his arms and with some effort carried her back through the tunnel to her room.

He put Alison on her bed and began shouting for Reba, but it was Roy who responded to his call.

"Where's your sister?" Chris asked anxiously.

"Home, down the path —"

"Get her, for God's sake move, Roy!"

Roy ran, and Chris dashed for the bathroom and soaked some towels in cold water. He began to bathe Alison's lovely face, and by the time Reba appeared, a frightened Roy behind her, Alison had begun to stir.

"Make some coffee, Reba. We have to

get her awake."

"What happened?" Reba asked.

"No time to explain now. Just do it, and do it in a hurry!"

Alison slowly became aware that someone was splashing cold water on her face, strong hands were rubbing her wrists, and someone else was holding coffee to her lips.

She struggled to open her eyes. Heavy weights were on her lids. Everything was hazy and the voices were far away.

"Open your eyes, darling," Chris was telling her. "That's it now, open your eyes!"

She heard the barking of the dog. Old Duggan. She finally got her eyes open and the room slowly came into focus.

"Thank God!" Chris said.

"I'll go get another cold cloth," Reba said.

She disappeared, and Alison reached out to clutch Chris's hand. "Where did you find me?"

"In the tunnel. Thanks to Old Duggan. I heard him whining in your closet so I knew you must be down there."

"Stone must have put me there."

"I don't understand what's happening. I found Roy. He said Salt had knocked him out!"

"That's right," Alison said, her head aching with the effort of speaking. "And I followed him into the tunnel and they caught me —"

"They?"

"They're leaving, all of them. Salt, Stone, the Meadowses — and they have the composition, Chris! Salt stole it from me. First Roy tried and then Salt —"

"Roy tried!" Chris said, nearly shouting.

"Ed Reeves was behind that, but there's no time to discuss it now. We have to stop them before they leave the island."

"I just can't believe that Salt —"

"It's Irene. I know now that she's the woman that Salt loved years ago. She's Miss Benson, Thordsen's secretary!"

"What!"

"You have to stop them, Chris. You can't let them leave."

"But how —"

"*The Maiden.* Salt is going to use *The Maiden* —"

Chris stared at her for a moment and reached out to brush back a lock of her hair.

"Will you be all right if I leave you?"

"Yes, yes, please —"

"I'll do what I can to detain them, at least until we can figure out what to do."

She heard Chris leave the room and dropped off again until Reba came back and revived her with another cold cloth.

"I don't know what's going on around here," Reba said. "Roy's out in the lobby sobbing his heart out, and Chris is talking about some tunnel I never heard of."

Old Duggan whined and put his head in Alison's lap. "Thanks, old pal, you really came through for me when I needed you."

Chris was back in a few minutes. He had fouled the motor of *The Maiden.*

"It will take even Salt a while to find out what's wrong. Now, I think I'd better get in touch with the police at Donnerville and ask them to come out."

"Yes, I'm afraid we must do that."

Chris went to make the call and they promised to come within the hour.

"What if Stone checks the tunnel and finds me missing?" Alison asked.

Chris nodded. "I've been thinking about that. We'd better take matters into our own hands. I have a pistol in the desk. I'll get it and go up to the house and hold them until help comes."

While he did that, Alison got up and went back to the music room. With a sigh of relief, she saw that her recorder with the cassette was still there. She tucked it firmly into her pocket. Chris was calling her and she went to join him. He looked grave and worried. It was a courageous and risky thing they were about to do, but Alison knew it was necessary.

Armed with the pistol, and sending Reba and Roy to the dock to intercept the police, they walked out into the bright sunlight and toward the Meadowses' house.

They went quietly to the door, which was unlocked, and slipped inside. Salt and Irene were arguing heatedly and Stone was berating both of them. When Alison and Chris burst into the living room, all of them registered shock.

"Alison!" Irene gasped. "How can you be here? Stone, I thought you —"

"I'd advise all of you to sit down very calmly. The police will be here shortly," Chris said.

"The police!" Salt thundered. "Why in hell did you call them, Chris?"

"There seems to be a matter of a stolen manuscript."

"You have no right to it!" Irene burst out. "It's mine. It belongs to me!"

Irene covered her face and began to cry. Salt went over to her and put his arms around her.

"It's all right, Irene. It's all right. Don't cry."

She leaned against his shoulder and wept. Alison and Chris exchanged a quick look.

"You were Miss Benson, weren't you?" Alison asked.

Irene dabbed at her eyes. "Yes. I was Miss Benson. I worked for Leighton as his secretary. Later, when we went to Venice, we were married shortly before his death."

"Married!" Alison said with surprise.

"Shut up, Irene," Salt said. "You don't have to tell everything."

Irene gave him a long look. "No. I suppose not." She glanced at David, who had sat through this looking dumb-founded, lost, and bewildered.

"Anyway, Miss Blair, the manuscript is rightfully mine. As Leighton's widow, it belongs to me," Irene said.

"Yes, I suppose it does," Alison agreed. "But why didn't you just tell us who you were, why keep it such a deep secret?"

"It seemed best, that's all," Irene said.

But it was an evasive answer and it did not satisfy Alison.

"Who is Stone?" she asked.

"My cousin. I hired him to help me with David. I can't handle him alone anymore. As you know, he is, well, not responsible."

"This has been very hard on him," Alison said with sympathy.

"Why don't you cancel that call to the police, Chris," Salt said. "Haven't these people suffered enough?"

Chris looked to Alison and then to Irene.

"Do you have proof that you're Thordsen's widow?" he asked.

"Of course," she replied. "I have all sorts of documents. I can show them to you. I keep them as mementos of happier days."

She searched through the luggage piled by the door and extracted a leather case. From it she drew out a wedding certificate bearing her name and Leighton Thordsen's.

"It's authentic, Chris. Believe me," Salt said. "I can vouch for it."

Chris looked into Irene's unhappy face and nodded. "I believe you, Irene."

David had watched and listened to all of this in a dull, disinterested way. Then he jumped to his feet and said he wanted to walk in the garden.

"Sit down," Stone said crossly.

Alison went over to him. "Let me go with him, please. I wouldn't mind at all. The poor dear is so confused and upset by all of this —"

"Let her go," Salt said. "Now, Chris, you're going to call Donnerville, aren't you? You're going to put that crazy pistol away —"

Alison left Chris to settle the matter and, taking David's thin arm, led him out to the garden behind the house. It was a warm day and the sky was clear with a few clouds floating overhead.

"Why don't we sit down here in the sun," Alison said.

"Yes, I'd like that," David replied.

"Tell me, David, where are you from?"

"I live here."

"But originally?"

"New York. I grew up in New York."

Alison gnawed anxiously at her lip. "And you've lived abroad too, haven't you?"

"Abroad? Yes, I think so. I'm not sure."

She took the tape recorder out of her pocket and turned it on.

"What's that?" he asked anxiously.

"Some music I played on the piano. I thought you'd like to hear it.

The clean, sweet notes rippled out, and David straightened as if hit by a thunderbolt. He stared at her and then he leaned back, listening, nodding his head in time, smiling to himself. Then he shook his head. "No, no. That's wrong. Those few notes are wrong —"

Alison's head was spinning and her heart was thumping hard. She didn't dare believe that her hunch was right, but she knew now why he had seemed familiar. Of course he had changed drastically — he was no longer robust, no longer young. It would be very hard to recognize him. Besides, who expected to speak with a man supposedly dead?

"You would know the notes were wrong, wouldn't you, Leighton?" she asked, holding her breath.

David Meadows went white. For a moment Alison thought he was going to bolt and run like a frightened deer. Then tears welled up in his eyes and he said, "It's been so long since I've heard my name. No one speaks it now, you know. It's not allowed."

"I, I can't believe that you're alive! They said you were dead!"

"Dead," he murmured. "Part of me is. Sometimes —" Then he broke off for a moment. "You must not tell Little Mouse, do you hear? You must not tell her that you know. Promise me — you must not tell!"

24

By the time Alison took David back into the house he was crying again, the tears trickling down his cheeks. When Stone saw them, he came to take David back to his room.

"Give him a sedative," Irene said.

When Stone had gone, David arguing every step of the way, Alison gave Irene a long look.

"I know the truth, Irene. I know that David is really Leighton Thordsen."

Irene closed her eyes and her face went chalky white. She began to weave back and forth, and Salt rushed to her.

"I knew it wouldn't work!" Irene said woefully. "I knew sometime we'd be caught."

Salt helped Irene to the couch and she put her head back, looking pathetically worn and tired. Chris stared at Alison, a dozen questions in his eyes.

"How did you guess?" Irene asked.

"From the beginning there was something familiar about him, but I could never put my finger on it."

"But he's *nothing* like the man he was!"

"No. But because I'd made a study of him, I probably was alert to some resemblances that others missed."

Irene covered her face with her shaking hands. "Do you know what it's like for me to see him like this, to have to live this way —"

"The question is, why are you doing it?" Chris asked gently. "As far as everyone knows, Leighton Thordsen died in Venice."

"You might as well tell them the whole story," Salt said.

"Yes," Irene nodded. "In a way, it will be a relief to tell it. For years now I've lived with this terrible secret, and believe me, it hasn't been easy. Even before we left Windswept for Venice, Leighton was ill —"

"That's why Salt took him secretly at night to see a doctor in Donnerville!" Alison said.

"Yes. He didn't want to see a doctor, but I kept urging him. Leighton was a high-strung, nervous man. He worked hard and played hard, and he found it difficult to accept his own failing health. It was a mental condition. The doctor at Donnerville suggested that we see a specialist in New York. We made a secret trip there and his diagnosis wasn't good. David would not get any better. So I arranged the trip to Venice, hoping we could stay out of the public eye and that way protect his reputation."

"He became even worse there," Salt said. "Irene wrote and told me."

"It was Stone who suggested we put out the news that he was dead. He arranged the phony papers, the fake private funeral, everything. We took on new identities. It's amazing what a little money in the right hands can do."

"But why would you want to put on such a charade?" Alison asked. "When the world loved him so much —"

"That's just it. Leighton was a proud man — *extremely* proud. You must have known that, Alison, if you learned anything about him at all. And so was I. I couldn't bear for the world to know that he was now only half a man, and in his lucid moments he didn't want it either. I didn't want him gossiped about or pitied. I wanted him to be remembered as the great man he really was."

The room fell silent. What Irene must have endured for the man she loved — the secrets, the lies, the fear of being discovered. The agony of it all must have eaten away at her every day.

"Why did you come back here?" Alison asked quietly.

"We loved it here. And I thought we would be safe. In Europe a few suspicious things had happened, and I was afraid we were about to be discovered. But Windswept was a small island where we could keep to ourselves, and Leighton wanted to come."

"And the music, the last composition —"

"Leighton composed entirely in his head. He seldom wrote down anything until he had the whole piece of music thought out. But when he grew ill, he couldn't remember well enough to put the music down again. It was hopelessly lost. I still don't know how you came upon it —"

Alison explained about the diary and how she had decoded the notes she'd found there. Irene smiled wistfully. "He liked to do things like that. It was a kind of game. He never told me he had done it."

"I just played him that composition on my tape recorder, and he remembered it well enough to know that I had two notes wrong," Alison said.

Irene smiled. "Yes, I know. Occasionally he remembers quite well. He has tried to put down the composition, but it only made him worse. It infuriated him so that we simply didn't even talk about it. One moment he can be as brilliant as he ever was, but the next —"

"It's gone," Alison said with sadness. "Oh, Irene, I don't know what to say to you. You can't imagine what a shock this has been to me —"

"And would be to the world. I must ask

you, all of you, to keep my secret."

They exchanged glances, and Alison saw the compassion in Chris's eyes. Salt reached out to hold Irene's hand tightly in his.

"My pet, you know I've kept this secret all these years, and I'll keep it until I die if you wish me to."

Irene patted his hand. "My dear Salt, I don't deserve your friendship after all that happened between us."

"There are still some things I don't understand," Alison said. "Why was a tunnel built between the inn and this house?"

"I lived here when Leighton lived in the inn. He constructed the tunnel so I could come and go at will, despite the weather. And then too, there were times he wanted to come and see me. We were discreet in those days because of gossiping servants and guests, and Leighton didn't want anyone to know that we cared for each other. I don't know why exactly — it was one of his quirks."

"I've been hearing strange noises in my room —"

"Leighton remembers the tunnel in his better moments, and there are times he slips away from us and goes there as he used to. I'm sorry if he frightened you."

"And once he sent me a note —"

"Yes, Stone discovered it, and he deliberately had to scare you away, Alison."

"The face in the window —"

Irene gave her another sad look. "Whenever you played, Leighton was drawn to the inn, especially if you played his music. It was very difficult for him, half-remembering, half-forgetting . . ."

"I understand," Alison said.

Chris got to his feet and offered his hand to Alison. "I think we should go now. They need to be alone for a while."

Alison gave Irene a smile and she returned it sadly, tearfully. The situation wrung Alison's heart. She felt deep admiration for Irene, who had endured so much.

Chris held the door for her and they walked silently out into the bright day and back to Greenwood. Chris left her momentarily to go find Reba and Roy.

"What will you tell them?" Alison asked.

"Nothing. Just that the matter has been settled peacefully."

"Will Reba believe that?"

Chris smiled. "Probably not, but that's all the information I'm going to give her."

"What about Roy?"

"That's up to you, Alison," Chris said with a frown. "But I think he's suffered quite a lot already. He knows he's done wrong. And poor Reba —"

"Yes," she said with a sigh. "I can forgive Roy, but I'd like to give Ed Reeves a piece of my mind!"

"No." Chris shook his head. "*I'll* do that — with pleasure!"

"Poor Leighton. How awful it must be for him," Alison said. "Do you know this is the most bizarre story I've ever come upon and I'm honorbound not to write a word of it!"

Chris came to put a kiss against her forehead. "I think they've earned their peace, darling."

"How can I end my book? How can I go on writing about a man I thought was dead when I know he's still alive?''

"For all purposes and intent, the man who was really Leighton Thordsen is dead. David Meadows is just a shell of Thordsen. Why don't you just finish the book as you started?''

"There seems little else I can do.''

"I wonder what they will do with the composition.''

"Irene will claim to have discovered it somewhere among Leighton's things. At least they should be able to earn some money from it.''

"What a fitting climax to the summer,'' Chris said. "I had no idea things would turn out like this!''

"I can finish my book at home now.''

A shadow went over Chris's face. "I see.''

"What about you and your old partner?'' Alison asked.

Chris moved away to stand at the window and made no answer. She sensed that his heart and his head were both in a turmoil. She left him there, feeling a sudden need to escape the inn, to leave all the confusion behind for a while.

She walked toward Joni's place, but the cottage was locked and the place looked empty. So Joni had really gone! Alison felt an ache in her heart for the aimless young girl.

Moving on, she came to Bob's house and saw him sitting on the front step, his chin in his hand, the sun putting a gloss on his blond hair. He lifted his head when he saw her coming.

"Hello!" he called happily.

She went to sit down beside him. "You look very ambitious."

"Terribly," he said. He lighted a cigarette and tossed the match away.

"Still no news?" she asked.

"Nothing good," he said.

"I'm sorry."

Bob lifted his shoulders in a shrug. "That's life."

"What's your next project?"

He laughed shortly. "Managing to eat and stay alive."

"Is it that bad?"

"No," he said. "Not really. I have my eye on a job in Donnerville as movie projectionist at the local theater. It will tide me over until I hear from Hollywood or until I decide to do something else with my life.''

''Does that mean you're leaving the island?''

''As soon as I can pack up my gear and go.'' Bob reached out and touched her hand. ''It's not going to work with us, is it?''

''No.''

''I never had a chance?''

''I wouldn't say that. You're a very nice person, Bob. Another time, another place — who knows? — the spark might have struck.''

''Yeah,'' he said. ''Well, you know Joni's gone, don't you?''

''Where?''

Bob shook his head. ''To Donnerville for a few days and then God knows where. And I just sat here and let her go, Alison. Sometimes I don't think I'm too bright.''

''Do you know what I think, Bob, I think you care more for Joni than you want to admit.''

There was a tortured look on his face.

"I'm a little afraid you're right."

"Why don't you do something about it?"

"Like what?"

"Catch up with her, follow her — don't let her leave." Alison got to her feet. "Get going!"

He rose too and kissed her cheek. "Thanks for clearing the fog in my head."

They smiled at each other, and then Alison walked away and turned back to wave. She had a feeling that it was the last time she would see Bob Beale.

Bob smoked the last of his cigarette, thinking, and then he crushed it out and went inside the house. It took a couple of hours to get his belongings together. Then he made several trips to take his things down to the boat. He began to feel hurried, anxious. Joni might change her plans and leave Donnerville sooner than she had planned. What if he missed her?

He broke out in a sweat and thought of phoning her, but that wasn't the way to handle it. For one thing, she probably would refuse to talk to him.

He was about to close and lock the door

for the last time when he was startled by the sound of the phone ringing. For days, weeks, months, he had waited for the damned thing to ring. He dashed for it.

"Bob Beale, please. Long distance is calling from Hollywood."

He closed his eyes and said a prayer, and in a moment he heard a man's voice on the other end of the line.

"Hello, Bob."

"Phil, you old devil! Good to hear your voice!"

"Bob, I've been running through your film and I think it's great. I have some people interested. How fast can you get out here?"

"As fast as you can wire me the money to get there."

Phil laughed. "Tell me where to send it."

"Donnerville. I'll hang out at the telegraph office until it gets in."

"You're on, fella. See you soon."

Then the line went dead and Bob hung up. His head was spinning. He felt weak and so sick with relief that he went to splash cold water on his face. But he had no time to waste.

He left the house, got in the boat and started across the lake toward Donnerville. Speed was of the essence, and he crashed over the water, the waves slapping angrily at the bow until, at last, he saw the dock ahead. Using the last of his money to get his car out of storage, he started to look for Joni.

He went to Lois Martin's house, but it was empty, and he reasoned that Joni was probably at the store.

When he got there he hurried inside. A bell tinkled overhead and Lois came to see what he wanted.

"Is Joni here?"

Her eyes went blank. "No, she isn't.

"Where is she? I have to find her."

"She's gone, Bob. She left this morning."

"What!"

There was a roaring in his head and a terrible ache in his heart. Suddenly nothing else mattered but Joni. Not the call from Hollywood or anything.

"I *have* to find her! Don't you understand? I must speak to her!"

"I'm awfully sorry, but you're just a few hours too late."

"Where was she heading?"

"Nowhere in particular. She said something about Texas or Florida. She said she wanted to be where it was warm."

"But not California?"

"No."

"It figures," Bob said glumly.

There was nothing to do but thank Lois, say good-bye, and go to the telegraph office to get his money. Joni would be thumbing a ride — she had no other way to go — and maybe he could still manage to catch up with her.

Texas or Florida? He made an educated guess. The Florida beaches would attract Joni, he was sure. He took the road south, but after an hour or two, he began to feel that he had made the wrong choice.

He stopped at a coffee shop on the way, asking if anyone had seen her, but the answer was negative. It was impossible to know where she was by then. Some trucker probably had picked her up. She could be miles ahead of him.

Still he pushed on, not willing to give up yet. It was early evening and the weather had turned unexpectedly bad. Rain came down in slashing torrents. If poor Joni was out alone in this . . .

Then he saw her! He would have known her anywhere, even if she did look like a drowned rat, with her blond hair soaked and stringy and her pathetic belongings wrapped in plastic and strapped to her back. The little fool . . .

He pulled up alongside her and pushed open the door.

"Don't you know you go west to get to California?" he said.

She stared at him, her chin set, her eyes fiery.

"I'm going to Florida."

"The hell you are," he said. "Get in here, Joni King, before I drag you in by the hair."

"Why should I?"

Bob drew a deep breath. "For starters, because I love you! Now get in here —"

She stared at him for a moment and then, with a little cry, she leaped inside and into his arms. Her wet cheek was against his, and he didn't know if it was tears or rain he felt against his face.

"Oh, Bob, Bob —"

He kissed her and then, with a laugh, he put the car in gear. Later he'd tell her about Hollywood and his good news. But right this moment, it took second place. He put his arm around her and pulled her close, and they drove on through the rain together, turning west to the waiting sun.

25

It had been a long and harrowing day, and Alison went to her room early that night. The time had come for her to decide what to do and when to go, but with all the dizzying events of the day she wasn't up to it.

Very early in the morning she thought she heard a boat, but sleep overcame her curiosity. It wasn't until the next morning that she learned the news from Salt.

"The Meadowses have gone."

"What! But I wanted to talk to Irene again, I wanted to ask more questions —"

"They've gone. I took them last night."

"Oh, Salt!"

He gave her a steady look. "I had to do what she asked. I owe her that much."

"But where, how —"

"I put them on a plane out of

Donnerville to Chicago. From there, I don't know. She wouldn't say and I couldn't ask."

"Oh, dear!"

"You left this in their garden," Salt said, handing her the tape recorder. "She asked me to return it to you."

Alison saw immediately that the cassette with her recording of Leighton's composition was gone! Her eyes widened.

"She took it," Alison gasped in disbelief.

"And the diary too," Salt said. "It belonged to them."

"But how —"

Salt gave her a winning smile. "The tunnel. They used the tunnel one last time while you were out walking yesterday."

Alison bowed her head. She had not expected that. She had no proof at all that she had discovered Thordsen's last composition. She felt sad and cheated.

"But *I* found it!" she cried. "I think I should have had a little credit in the matter. Is that too much to ask?"

"Irene is devoted to Leighton. She'll do

anything for him. You must know that by now."

She heard the raw emotion in Salt's face and knew that he too had suffered terribly from all of this. He still loved Irene passionately, he had loyally kept her secrets and given her a helping hand when she had needed it so desperately.

"You know, Salt, you're quite a man."

"No," he said with a shake of his head. "I'm just a fellow who runs an old rundown boat and tends bar here at the inn once in a while. I'm nobody. I'd like to stay that way."

She knew what he meant. He didn't want to be written into her book, and he would keep on protecting Irene for the rest of his life.

Alison leaned over and kissed him, her lips brushing the scar on his face.

"All right, Salt. But someday, when Leighton really is dead, I'm going to write a sequel to my book that will tell the *whole* truth, and it'll be a blockbuster."

"When that happens — go to it, girl. Go to it!"

It had rained in the night, but the sun had come out. The air was cool and the trees were decked in autumn color. It would not be long before the leaves began to tumble down and winter would set in with a vengeance. Alison decided it was time to go. She began to gather her things, and when she grew weary of packing, she took a long stroll around the island.

How quiet and empty it seemed with Joni's house closed and shuttered, and Bob's place empty too. The Meadowses' house looked the most forlorn of all, and Alison wondered about their journey. Where would they go this time? New York, back to Europe, Australia? Only God knew.

When she went back to Greenwood, it was lunchtime and Reba was waiting for her. Roy was there too, his head down and shy.

"Hello, Roy," Alison said gently.

He lifted his head and she thought he was going to run from the room, but finally he came over to her.

"You mad at Roy?" he asked fearfully.

She smiled. "Of course not."

"I didn't mean to hurt you."

"You didn't, Roy, so let's just forget about it, shall we?"

He smiled back at her. "Okay! Roy forget, just like that!"

Then he snapped his fingers and left the room, whistling.

Alison was about to leave her table when a local newscast on the dining room television caught her attention. There was an interview with Irene Meadows from O'Hare Airport in Chicago! Alison stared ·in fascination.

"I want to announce the discovery of my late husband's last composition that we all thought was lost. Alison Blair, an author who is writing a book about Leighton, found it hidden on Windswept Island where Leighton once lived. It will be published and offered to the musical world with my gratitude. This is a tremendous find, a joy for me, and I want to thank Miss Blair publicly for making it all possible."

For a long time, Alison sat at the table, touched by Irene's words. She had misjudged the woman after all.

Salt had heard it too, and when he came into the room his eyes were shining with pride.

"Now you see why she's such a great lady," he said, smiling.

Alison leaned back to bask in the moment, for she had found the focal point for her book. The climax would be the finding of the lost composition. While the rest of the story would have to wait until later, she knew she had a best-seller brewing, for the revelation that Thordsen had lived long after everyone thought he was dead would come as a bombshell to the music world that had loved him.

Irene's announcement gave Alison plenty of work to do, and with the summer over, it was time to go. She went back to her packing but her heart grew heavier with each item she put in her suitcase. When someone knocked at the door, she rushed to answer it and was relieved to find Chris. He looked at what she was doing and a scowl deepened on his face.

"The summer is over," she said simply.

"You can't go. We have to talk. Over dinner."

She smiled. "Well, you're the master here, so I shall obey."

His face softened at that, and she recognized the look of love in his eyes. When he had gone, Alison tried to analyze all that she had felt and done on this island all summer long. She was not the same woman who had come there. It had all started to change for her that foggy night, waiting for Salt to come and fetch her, when Chris Dumont had appeared, collar turned against the mist, a strange, quiet man with a heavy heart.

At dinnertime, she went to join Chris. There was no one else in the dining room and Reba discreetly left them alone after she served them. The breeze seemed cool and fresh as it came in the windows, and the autumn mood was all around them. Chris talked quietly about Irene and her surprise announcement, its effect on Alison's book, of Joni and Bob, of the island as it must be in the wintertime.

"You've decided to stay on," she said.

He nodded. "Yes, even though it won't be easy. I can't go back to Chicago, I belong here. I don't know when I've felt so right about anything. There's only one thing —"

"Yes."

"I don't want to stay alone."

"Reba and Roy will help you, and Salt will be here."

"That's not what I mean and you know it," he said.

His gray eyes met hers, and she studied his dear face and reached out to smooth back his dark hair. She loved him. It had become undeniable during the nightmarish events of the past few hours.

"Stay with me, darling," Chris implored. "Finish your book here. If the winter becomes too unbearable, we'll move to Donnerville. You know how much I love you!"

"Yes, I think I do," she said. "Nearly as much as I love you."

His eyes blazed and he reached for her and pulled her close.

"Can we live on love? We haven't much else," she pointed out laughingly.

"Our lives will be richer and fuller than you can imagine," he said.

"Yes, darling, I know."

The wine was forgotten, along with the sunset and the sighing wind at the windows as he kissed her for a long, burning moment.

"We have so much to talk about, so many plans to make —"

She laughed softly, knowing which road she was taking at last and longing to get started.

"I don't doubt that for a minute, but don't stop kissing me — not just yet . . ."